NO EXIT

NO EXIT

First published by Sort Of Books, 2026
Sort Of Books, PO Box 18678, London NW3 2FL

Distributed by Profile Books, 29 Cloth Fair, London NW3 2FL

Typeset in Palatino Linotype and Frutiger to a design by Henry Iles

A catalogue record for this book is available from the British Library

ISBN 978-1908745897

1

Printed and bound by CPI Group (UK) Ltd,
Croydon, CR0 4YY

GPSR details and contact
We make every effort to make sure our products are safe for the purpose for which
they are intended. For more information see our website (www.sortof.co.uk) or
contact our EU Authorised Representative:
EAS Project OU, Mustamäe tee 50, 10621, Tallinn, Estonia.
gpsr.requests@easproject.com

NO EXIT

SIMON LEWIS

Sort Of
BOOKS

For Noe and Hana

Contents

幸运日 LUCKY DAY

LUCKY DAY

1

Inspector Jian rapped his knuckles on the table to declare that he was out, and turned his tiles face up. He had collected four bamboos, four dragons and five rings. The other winds sagged and tutted and swept their tiles away as if they could no longer bear to look at them. They were playing on a tiger table, where one point equalled one English pound, so each now owed Jian a painful hundred and fifty in Queen's currency.

As they counted out notes, Jian yawned and stretched. No longer lasered in on his game, discomforts crowded his attention. The miasma of smoke and incense that hung over the tables stung his eyes. The plastic chair hurt his back. His throat felt sandpapered from multitudes of cigarettes, his stomach queasy from litres of weak green tea. There was a cloying stickiness to the air and a graininess to his vision. The din of the place struck him as discordant and rancorous, the incessant rattle of tiles like the static crackle of an untuned TV. His tablemates looked ugly and base and twitchy with need. He was suffering, he recognised, from the corrosion of the nerves that came from an excess of gambling. It was time to leave.

His winnings included a note he had not seen before, a big, bold fifty with a comely Queen in girly peach and pink. He explained to the other three winds that, although he greatly enjoyed their company and talents, other matters required his attention; he was glad to have been so fortunate, and positive that luck would be with them next time. No doubt the sulking men thought themselves unfairly deprived of the chance to win back their money. Jian had rinsed them ruthlessly. Some four,

five, or maybe six hours ago – his sense of time had slackened
– Jian had walked into the Lucky Day Leisure Association with
two hundred in British currency; now he had, he supposed,
over six thousand.

He was carrying a purse borrowed from his daughter. It
was pleather, decorated with hearts, and too small for this
meaty wad. His struggle to jam it in was watched with barely
suppressed agitation by the rest of the table. He succeeded,
but the only thing the purse contained was forced out: his
namecard.

It fluttered to rest among tiles and was snatched up by the
south wind. This sour, scrawny man was the session's biggest
loser. He had arrived with four cigarette packets jammed with
notes. Three were now empty and crushed at his feet. He played
in a slovenly manner, his wits blunted and temper heated by
the lagers he drank steadily and without relish. When the tiles
had started turning on him he had muttered his woes at his
captive audience, concerning the wife who had left him, the
chef job he had lost and the misery of his present occupation,
putting tarts' leaflets in phone boxes.

Now he held the namecard by a bottom corner, tilted his
head back to gaze down his nose at it and declaimed in a tone
of mock grandeur: '*Zhentan ducha*... Detective Inspector Ma
Jian... Qitaihe Public Security Bureau.'

A hush dropped over the scene. Hands travelling to or from
the tables froze. Jian, the only standing figure in the crowded
room, felt twenty or thirty curious gazes turn on him. He
heard murmurs, in English and Cantonese, which he could
not understand, and in Mandarin, which he could. 'A cop!
A mainlander cop! Look at him. What's he doing here? He's
dressed like a kitchen hand.'

The last remark stung, though Jian had to admit its accuracy.
He was stripped of all his habitual signifiers of status, and

sported trainers, sweatpants and sweatshirt, all unbranded and worn thin. He liked to think that his crisp accent, upright bearing and solid stature would hint that he amounted to more than he appeared: but was self-aware enough to know that maybe that was just vanity talking.

'So? What are you doing here?'

The question was repeated by the south wind. No doubt all were thinking it. The crowd demanded a response. Play had halted in anticipation. Jian affected nonchalance but cursed mentally. A cop would always be treated with suspicion in a place like this. No doubt at any future visit he would have to reassure, answer queries, allay suspicions. Few would want to play with him, and if they did they would become cautious and tight in his presence. He might even be barred. And all thanks to a sentimental attachment to a foxed old namecard of no possible use – not here, not now. It was foolish pride to have it on his person. Plucking it from the south wind's hand he resolved to stop carrying it around.

He said, cheerily and loud, *'wo zai duija...* I'm on holiday.'

'Feihua! Bullshit. How do I know you're lying? Cause you're a cop and your lips are moving. So I lost to a dirty cop. Of course I did.' The south wind crumpled his last cigarette packet. 'Now I know why you won,' he scoffed, wagging a finger. 'Policemen always cheat. You're a cheat.'

He tossed the packet at Jian then stood and grabbed one of his empty bottles. Clearly he had a characteristically ill-advised gamble in mind. The bottle swung and Jian stepped smartly aside, then snatched the wrist, rotated and yanked it. The man lurched, the bottle dropped. Foamy dregs spattered. With his free hand Jian pushed forcefully on a bony shoulder, and dunked the drunk back on his chair.

A loser was a dangerous beast but not a wild one, and could be disarmed with kindness. Jian dropped a note and suggested he get another drink, take a break, and cut his losses. The man flicked tiles about as anger faded into despondency. No doubt the game would break up now. No one would want to take his seat, the drunk would retire in a sulk, and the remaining two winds, already tired and demoralised, would cut their losses. The bottles and ashtrays would be cleared away, the table given a quick wipe, then a fresh set of eager players would claim the tiles. Gamblers came and went but the game never stopped for long.

All around, faces turned away, conversations resumed. Tiles moved and clicked once more. Jian headed for the exit, a battered metal door with strips of pasted characters either side wishing gamblers luck and advising good manners. A craving for sunlight, fresh air, and the company of people who were not sizing up his weaknesses increased. He realised how hungry he was – he needed something solid to soak up the tea. Mentally, he was already out of here, and waiting to be talked through the specials by a waitress. But here was someone else with something to say: a lad in a peaked American cap and sunglasses, snapping his fingers for attention.

'*Jingcha!*… Cop, come hustle with the big boys.'

He sat at the dragon table, which was set apart on a low platform, with a wooden rail around it. Players on this, the most exclusive game in the house, had more space, better chairs and that modern miracle, an automatic Mahjong table. The three winds, having just finished a hand, were noisily shovelling tiles into a hole at the centre of the baize.

The lad gestured at the table's empty chair. 'I always wanted to pit my wits against the force. Come play your tricks with us. Ten pounds a point.'

A set of notes bound with green paper bands was lined up before him. A fair number of similarly dressed wads nestled in the care of his opponents. These two were middle-aged men, blank-faced and haggard, with the dead fish eyes of professional gamblers. The lad's invitation was an attempt to break their flow and reverse his ill fortune.

Once the tiles were gone, the hole irised shut, a clacking came from the innards of the machine, then slots opened and the tiles rose to the surface as four neat walls. A perfect shuffle and set-up, all without human intervention: what a world we live in.

Jian aped humility. 'Your game's too rich for me.'

Another time he would be tempted. A win at the high table there would be glorious, for the ages. Ah, but... Jian had learned to play Mahjong from his grandmother. Sat on a hot kang, engulfed in an army coat, cracking seeds with her remaining teeth, she had taught him to play percentages, to calculate what other winds were building from their discards, and to break an opponent's concentration with chatter and cigarette smoke. And she had passed on the arcane art of tile tracking: how to use skilled fingers and gimlet gaze to follow a couple of major tiles all the way from shuffle to wall to hand, a slim but perceptible edge. That machine negated such an advantage, it would be wise to avoid it.

The chunky lad had the arrogant self-assurance and smooth rosy cheeks of a pampered little emperor. Above fat red trainers he wore baggy black trousers with many pockets and a black hooded sweatshirt far too big for him. He looked like an overfed crow: he cawed like one too. 'I know why you don't want to play. Over here, you can't arrest us if you lose. I'm disappointed. Didn't take you for a coward.'

Coward – *dan xiao gui* – an archaic term for a youth to use. And his accent was stilted. Jian supposed Mandarin was his second language, making him that curious hybrid, an overseas Chinese. Instead of grabbing the lad's head and stuffing those cheeks with tiles, which would have been satisfying but an inordinate effort, he said, 'Stop shooting for glamour hands, build solid combinations, and you won't have to talk tough. I'd stay to school you but idiots never learn.'

The lad pushed back his chair, stood and strode to the rail. Perhaps he was expecting to tower over Jian, with the help of the platform. When it turned out they were only face to face, uncertainty flickered in his eyes. He plunged his hands into his front sweatshirt pocket. Jian sharpened. The lad could be reaching for a weapon.

But as they squared up a figure squeezed between them. A pale, skinny man, middle-aged, with wet, red eyes. He made placating gestures and burbled conciliatory platitudes. The Manager: all afternoon he had prowled the tables, offering commiserations or congratulations, inquiring after people's health, or regretfully refusing lines of credit. The lad addressed him in English: a suggestion, Jian supposed, to have him thrown out or disciplined. There was invective, dismissive waves. Of course the lad was confident; in any dispute the higher roller would be backed. He finished by forming his hand into a gun shape and mock firing it with a jerk of the wrist. An acceptable degree of face restored, he returned to his chair. Jian, letting himself be escorted away, heard him apologising to his opponents, then the click of tiles as they started to play.

'You've won big,' hissed the Manager, 'why do you need to make trouble?' At his desk by the door he whispered, 'Don't cross that boy.' He nodded towards a figurine of Guandi, God of War, shown in knobbly armour, swiping a halberd, boggle-eyed and snarling. Jian understood the reference. The presence of the figurine meant tong affiliations; presumably the lad was connected. Jian knew that something about the seemingly random decorations near the door – the faded print of a bamboo forest, the dusty fan, the tatty calendar – would reveal which tong in particular. Jian couldn't read such signs: he was a northerner, and the old tongs were a southern phenomenon, he hadn't had many dealings with them.

'I do hope you enjoy your holiday, Inspector. Will you be with us long?'

'If I like it here.'

'So much to do. There are other schools in the city. You may want to explore them.'

As suspected, Jian was being told that he would not be welcome back. He paid a hundred pounds table fee. The man's smile widened, but didn't reach his eyes as he said apologetically, 'The same again, please. Rates double after a certain amount of time.'

Jian couldn't be bothered arguing. The money was tight in the stuffed purse, with no hope of getting the zip closed on it. He teased out notes and the wad, pleasingly, did not seem diminished. Flicking it was like thumbing the pages of an old book. But what a book – a transformative text.

Jian had been practically broke when he walked in. He felt the lifting of his money worries physically, as if a weight had been dropped. Standing tall, he luxuriated in lightness. First, pay the overdue rent. A feast to follow. What a pleasure it would be to see his daughter's face light up when he announced his intention to take her out. Fancy restaurants every day for a week. Plus treat her to whatever she wanted, however frivolous – clothes and shoes no doubt, also a proper purse, a decent phone. Following that – clothes for himself. How glorious to be smartly dressed once more, to catch his reflection in a mirror and approve. Then a period of calm contemplation, as the need to frantically scramble just to stay afloat lifted. With the benefit of a little breathing space he'd come up with plans to make everything better, and he'd have the capital to start working to realise his schemes. What a difference a bit of money made, what optimism it sparked. From these seeds a garden could bloom. Perhaps his misfortunes were at an end, and beautiful, prosperous times lay just around the corner.

The purse in his pocket weighted his tracksuit bottoms, dragging the waistband to his hips. He had seen such a slobbish arrangement affected as fashion on the streets. How could the tong kid back there, and his hooligan ilk, walk around all day like this? It was uncomfortable and inconvenient. He put a hand in his pocket to keep his trousers up and preserve his dignity and with the other reached to pull open the dull metal door.

It never got there. The door was shoved violently from the other side, smacking his arm away, and Jian was abruptly faced with another young man. This one wore baggy blue overalls with big yellow buttons, something like an oversize romper suit, with an element of fancy dress to it. But there was nothing clownish about the stocking pulled over his head, or the sawn-off shotgun aimed at Jian's face.

2

The knuckles of the hands holding the gun were pale with strain. A finger was stiff on the trigger. Jian stared down the quivering double barrel. It had been cut barely six inches from the stock. If he lost his head and that thing went off, a widening cone of shot would cause carnage.

The lad shouted in Mandarin. 'This is a robbery! *Na chu qian lai!*... Money out, all of it! Money! Money! Money!'

Another stilted accent: one more of these eccentric hybrids. He had neglected to cut or tie the foot of the stocking and it flopped about, getting in his eyes. He flicked his head to move it. A jittery amateur, hyped with adrenalin, fighting panic, a twitch of the finger from mass murder.

For hours the clicking of tiles had been a background murmur. Now it was replaced by gasps of surprise and moans of dismay. Heads turned and chairs scraped. Only the stooped old man whose job it was to walk round refilling cups and emptying ashtrays did not look. He stood gazing at the floor and his teapot shook.

Jian considered running, but before he had time to move a second hood came in and closed the door. This one wielded an automatic, held casually in one hand. A tall, rangy-looking man with a slight stoop. He was a white, the only one in the room. He wore dirty overalls, of the kind you might see on a butcher. His movements were more natural. Jian guessed he was older, more experienced. Jian supposed that he didn't speak any Chinese, that the younger one had been sent in first because he did.

The first hood was shouting himself hoarse. 'On the table, all cash and jewellery out! Put it on the table!'

Gamblers pulled out wallets and loose notes. On a cat table a woman sobbed as she emptied a jam jar of coins. The winds on the dragon table thumped thick bundles down. Jian pulled up an empty chair and sat. He put a hand in his pocket and pried a couple of notes from the weighty purse. He let them flutter to his lap where they could be easily seen and snatched away. Surely the robbers would take little notice of him, tired and worn in cheap clothes, and would never imagine he had more than these few pounds to his name. He waited and watched.

The first hood – the Romper – stood swivelling jerkily around, pointing but not aiming the gun. 'Hands on the table, hands where we can see them. Don't move. Don't look.'

The Butcher put his gun in his apron pouch and took out a red pillowcase. He started hurriedly stuffing it with money and valuables. What a team, thought Jian, a mad dog and a skittish kid. He wondered how they had got in. The gambling den was on the third storey of a nondescript brick building. The entrance was an unmarked door at the back of a herbalist store. In the dim corridor just beyond, a doorman lounged on packing cases. There was an alarm switch on the wall. If he'd jabbed that button before being overpowered, a gang of tong hatchetmen would soon arrive. A gunfight here would be a massacre.

On the tables, cash and valuables mixed with ashtrays, cigarette packets, bottles. The Butcher grabbed and stuffed. The pillowcase had a racing car design, cartoon sports cars with smiling drivers, the sort you'd buy a child. Why bother at all with the cat tables? The dragon table held more money than the others put together; pros would just clear that and leave. It was long seconds before the Butcher got there. He whooped and chuckled as he snatched stout bundles. The fat lad in the baseball cap scowled. The older gamblers looked frozen, one even had his eyes closed. Perhaps it was not their first time, and they considered this merely an occupational inconvenience.

The Butcher jumped from the platform and skidded to the last uncleared table, a cat, where a little jade and gold glimmered among coins. He began plucking jewellery, and ladies sniffed and gasped. The Romper moaned, his gun jerked even more erratically, then his nerve broke, and he dashed forward and yanked at his colleague's arm, imploring. Brief words were exchanged, then they hurried away, splashing tea.

The Romper was out first. The Butcher seemed set to follow but halted suddenly in the doorway, and turned to consider Jian. Jian looked levelly back. The man's face was thin and sharp, and the mesh squashed his nose into a beak. He grinned, revealing crooked teeth, and said something to the unseen Romper.

He put the pillowcase between his teeth and held it with clenched jaw. Then with one hand he kept his gun trained on Jian's head. He thrust the other into Jian's pocket and yanked the fat purse out. He must have seen its shape, how its weight distorted the fabric.

Jian could take the hood, right now. Rising, one hand to grab the gun and turn it, an elbow to ram that vulpine face. But who knew what his twitchy companion would do with that cannon?

The moment passed and Jian watched the girly purse, straining at the seams from its burden, drop into the pillowcase. What shitty luck. The robber had missed plenty of less well concealed valuables. He took a long blink, and in that moment of mottled darkness saw his winnings as a fluttering flock. The notes looked exotic, sparkling. They flew away.

The door was swinging shut. The thieves' receding footsteps could be heard, in the corridor, then on the stairs. Smoke clouds that had parted as they ran around began to close. Hands rubbed faces or snatched back jewellery. Ladies quivered and sobbed. A fist banged on a table, making tiles jump.

Jian stood up, rolled aching shoulders, and stalked out.

3)

There were two ways out of the building: the little herbalist store at the front or the fire exit in the corridor at the back. Jian guessed the thieves would go for the latter. He closed his eyes and worked up a mental map of the building. Details were hazy but he recollected the basics – flights of steps, the rough length of rooms. He turned away from the stairs, along a dim corridor, and opened a door.

He entered a dark, dusty storeroom cluttered with stacked chairs, cups and trays, boxes of Mahjong tiles. The windows, as in the main room, had been painted over. A sloppy job, streaky on the glass and with blobs of paint spattering sill and frame. Jian grabbed a couple of boxes. They were tin, marked with a faded brand name in long-form characters, about the size of two bricks and, with one hundred and forty-four plastic tiles in each, about as heavy. He used them to smash the furthest window from the door, sweeping back and forth to clear tinkling glass from the pane. Daylight streamed in. It was the first natural light Jian had seen for hours and it jolted him from the static, airless world of the gaming den into a sense of passing time and the world outside.

The sun was low and weak in a steely sky. It must be late afternoon already, he had tarried even longer than he thought. His daughter, on the other side of the alien city, would be preparing dinner, washing rice and setting it to boil, opening tins and chopping veg. She would be beginning to wonder where he had got to.

He dragged a chair over, stood on it, and poked his head out. He was looking down at a little fenced yard at the back of the building. It was empty but for a parked blue car. It seemed a neglected space, and very private: the only building which overlooked it, on the far side, had its windows bricked up.

As calculated, he was right above his building's emergency exit. The fire door directly below was opening. Jian dropped the first box.

It plummeted, turned, and detonated with a crack on the Romper's shoulder. Tiles sprayed like shrapnel and the lad went down hard, sprawling, arms wide. The Butcher came out after him, and Jian dropped the second box. But the man had seen what had happened to his colleague and lurched aside. The box exploded on tarmac. He looked up at Jian, down at his fallen colleague, then sprinted away. The laden pillowcase bumped his thigh as he exited an opening in the wooden fence, into the alley beyond.

To have taken one thief out seemed a fair result, though he wished he'd got the one with the spoils. Leaving, he was surprised to see the Manager hurrying ahead of him, rushing down the stairs three at a time, his shirt tails fluttering behind. He seemed in a state approaching frenzy, in danger of tumbling at any moment. He must have been spurred into action by the banging sound, realised something was developing, and was now determined not to be caught on the backfoot a second time.

At ground level a dim corridor was made into an obstacle course by piles of cardboard boxes and packing cases with medicinal labels. The Manager slalomed around them and headed without pause out of the open fire exit doorway. Jian followed.

The Romper was prone on knees and uninjured arm. He shook his head to clear it before rising groggily to his feet. He reached for his dropped gun, which lay among the scatttering of tiles.

The Manager launched himself at the lad, knocked him down, and started hitting with his fists, shouting in English and Mandarin. 'I got you, thief. I got you.' The dazed thief flapped ineffectually. Disappointed perhaps at the slackness of his punches, or wishing to spare his hands, the Manager changed to slapping and kicking. He paused, breathing heavily, and pulled out a set of car keys. 'Going to gouge your eyes out, how would you like that?' He jabbed, the lad parried, then, farcically, the car behind beeped as it unlocked.

Jian's knees were sore, the sudden exertions after prolonged sitting having set off an old persistent ache. If he'd left an hour earlier, he would not be hurting now, he would still have his winnings and he wouldn't be dealing with this nonsense. He picked up the sawn-off shotgun. It was far too light. A fake, made of plastic and skilfully painted to resemble steel and wood. Very convincing in appearance but in the hand it felt like a toy. Still, it had served the lad's purpose, and it would do for his now. He held it by the barrel and smacked the Manager around the head a couple of times with the butt.

'What are you doing?' His tone was outraged. He seemed more surprised than hurt. The thief was his captive, no one else's, not that Jian felt the need to explain. Jian gave him one more hit to knock him prone. He took a deep breath, dizzied by all this light, fresh air and exercise. Then he grabbed the car keys.

This was working out. Perhaps the luck gods were playing their own game, feting and damning him in quick succession. Jian grabbed the Romper, yanked him round and pulled the stocking off his head. The terrified face blinking back at him was that of a callow youth, at least partially Asian, with delicate features. He was slim and lanky with, usefully, long hair tied in a ponytail. Jian grabbed it and started pulling. 'You're coming with me.'

The stricken lad looked puppyish in his helplessness and confusion. 'Please don't hurt me.'

'I won't. If you do what I say.'

4

The car was a big blue Treasure Horse. Jian manhandled his captive into the passenger seat, gave him a squeeze on the injured shoulder to keep him honest, then secured the lad's seat belt and locked the door. The fake shotgun, now dented, bent and chipped, fitted neatly in the front seat pocket. He got the hefty German car started and manouevred it through the gap in the fence and out into an alleyway.

He drove rapidly away, taking turns at random. The car was a good ride, with a throaty purr to the engine, gears easy to find, a pleasing firmness to the brakes and a spongy clutch. It was an old model, which meant not too many baffling features and icons on the walnut dashboard. His spirits rose: you always felt in charge of your own destiny when you were at the wheel.

After some fifteen minutes he found himself in a residential district of low-rise houses and blocks of flats, wide tree-lined pavements and few pedestrians. Satisfied that he was not being pursued, and could not be easily found, he continued till he found a quiet dead end and pulled up.

He looked his captive over. Blood oozed from cuts on his forehead and lip – from the fall rather than the strike – so superficial and of no concern. The open, pretty face, with its full lips and wide, glassy eyes, suggested sensitivity rather than aggression. His hands were soft and nails clean, probably he had never done honest work or thrown a punch. A good reach perhaps, but no muscle in him. And so young – he should be in a classroom. Give him credit though, heisting a gambling den with a replica gun took balls of iron. He was not to be underestimated. Jian rummaged in the lad's pockets and found cigarettes, lighter, phone.

Jian leaned in and laid it on thick. 'That place was a tong den. If they get hold of you... they'll torture you until you've told them your mate's name and address. Then they'll go get him, and then they'll kill both of you in some disgusting and horrible way. They're animals when they're roused. Understand?'

The lad looked suitably appalled.

'But none of that has to happen.' Jian patted his thigh reassuringly. 'I'm going to sell you to your friend. He returns my money, I let you go. Six thousand British pounds, or thereabouts. In a girly pink purse with hearts on it. That's all I want. Then you are both free, happy and rich.'

'But...'

Jian grabbed the lad's ponytail, pulled his head right back. 'If I don't get my money, I take you back there and sell you, for the aforementioned six thousand, to those horrible, awful people. I get what's mine. You get to choose how I get it. Do you understand?'

'Yes.'

'What's your name?'

The lad mumbled something, it sounded like To-Mu.

'You haven't got a proper name?'

'I'm English.'

'The other robber, is he English?'

'Yes.'

'Speaks Mandarin?'

'No.'

He tossed the lad's phone into his lap. 'Call your friend and explain, To-Mu. Better get him to see that giving me my money is his best option as well as yours. It needn't be difficult, we can get it all done in a couple of minutes, then you're free to take off and divvy your haul.'

Jian lit one of the lad's cigarettes. It was a lady smoke with no kick to it. The lad seemed to have largely returned to his senses, though his shoulder was causing him pain, as pressing the screen made him wince. His call was connected, and the phone buzzed, steady and insistent, on and on, eating all attention. The lad started muttering, a prayer perhaps. Then the call was answered and he gabbled a great gushing stream of English.

It annoyed Jian that he didn't understand. His captive could be talking to anyone – perhaps asking thuggish friends to come and save him. But the worry was allayed as the call went on, for the lad sounded very like someone arguing an urgent point with a sceptic.

To-Mu turned to him and said, in his oddly accented Mandarin, 'How much was it again?'

'Let's call it six thousand. In a fat pink purse with hearts on it.'

'He keeps asking, how does he know this isn't a trap?'

'Tell him I'm a gambler who's violent and insane but with limited ambitions. Tell him to look for the purse. Tell him about how I beat you up and stole this car. Go into detail. Your life right now depends on convincing him that I'm a nutter working alone.'

More gabble, then Jian was heartened to hear the lad make affirmative noises and sob with relief. Some short assertions, what sounded like a pledge of heartfelt thanks, then he ended the call and dropped the mobile in his lap.

'He says he's coming now.'

'Good.'

'He's in a van. I gave him the street name, a description of the car. he says he'll be a couple of minutes. He says if he sees anything suspicious, like if he sees any Asians hanging around, it's off.'

'We'd better hope no one's ordered Chinese.'

There were depots or warehouses on one side of the street, a strip of fenced-off waste ground on the other. No vehicles had come down while they'd been here and he'd not seen one pedestrian. It was a good enough spot for his purpose, quiet and discreet, though he would have liked more exit routes. He got the car turned around so that they faced the T-junction about seventy metres ahead.

'What's your mate driving?'

'A dirty yellow minibus.'

'That's your getaway vehicle? What's wrong with a motorbike? You two are idiots. Is his gun fake as well?'

'Yes.'

'You've got rocks for balls, I'll give you that. Rocks for brains too, unfortunately.'

He lit another cigarette, gave it to the lad. His hand shook and he dropped it in his lap. Trying to pick it up he knocked it into the footwell, then stamped like there was a snake down there till it was out. Jian gave him another. His phone started up, blaring a snatch of dramatic music. The lad whipped it up and frowned.

'It's not him?'

'It's my mother.' He let it blare on while looking sightlessly up. He didn't want to look at the screen, see the name. 'She's going out of her mind with worry.'

'I should think so, with an armed robber in the family.'

'She doesn't know anything. It would kill her.'

'You couldn't have a normal ringing sound?'

'It's from a film.'

The looping refrain ceased and they sat in silence till he suddenly blurted out, 'They looked so frightened. Old ladies. Crying. That old man with the teapot. It was horrible.'

'Thoughts of your dear old mama pricked your conscience? Too late. You ruined a lot of people's lives, you little shit.'

'I haven't eaten for days,' said the lad. 'Don't even know if I could. But I'm smoking like a bonfire. Can't get enough. I finish one then start the next.'

'Take up a quieter profession, you haven't the stomach for this one.'

'Your accent. You're a mainlander, right? A northerner?'

'Yes.'

'I'm a northerner too.'

'No you're not, you're English.'

'My dad is English, my mum is from Shandong. She took me there. I went to her hometown, Qingdao. You know it? I saw my family. Lots of them there. I went to Beijing. I liked it. I liked the… Forbidden City, Temple of Heaven, other temples… I liked the friendly people. Great food… noodles, duck.'

He was babbling, one word bleeding into the next, his tones flattening. 'I watched a man write characters in a park, with a big brush and water, he drew beautiful characters on the ground that would fade in moments. I wanted to stay longer. Find out what it really means to be Chinese. When I came back here I started learning calligraphy, to improve my written Chinese. I got into running script. The freedom of it. Like doing tai ji on paper. Mum says it's really coming on.'

The lad finished his cigarette. Jian cracked his window to let out the smoke. The light was beginning to dim. Trees were ranked along the road. The leaves were yellowing as autumn bit. In a few weeks the branches would be bare, the temperature would plunge. Winter was when you felt your money. Or lack of it.

He stared at the junction ahead and willed the Butcher to appear. The more delay, the more likely this was to screw up. An off-the-cuff plan like this depended on keeping the principals off balance and scurrying around. Give them time to think and they'd start exploring their options.

The lad said emphatically, 'I'm not a criminal.'

'Sure.'

Dipping his head like a supplicant, he grabbed Jian's arm.

'Really, I'm not. I've never done anything like this. Never done anything illegal. I'm a student. I'm at college. I'm studying computer aided design. I should be... Saturday night, I should be drinking with my friends, I should be at a karaoke party in Shoreditch... instead I'm here, with a...'

Jian shucked his arm away. 'I know what you're doing. You want me to see you as a fellow Chinaman, rich human being and decent citizen, so I'll feel some sympathy. And maybe I won't have the heart to sell you to the tong if your mate doesn't come through. It won't work. All you are doing with your talk is annoying me.'

The lad's phone started off. But after looking at the screen he winced and let it ring.

'Your mother again? Seems she's worried about you. She should be. I'd say you've really gone off the rails.'

'Don't take me back, please. Don't do that to me, I don't deserve that, no one does.'

'When your friend turns up you can go.'

'Honestly...' He gave a juddering sigh. 'I have no confidence in that guy.'

'You worked with him before? Robbed a lot of places?'

'I said, I've never done anything illegal, I've never robbed anyone. I barely know that guy.'

'Would you describe this untrustworthy stranger as rational and level-headed?'

'No. Not really. I'd probably say the opposite.'

'Even a mad dog knows not to run in the road. Surely he would look at this arrangement and see it's in his interests to go along with it? Yes? What do you think? You think I should give up on him, drive you back to face the people you robbed?'

He couldn't look Jian in the eye. He mumbled into his lap, where the phone lay. It was now smeared with sweat from the lad's palms.

'No, not that, please no. Stop it.' He was suddenly earnest. 'Look, I think – you should know – the reason I robbed that place – you need to understand...'

Jian clicked his fingers and pointed.

'Is that him?'

A yellow van had turned into the road and was slowly approaching. It was of unfamiliar design: boxy, with a flat squashed face like a lion dog. It seemed a rather unserious vehicle, surely inappropriate for the matter in hand. It was also very dirty. Someone had doodled with a finger in the grime on the bonnet and side – a smiling face, and some kind of sigil, a rough triangle in a circle.

The lad almost sobbed with relief. 'Yes, it's him, it's him.'

His phone rang.

Jian got the car into first and rode the clutch.

He said, 'Explain carefully. He drives alongside, stops his engine. He hands the money across to me through the window. Any dumb moves and I drive off. When I'm happy you get out, fuck off, I never see either of you again.'

'Yes, okay yes.' Then he was gabbling in English on the phone.

Jian brought his window three quarters down and a breeze chilled his face. He took firm hold of his captive's ponytail at its root and watched the van come closer.

The driver was hunched low over the wheel. Again he wore the stocking over his face.

'He says he's got the money, and he's going to do what you say.' The lad shifted.

The driver put his phone down out of sight and the van drew up alongside. The passenger window was open. The driver reached across and threw something down. A pink blur came through the window, bounced on the windscreen and slid into the footwell. His daughter's purse.

'That's it,' shouted the lad, 'That's your money. Let me go, let me go.'

Jian picked the purse out. It had a weight and heft that felt pleasingly familiar. He spotted the peachy fifty poking out from the furled notes. It was all there.

He let go of the lad. Immediately a seat belt snapped back, then the passenger door opened and the lad scrambled out in a flurry of limbs.

The van reversed and stopped. To-Mu picked himself up and hurried towards it, looking gangly and earnest. Suddenly it lurched forward, roaring, barrelling straight at him. Its dumb flat face ate up the space between them. A crunchy impact seemed certain and Jian tightened. The lad screamed and hurled himself back and away, arms flying up behind his head. He seemed for a moment to flicker like a ribbon right at the edge of the bonnet. He was missed by the tightest of margins. The van swept on, past him, swerved, rammed Jian's door and came to a halt. Jian lurched as the car was struck. His window shattered with a crack. Glass cascaded.

As Jian gathered his senses the van began to reverse. It had a dent on the bumper but seemed otherwise unharmed. Jian supposed his car had come off worse in the encounter. He curved into a right angle and stopped. Jian wondered if he was going to come again – in which case the lad had better get himself up. But when the van started moving again it began to turn in the other direction, beginning a ponderous getaway up the street. The Butcher was twisted round, looking through his back window.

Jian's door was warped by the crash and wouldn't open; he had to slide over the seats and exit from the passenger side.

The lad was still on the road, sitting on his haunches. 'He… he tried to kill me,' he said. He had such an abject expression of dismay that Jian almost felt sorry for him.

'A mad dog indeed. Wanted you out of my hands. And out of the way. Guess he doesn't want to share the spoils.'

He considered offering a few words of solace, perhaps a cigarette, but the lad did not know when he was beaten. To Jian's surprise he stood and sprinted away after the van.

Jian watched him go. He was a good runner for a lanky kid, some good lungs on him. Not that he would be catching up that van any time soon.

Jian watched till he was out of sight. Criminals and their antics – if they were not tragic, they would be amusing. Well, the whole sordid incident had been brought to a satisfactory conclusion. He had his money, and the incident was over. With luck he would see none of those characters again, and he'd be giving Mahjong schools a wide berth for a while.

Jian took stock and tried to work out how he would get home. The gambling den was in an undistinguished suburb in the south and east of the city, some four kilometres from the big river and a ten-minute walk from a certain stop on a certain bus route. He was some fifteen minutes in a car from there – and that was all he knew about where he was. He wanted to get away from the area but was loath to spend any more time in the stolen car. He decided to walk, then ride a random bus till he spotted a Chinese restaurant, then ask his way from there. He carried a pocket map book, with all the places he needed to know marked. He only had to jab a finger at the dot for home.

He looked forward to surprising his daughter with his good news. There had been little enough of that lately. He rifled the wad. No clever substitutions, no packets of paper: all there. No. He stopped, checked again. His namecard was gone – once more, the troublesome thing had slipped out at an inconvenient moment. The paper notes tended to adhere to one another, but the card, with its slicker texture, would slide at any sudden jolt. So either it had fallen out in the pillowcase or when the purse was tossed into the car. The thought that it was right now lying by the pedals niggled. It was a link to the vehicle that he did not want discovered.

He returned to the car to check, but found only glass bits in the footwell. He had to accept the card was gone and that was probably for the best. As he was exiting the passenger door a black SUV roared up. It screeched to a stop, each of the doors flew open and Asian lads, some barefoot, some bare-chested, barrelled out and came at him. All shouting, raising coshes, cleavers, stun guns. Another car arrived, disgorged more of the same.

There was nowhere to run. Jian closed up, with chin tucked, arms raised and fists clenched.

5)

David Yip, manager of the Lucky Day Leisure Association, sat on his knees on the floor between gaming tables. The imminent arrival of Uncle Seven, Incense Master, occupied him completely, and he was barely conscious of the Mahjong tiles digging at his legs and the cold tea seeping into his trousers. The tong boss would see the robbery as a terrible loss of face, and who knew where his wrath would strike? Vital, then, to hit the right tone: deferential, apologetic, submissive but not supplicating. Aim to come over as unlucky rather than incompetent. Culpability should fall on the doorman as the weak human factor in an otherwise flawless security system. A reconstruction would show how simple it would have been for the lad to ring the alarm when confronted.

At least he had been able to help: to open the CARTRACKA app on his mobile and watch the pulsing dot that represented his beautiful BMW gliding through the streets of Wanstead and settling in a cul-de-sac less than two miles away; to dictate this location over the phone to a red pole. That was a tick in his favour, surely. He hoped the thief had been caught in the car, along with the mainland cop.

Indignity had been piled on indignity. To be robbed, then see his car stolen, then watch his irate customers flee. They had rubbed at bare fingers, plucked at empty pockets. One had joked that, after all, this robbery was not really of note, he had just been cleaned out a few hours earlier than anticipated. But most were far less sanguine, and shot him foul looks or muttered curses. 'Such a shame.' 'Where was the security?'

'What kind of place is this?' 'Will we get our money back?' 'Shocking, shocking, I hope they catch them.' Anyone inquiring about compensation was given a namecard. He knew many would never return. They would go instead to his rivals, to the Jumping Tiger or the East Wind School, and never mind that those places charged for tea and the tables were too close together.

But he was not quite alone: one customer had stayed. The lad in the red baseball cap who now sat at the dragon table, building a tower out of tiles. It fell and he started piling them up again. He seemed entirely unconcerned, tapping his feet to some tune coming through his headphones.

The lad's phone vibrated and he studied it a moment then called over, 'Look sharp. He's here. Why don't you put your head down, in a proper kowtow, when he comes in? My Dad will like that.'

6

The door was flung open, with as much force as the robbers had used, and Uncle Seven strode in. David, kowtowing as the lad had suggested, saw two feet in disposable hotel slippers. A dressing gown of white towelling billowed behind him, the belt trailing like a tail.

'Honoured master.'

Uncle Seven ignored him. He strode over to his son. David could not see but he listened carefully, anxious to judge how angry Uncle Seven was. He heard a slap.

'Dad!'

'Don't dad at me. You think I can't hit my own son? The fuck are you doing here?'

'What do you think? Gambling.'

'And you got robbed. Who would do it? Who would rob one of my places? Who would dare?'

'Scum.'

'You are right. Only scum would do it. What does that make you? When I was a lad a robber pointed a gun at me. So I went at him and I took the gun off him. Then I had to teach him, and everyone else. So I shot him in the leg. Then the other leg. The arm. The other arm. I wanted to see how long it would take a man to die, who had a bullet in each limb.'

'And how long did it take?'

'I got bored of his moaning and put a bullet in his face, so I never found out. How often are you in here? All the time, I expect. Drinking and gambling. How much money did you let them take from you?'

'I had no choice. They'd have killed customers... about seven thousand pounds.'

'I let you run around and this is what happens. You have exams soon. Go down and get in the car and wait for me. No more fun for you this weekend, you're studying. And you'll be sticking by me, so I see you do it. Well?'

'Well what?'

'Say "Yes, Dad." Go on.'

The lad mumbled something, then stalked off, stepping carefully around the tea puddles, anxious not to get his fancy trainers dirty.

Uncle Seven's slippers arrived at the edge of David's eye-line.

'When times are good, people grow soft. Look at us. We thought, just because of who we were, no one will touch us. This has been proved wrong. Now everyone will know they can take from us.'

He was addressing the figurine of Guandi: the God of War, with his armour and halberd, his comically overdone fierceness – a red face and a snarl, beetle-brows over popping eyes. The thing didn't mean much to David, but you put it up and everyone knew: knew not to make a fuss, start fights, argue about the cut. They knew, or should know, not to rip the place off with guns.

'You. Get up. Sit.'

David obeyed. Uncle Seven stood with his hands on his hips. His muscular chest was bare, hairless, with a black circle, about six inches in diameter, tattooed in the centre. All he had on was the dressing gown and underpants. David couldn't help but recall the stories he had heard. How as a red pole in Hong Kong, he had fought for control of drug markets, kidnapped businessmen, robbed jewellery shops with grenades. During the tong wars in Macau, it was whispered, he shot men from the pillion seat of a motorbike, and chopped a colleague to death for losing him a deal. But all that was long ago, in another country. Surely age had mellowed him.

David coughed and began his speech. 'Honoured master… this tragedy was terrible, and so much the worse for being avoidable. Such a shame that the security system was not given a chance to work. If only my doorman, downstairs, had pressed the button beside him, which locks this heavy door, none of this would ever have happened. I…'

The tong cut him off 'My lazy son is supposed to be studying business. But he doesn't make an effort. I believe I have discovered why. How often is he in here?'

David said, carefully, 'I could not rightly say.'

'Every night?'

'Many nights. Not every night.'

'You give him booze? You keep him entertained?'

David wanted to plead, what was I supposed to do? He's your son. I can't not give him everything he wants. Instead he said, 'I give him what he asks for. But advise caution.'

'He is the weak wind, and sharks come to take his money?'

A degree of candour here might help his cause. 'I keep an eye on him. I'd say he wins nearly as much as he loses. And recently, I would say, his game has improved. He takes it seriously and does not drink too much. I think people are afraid of winning big against him. Because of who he is. When they are up a little, they leave. I was going to tell you. I thought, if he starts losing big I will tell his father.'

'He pays you his cut?'

'I waive that.'

'You've been encouraging him then, haven't you?'

Impossible to tell what Uncle Seven was thinking. The chunky glasses, which seemed wilfully archaic, helped to conceal his expression. Everything he said was in the same even tone. He would make a good gambler, probably better than his son.

'He came to me with a scheme. He would put marks on the back of the tiles, invisible to the normal eye but if you wore certain contact lenses you would see them. I said no.'

'Quite right.'

'But I thought that if he lost too much, I would let him use them, until he got his money back.'

'What a position he put you in! Quite tricky. Well, this man who took your car...'

'Did you catch him?'

'He has been caught. He is being brought here.'

'Here? Oh… and the thief?'

'The thief had already gone.'

'You are so clever. The cop might know where he is. Yes, he might have learned a great deal.' That cockroach. The robbers were reprehensible of course, but at least there was sense behind their actions. Taking a man's car just because you wanted a ride was a whole other level of shitty behaviour.

'You know anything about him?'

'Name of Ma Jian. A cop from the mainland, place called Qitaihe. He won pretty big, I guess he was trying to get his money back.'

'Beat cop? You know what they're like out there, they'll give any thug a uniform.'

'An Inspector, I believe. Crisp accent, like a newsreader.'

Uncle Seven was looking at a map on his phone. 'It's way up north. They do speak well up there, don't they? Clear as melted snow. Nice women too. Tall and white.'

'Some class about him. But dressed down.'

'So why is he here?'

All these irrelevant queries. Had the Incense Master become slow? But David was careful to answer as helpfully as he could. 'Said he was on vacation. But that didn't seem likely. You know how mainlanders dress up when they're abroad. He looked like a kitchen hand with twenty quid to blow.'

'How much did he win?'

'About six thousand.'

'So this important Chinese citizen, a man of status and privilege, bastion of the law, is so desperate to get back a few thousand in gambling winnings that he starts some spur of the moment scheme involving what, assault, car theft, kidnap? In a foreign country where his position counts for nothing?'

'Perhaps it's face. A man like that must be used to doing whatever he wants. Yes sir, no sir, all day long. A hood aiming a gun at him, the indignity of being robbed – it knocked him over the edge, drove him crazy.'

'Possibly.' Uncle Seven was back on his phone again. David tried to steer him gently back to the issue at hand. 'He'll not only know what the lad looked like, he might have talked to him too. He might know where they were going, what they plan to do with the money.'

Uncle Seven stroked under his chin. It looked like thought, but there was also something sinister about the gesture, as if he was stroking his vulnerable area because he was thinking about yours. David told himself to get a grip, his fancy was running away with him. The problem was the man was so hard to read you interpreted the smallest movement.

He said he wanted to make some calls so David retreated to the litle kitchen to give him privacy. What could he say to prove his strength of character, integrity, and lack of culpability? Whatever it was, he had not said it yet. He had been shaky so far, very shaky. He would have to shape up fast.

This was not much of a place. Chipped floor tiles, plastic furniture, strip-lights. But he had made an effort to brighten it up with prints, paper fans, fake flowers. The ashtrays were collected from all over, no two the same. It was not much, but he had thought it his. It wasn't, of course. The man in the dressing gown could take everything with a word.

A little paint had chipped off the kitchen window. He heard vehicles arrive below, and peeked. He saw his BMW and a couple of black SUVs come to a halt in the car park.

A couple of guys hurried from the SUV and tugged and pushed at a package on the back seat. He glimpsed something substantial, wrapped up in tape. It slid and jerked. David realised it was the mainlander and retreated, shaken by the sight. Really, he reminded himself, it was good news: the mainlander would lead to the thieves and their loot, and the BMW was only the first in a long chain of returns. He listened to the burden being lugged up the stairs, and came out to see when it was brought into the room.

Tables were cleared to the side, and the red poles dumped the cop on the floor. He was wrapped with silver duct tape, arms trussed behind his back, legs fast together. His sweatshirt hood was drawn over his head and taped down across his eyes, and more tape smothered his mouth. Of his face, only his nose was visible. The men had obviously rushed out, as Uncle Seven had. Some were barefoot and one was in a waiter's black suit.

'Look what we caught.'

'Shines like a fish.'

One man rubbed an arm.

'But kicks like a donkey.'

Uncle Seven told the red poles to wait downstairs. David wished he could have gone with them. He supposed there would soon be screaming and unpleasantness, and mess that would be hard and distressing to clean up.

He wanted to say, I am only a man of business, I can be no help here, could I not too be dismissed? He suspected he knew what was going to happen now. As punishment or test, Uncle Seven was going to ask him to help with some forceful questioning. The idea made him queasy.

He realised with a start that Uncle Seven had a gun, a little black revolver with a short barrel, no bigger than a starting pistol. One of the red poles must have given it to him. He held it loosely by his side.

'What did you do,' said Uncle Seven, 'back in the territory?'

Again this oblique approach. 'I ran a bookies.'

'Everything written on rice paper, so you could eat it if the police raided. You were never robbed?'

'No.'

'Because everybody knew, it's not worth it. Don't cross a tong. But they don't know any more. Maybe they are right to test us. That is what young people do. Test, and see if there is weakness. So. It is time for the new generation to learn its lesson.'

'Yes. I see.' He didn't though. The gun made David nervous and he didn't like to look at it. 'I think you need to talk to him... find out what he knows... I don't...'

'Be quiet.'

David felt immedlately contrite and, head down, mumbled an apology. If the Incense Master had decided the cop was to die, he was in no place to object. 'Of course, I'm sorry.'

Maybe he would be expected to do the shooting? As a form of punishment. In which case the secret was probably not to think about it overmuch. Pulling a trigger was merely a little twitch. He could look away at the decisive moment. It would be painful but at least that would be the end of it.

'If you would like, I can do the...' He couldn't bring himself to say the word. 'Use the gun.'

'You'll be happy to do it, I see. But that will not be neccessary.'

The tone was light, even mocking. David looked up. The gun was aimed at him. Uncle Seven's grip on it was firm, and the thought struck David that perhaps something appalling was about to happen to him.

'I… Sir…'

He fumbled for the right way to seek clarification without sounding rude, but before he could speak another syllable there was a tremendous noise and he was kicked so hard in the chest that he fell down on his back. He tried to right himself and failed, as all his strength had suddenly gone. His shirt was hot and wet. Blood was spilling all over the floor: what a mess it would be to clean it. He looked up and the gun fired again.

7

The bangs made Jian's ears buzz. He had identified the Manager by his voice, though had not understood what was said, as he and the other man had talked in Cantonese. Judging by the Manager's supplicating tone, he had been explaining himself to a displeased superior. Who had shot him. And for the crime of being robbed. Typical gang politics. Gratuitous violence was a crude but effective way to cow and control. A chicken was killed to frighten the monkeys. Now all would know the price of failure.

Something just as terminal seemed likely to be about to happen to him. Whatever occurred, he had to keep his daughter out of it, must not even admit to her existence. He mentally examined his possessions for anything that might lead to her. Her number was in his phone, but with no name attached. A red dot on a page of his map book marked where they were staying. But it was not labelled, and there was nothing to distinguish it from other dots marking bus stops, shops, Chinese restaurants, gambling dens and so on. It should be okay.

When they tortured him, he would quickly give up everything he knew about To-Mu, the robber. Then the trick would be to convince them he was broken, with nothing more to reveal, and could be safely despatched. He was glad about the gun, it suggested that at the end he'd have a quick exit. Perhaps he could anger the tong boss, get him to fire off in a snatch of temper. The whole business to be concluded with no risk to his girl: that was the plan. He was set. He could take his bullet.

A scraping sound started, grew louder. A chair was being dragged across the floor towards him. He had done the same. Nothing like it for getting a suspect on edge. He concentrated on breathing steadily, clearing his mind, unwinding his body.

Tape was peeled away, his hood was yanked off, the gag tugged down. He was, as he had suspected, back in the Lucky Day gambling den, on the floor, among scattered tiles. The body of the Manager lay close enough to smell. A slick pool of blood welled beneath him. His face held an expression of frozen consternation.

A stocky man wrapped in a loose towelling dressing gown sat backwards on a chair, legs apart, arms resting on top of the chair back, revolver held lightly in one hand. He was in well-preserved middle age, with a wide, impassive face, very short bristly hair and thick glasses. His tone was conversational. 'Hello Inspector Ma Jian. You can call me Uncle Seven.'

A native Mandarin speaker from the sound of it, with a touch of Hunan gravel in the accent. It would be Hunan. After politicians and spicy food, gangsters were that province's main export.

Jian spat blood. 'How did you get that nickname? Suck seven cocks in one sitting?'

'Crude.'

'You were born under a peach tree?'

'How did you guess?'

It was slang: it meant you were a tong. Jian went on. 'My Gran had a peach tree in her garden. It was rotten. When I grew up I cut it down. I chopped it into pieces. I burnt it.' He cleared his throat. 'Then I pissed on it.'

The gangsters Jian had dealt with in the past would have flown into a rage by now, and started blasting. But this one did not react at all, it was as if he hadn't heard.

'I was supposed to be taking the weekend off, spending a couple of days with a convivial air hostess,' Uncle Seven said. 'Now my simple pleasures have been ruined... I rang your station – Qitaihe. I talked to your boss, Inspector. I told him I was a representative of the police over here with a few inquiries. He was quite forthcoming. He told me the story.'

Jian did not like his business known by anyone, least of all criminals. The loose-lipped DI had no doubt enjoyed filling the man in. Jian's unfortunate circumstances were hardly a state secret, but still, it felt like a betrayal.

'For someone in your position, I imagine six thousand is a considerable loss. No wonder you were so desperate to get it back.' He was rubbing the gun with his dressing gown belt. 'So. I know about you. Let me tell you about me. I am Incense Master for the Big Circle Boys. You may know the name.'

Jian had heard it a couple of times. One of the tongs that flourished like weeds in Hong Kong in the last century, when it was under the yoke of the British colonials. Unusual for having strong links with the mainland. But he had not heard the name for many years. Perhaps they had moved operations abroad.

'We were started by ex-Red Guards. I grew up on the Chairman's dictums. We all did, didn't we? They are burnt into our hearts. *The people are the sea in which the revolution swims.* Let me tell you my favourite. No flowery language. A simple phrase and a guide to action. *Make one thing serve two purposes.* I will give you an example of the practical application of this thinking.'

Uncle Seven stood and went behind him and Jian felt metal being pressed against his hands and fingers. Then the man came back around and now he was holding the gun delicately, through the material of his dressing gown.

'Your fingerprints are all over this gun, Inspector. It will be stored, along with this unlucky failure.' He gestured at the body. 'Any time I like, an anonymous phone call can be made to the British police, telling them where to find a shallow grave containing both body and gun. Then witnesses will come forward to tell how you quarrelled with this man, then went and got a gun and shot him. The police here are very motivated when it comes to catching murderers and locking them in prison. Even when the victim, like this one, was a person of no great import. If they want you, you will not stay out of their grasp for long, however well you hide.'

The man stepped away and came back with a knife. He began to slice at Jian's bindings.

'But that doesn't have to happen. Your boss told me you were good. Show me how good. Find the robbers and bring them to me. In return, this unfortunate will vanish, so will the gun, no call will be made to the police, all witnesses will stay silent, and you'll get your six thousand pounds back.'

Jian's hands were free. Uncle Seven gave him the knife and he slashed at the tape around his legs.

'A failed subordinate is punished, an investigator commissioned. One thing, two purposes. Let's make it good sport. I'll give you the rest of the weekend.'

Jian was rubbing his wrists, squeezing circulation back into stinging hands. He wiped blood off his lips, said, 'I'll need the car.'

TIGERS AND FLIES

老虎和苍蝇

8

Get the English tea ceremony right and the results were most refreshing. WeiWei added milk to a mug of boiled water, then smushed the teabag on the mug's side with a spoon until the drink darkened to warm beige. She slung the bag into the sink with a wrist flick as graceful as a dancer's.

It was brewed hotter than normal tea, so preparation was followed by a cool down period that formed a pause for contemplation. She held mug high, so steam caressed her face as she closed her eyes and dwelt enjoyably on future plans. When she got back to China she was going to start a boutique. She would nurture bold young designers, hone fashion's cutting edge, offer the smart and deserving affordably priced elite chic. She imagined a cool, white space, more art gallery than shop, fragranced and delightful, a haven of beauty.

Soon she would broach the subject with her father. She rehearsed her spiel. First, remind him what a filial daughter she had been of late, so dutiful and responsible – enduring their squalid circumstances without complaint, cooking and cleaning and laundering every day. Then unfurl her grand design. Show it was no idle dream. Demonstrate shrewdness and practicality by discoursing on marketing, footfall, supplementary revenue streams. Then, crucially, reveal how inexpensive it would actually be. A hundred thousand yuan, that's all she needed. It wasn't that much, was it? She was sure he'd financed wilder schemes, for greater amounts, by mistresses she wasn't supposed to know about.

A knock at the door curtailed her ruminations and she opened her eyes to gritty reality. She was leaning against the kitchen unit in a cramped and dismal London bedsit, looking at a spattering of mould on the wall, a frayed curtain failing to reach the sill, a pair of sagging beds.

The knock came again and she continued ignoring it. If it was not her father – and he had his own key, so it wouldn't be – it could be no one she wanted to talk to.

'Hello? I know you're in there.' Their landlord, the Captain, speaking his slurry, accented English. 'We need to have a chat.'

He would be after the rent, as he had been the last two times they had talked. It was overdue. But this was her father's business, not hers. She shouted, 'My father's not here. He'll be back later.'

Outrageously, the door was unlocked and opened. She knew he had a key but to see him use it was disturbing. Any sense that this was her private space was an illusion.

The Captain was a chubby man whose stubby hands were always moving. Now they were running up and down his sides, as if to smooth out the wrinkles in his usual outfit of military fatigues. Despite those, and the title he insisted on, she could not believe he'd ever served in any armed forces, he was too slovenly and out of shape. She could tell he wasn't native, but could not place where he might be from – Eastern Europe, the Middle East, South America? And she would never ask, as she didn't want to encourage the idea that she might be at all interested in him personally.

He said sombrely, 'I'm afraid we need to have words.' Why was he afraid? In their dealings, he had all the power. If anyone should be afraid, it should be her.

He looked her up and down, and she wished she was wearing more than yoga pants and a hoodie. 'Way. Way Way

Way. Don't Chinese people usually take an English name here? Coco. Joy. Daisy. You'd make a good Daisy.'

These did not seem the words he was afraid to have, but she was in no hurry to hear those, so indulged this lame attempt at conversation. 'They do that as they have names that are difficult for English people to say. My name is not difficult though.'

'As in, Way of the Fist. Way of the Dragon...' He smirked. 'Way of All Flesh.'

Had he made a joke? She sipped her tea. The first sip was normally treasured but she found she could not enjoy it now. 'I'm sure you want to speak to my father. He will be back at any moment. He is at the bank getting money.'

'Is he applying for a loan?'

'No, he is getting his money. He has money. Lots of money. It's just getting hold of it that is a difficulty. He's a top policeman.'

Should she have said that? Perhaps it was not wise to volunteer information in circumstances like these. But back home, such a revelation would ensure good treatment and there was something reflexive to letting it slip out in times of insecurity. Well, it couldn't harm their cause, could it, for him to understand that they had some weight of authority, albeit a far distant one, behind them?

'Course he's a top policeman.' She had difficulty with irony and sarcasm in English, but was pretty sure that was an example of it. 'A top China cop, if you say so, and his fetching daughter. Rich, apparently. But with out of date visas and money troubles, holed up in a budget bedsit they're having difficulty paying for. What's the story, as a matter of interest?'

WeiWei had come to the UK to study, just over a year ago. She had dropped out of college and dated a gangster, and after seeing things she shouldn't, he'd tried to kill her. She'd got a message to her father, and he had rushed to the UK to help. Once that traumatic business had been concluded they had tried to return home. But at the airport, her father couldn't buy tickets: his cards were rejected. He'd made her wait in a café while he called home to see what was up. Some hours later he'd come and told her: his accounts had been frozen by the bank and he had no access to any funds. Just a mistake, he reassured her, a bureaucratic error caused by an overzealous computer. But they had better find somewhere to crash till his funds were released. The only money they had was the little that was in her British account, so it would have to be the cheapest room they could find, with a landlord prepared to overlook an expired visa.

She had found this place from a handwritten sign in a newsagent's window. Jian insisted they look on the bright side. Sharing a room they would really get to know each other: she should see this as a brief, character-building time of hard living, like being sent to the country, referring to when he'd been forced to work on a farm as a youth.

That had been three weeks ago. Bafflingly, aggravatingly, this dreary interlude, as meaningless as an airport layover and even more uncomfortable, was just going on and on. His tourist visa had run out and he had joined her in being technically an illegal immigrant. She had, as he had said, got to know him better: learning, for example, how little they had to say to each other, how uncouth his manners were, how loud he snored, and the state of his underwear. No progress had been made in unfreezing his funds, as far as she could tell. When questioned, her father always had an explanation, reassuring but confusing, concerning the ineffable workings of China's banking apparatus. Some cash was coming in, enough to get by on. Supposedly it was special compensation sent to last them till the corrections were worked through the system, though she suspected it was being donated by well-wishers back home, and he was too proud to admit taking charity.

But she was not about to reveal any of this to the creepy Captain. She said, 'We're on holiday.'

He smiled indulgently, telling her that he didn't believe her but wasn't going to push it. 'What it is... I look at you, and I think, here's someone who knows which side her bread is buttered.'

Another opportunity to avoid getting towards his point. 'What a good idiom. I will have to write it down.' Any new phrase she heard, she wrote in the back of her notebook. When she had scribbled it he took the book off her and read aloud. 'By and by. Soy face. Air of condescension.' He opened it at the front, where she wrote her research. 'This season's colours are puce and yellow. These are flattering and elegant and work like neutrals so are easy to... bend? Blend... You write this yourself?'

She wanted to snatch it off him. Even her father wasn't allowed to look at it.

'I copy out of magazines.'

'You little scholar.'

He held the book out. As she took it he moved his hand so that his clammy fingers covered hers. He must have seen the distaste in her face, for his tone grew abruptly formal, and he came to his point. 'It is an unfortunate fact that you're in breach of contract, and my patience is at an end.'

'I said, my father will be here any minute and he can help you then.'

'He's not here now though. And I need payment. What I think is, in the absence of a monetary satisfaction...' – he stepped towards her and spoke breathily – 'we're going to have to come to an alternative arrangement.'

He smelled strongly of stale tobacco with topnotes of sweet sickliness, from that apple beer he drank. 'It's quite normal, and other tenants find it useful, when they are in difficulty.' His matter-of-factness, his obliqueness, the difficulty of understanding his accented English, meant that she took a moment to grasp what was being proposed. He stepped closer and leered.

He put a hand on her shoulder and made a kind of purring noise. The rough palm moved up her rigid shoulder and his fingers touched her neck. She said, 'Excuse me. Actually, no.' She was going to throw scalding tea at him if he went any further. Any moment now, if this couldn't be stopped by any other means. Now his fingers were in her hair—

She heard a familiar coughing in the corridor. 'Here is my father now,' shouted WeiWei with relief. 'My father is home.'

The Captain stepped back. He cracked his knuckles and crossed his arms. In a confrontation he was no match for her father. But he didn't have to be, did he? He had many friends and they had none.

The door creaked open. When WeiWei saw her father her relief flipped into alarm. His face was mottled with bruises and spattered with blood. His clothes were filthy and a grazed knee showed through a rip in his sweatpants.

She shrieked, 'Dad! What happened?'

'I got robbed.' He frowned at the Captain. 'What is he doing here?'

The Captain declaimed loud and slow. 'Rent. Overdue.' He slapped the fingers of one hand into the palm of the other. 'Pay money money money.'

Why was this lecher still banging on about his petty concerns? WeiWei turned on him, emboldened by outrage and concern. 'Oh come on,' she snapped. 'Look at him. Can't you see he's just been assaulted? He's bleeding, look. Leave it. Come back later.'

She wet a dishcloth in the sink and started wiping her father's face. 'Have some… heartness.' Not the exact word she was looking for, but something like it. 'For heaven sake. He's been robbed. He had the money but it's been stolen. Surely you can see that.'

'Some policeman.' The Captain sighed and let his arms drop. 'Alright, I'll let it go. For one day. But you lay it out for the big man, yes? I'm not messing about here. I'm coming round again this time tomorrow. You sort it then, one way or the other…' He gave her a sly, shifty look. 'Otherwise you're out. Don't think I won't make good. Have to be harsh, the people I deal with. Warn you, I'll be turning up mob-handed. You know, with others. Mates.'

'You will get the money. Thank you.'

She could still smell him after he had gone.

Jian took the cloth off her and dropped it in the sink. 'Wanted rent did he? Don't worry about him. I'll pay him, and we'll be out of here in no time, shack up somewhere much nicer.' He took off his joggers and sweatshirt, revealing bruising on thighs and upper arm. 'Just got a job to do first.'

'You should go to a doctor.'

'I'm fine.'

'I'll go and get some plasters, get in the shower and…'

'No, I'm off out and I need your help.'

He pulled on his other joggers and a T-shirt and hoodie. It was all charity shop gear, picked solely on price. The T-shirt proclaimed him a ROCK GOD.

'At least drink something.' She offered her tea.

'When I start drinking that muck, that's when you'll know there's something wrong with me. Oil up! Let's go.'

'Right now? But…'

'Come on.'

Their flat was on the top floor of a block. There was a lift at

57

the end of the corridor, but it rattled and the light flickered, and they didn't trust it. She followed her father down flights of stairs. She caught whiffs of curry and skunk. 'So what happened? You got robbed in the street? After you'd been to the bank? Where?'

'I don't know. You know how I get lost.'

The block had been converted from offices, and traces of its former life remained in the fluorescent strip-lights, fibre ceiling boards, and grey carpet tiles. Behind an old reception desk in the lobby, a board held faded names of forgotten businesses. Their floor had once been OLYMPUS NETWORK SOLUTIONS. She hurried after him, across pocked tarmac, past big metal bins, onto the narrow pavement flanking a dual carriageway.

'They must have looked at you and thought, oh yes, a kitchen hand, easy target. Robbers target Chinese people, because they know they get paid in cash.'

'Why does everyone think I look like a kitchen hand?'

'You want to be the big tough guy, and so you think, I can't let myself get robbed, but that's not how you have to think, you really have to be sensible, you have to be smart about it, and not try to fight, but instead, just give them what they want, and walk away. Because they might have a gun or a knife and kill you just like that. This is a dangerous city. I know like you don't, from the newspapers. Gangs of wild young men rob and stab. You're actually lucky it wasn't worse. Slow down please, and tell me what is going on.'

They had arrived at a strip of shops: for groceries and alcohol, for betting, for vapes and coffee. He led her to the last, a cramped internet café. She came here every day. It was run by black men who drank coffee from tiny cups, and sometimes knelt to pray on mats put down in the phone booths. Posters advertised remittance services and handwritten signs read

NO PORNO. She would spend 50p for half an hour and read blogs and Weibo, browse dating shows and fashion on Youku, or watch a subtitled Korean soap at double speed. What she really wanted to do was check her WeChat, but it wasn't even installed on the grimy computers. Her father got them a stall.

'So?'

'Finding someone. Young student name of To-Mu. His friends are in a karaoke bar at the moment. In a district that begins with a *sh* sound. Definitely *di-che*, hard, at the end. Shi-wo-li-di-che. Something like that.'

'And we ask them where he is.'

'Exactly.'

'Is he missing?'

'Not really.'

'You're finding him for?'

'Concerned parties would like a word.'

'So you're like a private detective? Getting paid?'

'That's the good news.'

She found a London map and read out names. 'Shadwell, Shepherd's Bush, Shirley, Shooters Hill, Shoreditch.'

'That's it.'

'I'll look on Google.'

'What's that?'

'It's what they have instead of Baidu. Shoreditch is a trendy area.'

'There might be a thousand karaoke venues.'

'We're not in China now.' She pointed at the screen. 'There's only three. So who is paying you?'

'Concerned parties.'

'You won't tell me.'

'Just help me and don't ask questions.'

WeiWei wanted to exclaim: for heaven's sake, is this any way to treat your daughter? Under normal circumstances she would storm out at this point: let him find this lad his own way. But thought of her future plans gave her pause. To do as she was told – what a favour he would owe in return. She swallowed annoyance, curiosity and concern, and started opening links.

'They don't do karaoke much here. Or they do, but it's different, like a talent show, so it's mostly just show-offs making fools of themselves. Let me see... That one's closed... That one's more of a restaurant, it's probably not there... this looks promising...'

The internet was slow. She watched the buffering circle spin round and round and thought it a metaphor for her condition. When the site finally opened she read aloud in English, never mind that he wouldn't understand: 'All-Stars. London's premier karaoke venue. Fifteen luxury booths and two super deluxe. Caters to all special occasions. Tens of thousands of tunes available on our state-of-the-art audio-visual systems.' There were pictures of the neon-lit exterior, the song rooms, the audio equipment, food platters, cocktails. She returned to Chinese. 'This'll be the one. I'll look up bus routes.'

'No need, I borrowed a car.'

'I'm sure we'll find this lad in no time at all.'

9

Shan Xiang was heading home from Sutton train station. The dull walk down placid suburban streets, so familiar she could do it with her eyes closed, helped slough away the stresses off her workday and reclaim her domestic self. She wondered whether she could be bothered to cook the fish in the freezer. She would have to do potatoes as well. Or she could order a curry. She was tired after work and wanted an easy night. She decided she would cook if her son Tom was there to join her.

So she called him. Still no reply. Probably he was asleep or wearing headphones or engrossed in some comic or film. She'd called a couple of times yesterday, and four or five times today, and got no answer, and not a word in return.

Was it too much to ask for a quick 'Hi Mum'? Or a text to say hello and yes he would be wanting dinner or no actually he wouldn't. She resolved to have a quiet word, when she finally achieved contact, about the responsibility to communicate, the need for a bit more back and forth. The rule, at least in her mind – perhaps it had not been well articulated – was that he was allowed to come and go as he pleased, as long as he let her know where he was. Clearly it was not as well understood as she had thought. I am modern, I am flexible, I am not unreasonable, I am happy for you to have lots of freedom, of course I am, but a mother needs to know where her boy is. Don't shut me out.

She opened the front door and called him. No reply came. The house felt empty, she could sense that he wasn't there, though she checked anyway. His bed had not been slept in.

That was unusual, and gave her pause. She had seen him last on Thursday morning. He went for a jog, neglected to eat breakfast, ran for his train. All as usual. In the evening he had called to say he was going out to eat with friends. He hadn't come home Thursday night, had he? And, it seems, Friday night he hadn't come home either, and now most of Saturday was gone too… he'd been gone for three whole days. And all without telling her where he was. Nothing seemed missing, his bag was where he usually left it. She looked in the bathroom. His toothbrush was still there, and the supplements he was religious about taking.

The LED on the house phone in the hall was flashing, a message was waiting. Almost no one called that number except her relatives back home, and they always hung up if there was no reply. She played it.

'Mum? I've got something I have to do. I… it's going to be fine. But I can't talk about it right now.' Then a long pause. 'Don't call me. I'll see you in a couple of days… Monday, I think. I'll see you on Monday. Bye.'

She listened to the message twice more. The nonchalance was affected, there was strain beneath it. That catch in his voice when he said 'fine' – was he in pain? Why did he sound out of breath? Why say it was fine? That's not what you would say if it was fine. It's what you would say if it wasn't and you didn't want your mother to know. Why leave a voicemail on that phone, a phone he never used? When he knew her mobile number perfectly well. He must have done it because he knew she would be out, and wouldn't pick up. He did it because he didn't want to talk to her.

This was all so out of character. He was not some stormy teen who lashed out and looked for trouble. He was quiet, conscientious and careful. She had always worried that he was too nerdy, too bookish, too timid, too bound to home and screen. If he went out at all, it was to cosplay conventions, or to his friends' houses, where they played role-playing games. He spent his evenings watching TV, if his homework was done. He owned a sewing machine, for heaven's sake.

She sat on the stairs and rang his mobile again. Still no answer. She sent a text: 'I GOT YR MESSAGE. WHAT'S GOING ON? R U IN TROUBLE?

A few minutes later she sent another: I DONT CARE WHAT IT IS. YOU CAN TALK TO ME ABOUT IT

She had no appetite. Something was wrong, and she was not going to rest till she had got to the bottom of it.

10)

WeiWei liked Shoreditch: lively, fashion-forward, a good example of 'shabby chic' and 'post-modern urban cool'. Luridly decorated bars and cafés lined streets busy with a boisterous Saturday night crowd. A lot of the girls looked a bit like boys and the boys a bit like girls and they all had tattoos. It would be fun to live around here, and great for her research. Her father, in contrast, was unimpressed, tutting at the sight of grown men riding skateboards, wondering aloud why the graffiti wasn't cleaned off.

WeiWei caught their reflection in the glass of the All-Stars door. They looked a trashy duo: a middle-aged lout and a hot mess of a girl with no make-up, unkempt hair, dressed in clothes barely suitable for a trip to the supermarket. Fortunately it was pretty dark inside. Giggly ladies in sashes trotted past. A barman was making a show out of shaking up a cocktail. WeiWei smiled at a receptionist, told him she was here for a birthday party, she was late, her phone was out of charge, where were they please? There was only one party tonight, they were in SUPERNOVA.

In a dim, red-lit corridor they heard faint snatches of song from behind padded doors. At SUPERNOVA she peered through a porthole, at the usual scene. Ten to fifteen youths, some standing and swaying, most sitting. A girl and a guy crooned into microphones. She knew the song they were killing, an oldie: Loving You by SHE.

Jian said, 'Why they're all Chinese! I thought they'd be *laowai*. Go back to the car. I can deal with it from here.'

She stopped him with a hand on his chest. 'They won't help you. Even if you tell them you're a cop. Actually, especially then. I know the modern youth. They don't trust authority. They'll clam up soon as you start asking questions. Then what are you going to do, smack them around? You're not at home now. This job requires a delicate touch. Let me go in there.'

'I don't...'

'They might be English Chinese and speak no Mandarin, or Hong Kong Chinese who only speak Cantonese. I can charm the information out of them, in English if necessary. Come on, I've had nothing to do for weeks. I want a challenge.' Plus, what a favour he was going to owe. He could not refuse her after this.

'Alright. To-Mu studies computer design. Tall, skinny, ponytail, earring in left ear. Half-Chinese, mother from Shandong, English-born. He was invited out tonight but he couldn't make it.'

WeiWei had long noted how westerners, in certain environments, socialised freely with strangers. In pub or club it was acceptable, even encouraged, to chat to fellow revellers. The Chinese were more circumspect, and the groups they went out in were invitation only.

'We'll need a plan.'

11)

WeiWei watched her father barge the SUPERNOVA door open. He was waving a bottle of beer and slurring, 'Happy Birthday! It's my birthday too!' She'd seen that boorish side before, and he hadn't been acting then. The door closed behind him and through the porthole she watched him lunge and shout. The singing stopped.

She closed her eyes and counted to twenty, then followed him in. He'd got hold of the microphone and was yelling, 'Sing a birthday song! All together! *Yi er san si*!' The mike screeched with feedback and booze looped from his bottle to spatter mortified and hostile youths. A lad rose to challenge him. Jian swung the bottle in blind merriment and nearly caught him, and he thought better of it and sat down.

'Dad, get out of there! You're drunk! Get out!' She put as much vigour into her performance as he was putting into his: there was plenty of backed-up frustration to draw on. She stamped her foot and said with secret relish, 'You're an idiot! I'm so ashamed!'

The music was drowned out by Jian's drunken barks and WeiWei's yells.

'It's birthday time! Sing a song!'

'Dad, get out of there, get out! Oh, I'm so sorry!'

She grabbed him by the arm, and he stumbled into a table, and a beer bottle toppled. Trying to right it, Jian knocked over two more. Trying to catch them, he upended a popcorn dish. Then he collapsed, onto three or four shrieking girls. She helped him to stand in a frothing beer puddle.

'Sorry, so sorry!'

WeiWei got him turned and aimed. She coaxed him forward, opened the door, then got behind and shoved. He advanced, pirouetted, then lurched into the corridor, where he could be heard singing tunelessly until the padded door closed with a sigh. A couple of boys rushed to the door, to see the intruder safely away. A girl brushed popcorn off her dress and another tapped the wet microphone to see if it still worked.

'Oh, I'm so sorry! I'll pay for any damage!' WeiWei tugged a hunk of tissues from a dispenser and got down on her knees to help mop fizzing booze. 'I'm so embarrassed. Please don't get him thrown out! He won't trouble you again. I'm so sorry. If he's done any damage I'll pay for it. He's been drinking all day, and I told him he can't hold it.'

She blinked, and tears flowed. 'I just... I can't believe it. He makes me so mad. The whole time he's here he's acted up and I'm totally sick of it.'

A lad said, 'Don't worry about it. My father's the same.' Another went to get more tissues from the bathroom and a third reassured her that they weren't going to make a complaint and didn't want her money. The girls fussed with their clothes.

WeiWei rocked on her heels and wiped her eyes. She raised her voice, knowing that despite how she looked, her pure, sharp accent projected her high-class origins and showed that she was one of them. 'Oh, you're so nice. I can't thank you enough. You're so... civilised.'

She had a feeling for atmospheres: this one could still go either way. More manipulation was required. Making sure none of the girls saw, she touched the knee of one bespectacled lad. Standing, she touched the shoulder of another and breathed, 'Oh you're too kind,' to a third.

She said to the group, 'I miss civilised. You know who he's got in the room with him? This old whore. Both shouting and

67

drinking, it's awful. It's humiliating. It's too much, really.' The song finished and the room was silent. She slid sopping tissue away with her feet, so she was looking down when she said, 'I don't want to go back there.'

A pause: perhaps she had been too hasty. The microphone crackled as it was put down. Someone turned a page of a songbook. She sensed that looks were being exchanged.

The three lads with glasses said, pretty much simultaneously, 'Uh, you could hang out here for a while. Why don't you stay a bit? There's room for one more.'

She acted as if the guy beside her had said it too: a smile just for him. Then she aimed her attention rapidly around, giving each head a sentence. 'Is that okay? Thanks. Oh, you're so kind. Maybe just for a minute. Oh, such a relief.'

A space was made for her, and she wiggled onto the sofa.

12)

There were painted planets on the walls and model rockets in niches by the TV. The popcorn container was shaped like an astronaut's helmet. Glittering stars hanging from the ceiling rotated in the breeze from the air conditioning unit.

Introductions were made. What a relief, after so many months of complicated western names, to be given ones that were easy to say and remember. They were, as she had guessed, east coast big city types, students of either international trade or art and design.

WeiWei thought she knew rich kids. The *tuhao*, or 'new rich', that she met back home, the children of oil magnates, bureaucrats or factory owners, wore head-to-toe designer labels. They flourished chunky watches and their home-screen was a picture of their sleek car. This lot were – what – subtler, more refined, in disguise? Many of the girls styled themselves in a way that seemed wilfully perverse, with, for example, short dyed hair, chunky glasses, and flat, mannish shoes. The boys were in street-style gear, mostly black with discreet or absent logos, and not one wore a shirt, shiny shoes or a watch.

She might have wheedled the invite off the boys, but she ignored them now, aware that she was only allowed on the sufferance of the girls. She set about befriending a pair. One showed off her new tattoo, of the Indian God Ganesh. When she went home, she'd buy long-sleeved clothes, she was confident her parents would never find out. The other wanted to tell WeiWei about her food blog. Then a lad gave her a microphone, told her she couldn't stay unless she sang.

To showcase her English ability, she picked a song called 'Panic' by a novelty band called The Smiths. Standing and crooning, flicking her hair, swinging her hips, she felt the currents in the room shift and the chatter still. Her powers had not been used recently – she did not count the creepy Captain – and deploying them was satisfying. She derived a craftman's pleasure from the demonstration of exceptional skill. But of course, she must be careful, or the girls would start to resent her. So she missed a note, fumbled the mike, and tried to look awkward. Nope, that didn't work, they just liked her even more: they were puppies every one. She sat to finish the song then relinquished the mike.

Someone asked her, 'Why is your father here?'

'He's on a fact-finding mission. Government-sponsored, of course.'

'I know just the type. Has he found a lot of facts?'

'Probably not the ones he's supposed to.'

She tuned into a conversation about college. 'The first year I worked so hard I thought my hair was going to fall out. Then I discovered that the professors are instructed never to fail an overseas Chinese. Because the colleges can't afford to lose our money. So I thought, well, what is the point? I just stopped working. Now I have fun. And I still pass all my courses!'

'But you have to avoid the Indian and Chinese tutors. They're old-fashioned, they don't understand the way things are, they can make trouble.'

'Everybody wins. The colleges get money, we get qualifications, and we get away from home.'

'We're pawns in our parents' money-laundering schemes, don't forget that.'

'Some of us! Don't talk about that!'

'Come on, admit it. Dad needs to get money out of the country, what better way than to send a brat abroad then fill up their bank account. Who doesn't love being a "white glove"? The perks are good.'

This would bolster her cover. WeiWei jumped in. 'Tell me about it. It just makes me feel a bit used though, you know?'

'Not you too!'

This was easy. Everyone wanted to be her friend. She was having fun. She should be among people like these, it was her rightful place, she had almost forgotten.

Her phone vibrated in her sweatshirt pocket, signalling an arriving text. It was the shittest form of phone available to humanity, a rock with a keypad and a two-tone screen. It did almost literally nothing, just text and call. To slip that thing out in this company would destroy her credibility. Fortunately she did not need to take it out, as she knew who it was. There was only one number in Contacts, that of her father's identical shitty phone. And she knew what his message was too. As neither device was capable of displaying Chinese characters, and his command of pinyin was not good, his missive would be, as usual, a string of random letters, designed not to communicate but just to remind her of his presence.

A tall guy stepped out of the shadows, asked her to repeat where she was from. Good hair, an air of louche detachment and an insolent smile – she was surprised not to have marked him before. He introduced himself as HuaGua and they fell into conversation. He explained that they were a gang of expat students who called themselves the Red Scholars, which was tongue in cheek, as they were dedicated to adventurous good times. That seemed an easy way in. 'I think I've heard my friend Tom talk about you lot. But he's not an overseas student. He's English Chinese, studies computers.'

'Ponytail, cosplay, that Tom? Joined at the hip with Butterfly?'

'That's him.'

'Saw them a few days ago. At that Xinjiang restaurant in Camberwell, you know it?'

'Of course. So… how was he?'

'Such a cute pair. They were talking about dressing up as the Mario Brothers at some convention. They should be here.'

She considered a direct approach: Tom had asked her to help with dressing up, but she'd lost his address, did he have it? It seemed tenuous. Why would she not have a phone number or an email? No, she could not risk such boldness until she was better embedded and they were drunker. She would keep poking around for now. 'Have you been to his house, in that area, what's it called...?'

But the conversation was derailed, as someone shouted, 'Bored! Want to go clubbing!' And that became the group topic. The idea received enthusiastic consent. HuaGua invited her along.

She pouted. 'But I haven't brought any money. My father's out there using my card, so none of this shows up on his. I can't bear to go and get it from him. He makes me sick sometimes.'

'It's my birthday, I'll treat you.'

The phone buzzed again. Yes, yes, thank you, I know you're there. She imagined him sitting in the parked car, drumming his fingers on the wheel. Sighing and grumbling, like he did when he was trying to sleep. The dismissive way these kids talked of their parents gave her licence to vent her irritations. He was making her live in a slum, exposing her to lecherous advances, ordering her about like she was one of his flunkeys, all without satisfactory explanation. Well, it wouldn't hurt to give him a little of his own treatment: keep him buffering a little while. She'd find out what he needed to know, but she'd do it in her own time, and ring back when she was ready.

'Sure. Why not?'

She figured she wouldn't get to eat tonight so she grabbed a handful of popcorn. The other hand went in her pocket and turned her phone off. Couldn't have it buzzing all night.

13)

Hotpot. The four simmerings. Dongbei hotchpotch. Buckwheat noodles. Pork ribs... no, pork cheeks. Jian was known for tremendous patience at stakeouts, but those were always conducted on a full stomach. This was a new kind of trial. Wholesome dumplings, white and steaming.

He sat in the Treasure Horse. The chill breeze blowing through the broken window helped him stay awake. He was parked within sight of the entrance of a nightclub. The other vehicles around were taxis and the drivers chattered to each other and called at the youngsters coming and going. He knew it was a club because of the bass that he could hear even out here, it thumped like a headache.

Over three hours ago, WeiWei and the other Chinese kids had spilled out of the karaoke venue and hailed bowler hat taxis. They looked to be having a riotous time. She seemed to be well integrated into the group, which was fine, as after all that was her assignment, but he would have liked her not to be quite so touchy. The gang had come here and here they had stayed. Every half an hour or so he sent her a message. No reply. How much effort would it be to send a text? He just wanted to know that she was okay. It was very unprofessional of her.

It was morning back home. Now would be a safe time to call. He rang a number in China.

'Jian. How's England?' Chief Inspector Bo's voice came clear.

'The air is clean.'

'Where are you, right now?'

They were both raising their voices. Not because the line was bad, but because of the delay, and because it was their habit.

'Posh hotel. Fancy wallpaper. Big bed, too soft, lots of pillows. A bottle of Johnny Walker.'

'Is that a shower?'

The Chief had heard the hum of traffic and jumped to the wrong conclusion, which wouldn't be a first.

'It might be.'

'Some honey washing your muck off her stomach. You dog. What's it like, riding the white horse?'

'Chinese girls are best.'

'No problem getting proper food over there?'

'It's never quite right. I don't know what it is… the rice is wrong, the sauces. How's the district?'

'Falling to pieces, as usual. A rash of pickpocketing.'

'Go to Lanzhou Noodles at the corner of Genxing and Fuhua. Aygul will be upstairs. His wife's pregnant, give him a red envelope. Tell him to get his Xinjiang lads under control or you'll crack down on illegal street trading… So what it is, I think the department had a call about me.'

'Yes, in the middle of the night. A superintendent from the Foreign Affairs Department of the Capital Police, over there in England. Wanted to know your situation.'

'I've spoken to him since, as a matter of fact. Nothing of concern. I have a question for you. What was he told?'

'Talked to him myself. I was overnighting in the office. I told the truth.'

'Why would you do that?'

'It's not a state secret. They could find it off Baidu. To start they got through to the PR bureau, you're lucky it was passed to me, cause you get those old ladies talking, they'll say all sorts. I gave them bare bones and a positive spin.'

'And did you tell him I had a daughter?'

'Of course not.'

'If anyone ever rings back, keep her out of it.'

'Of course. Jian? He asked if you were good. I said you were first class.'

So his boss had given him up to Uncle Seven with no prompting at all. Jian would like to have called the man a moron. Instead he lowered his voice. He was aware that his next inquiry would cause awkwardness for them both. He said, 'How's the investigation going?'

There was a silence, during which Jian could picture his superior clearly, talking on his red telephone, swivelling in his orthopaedic chair. A newspaper on his desk. Pennants on the wall behind: SERVE THE PEOPLE. BETTER POLICE BETTER CITY. LOYALTY! DISCIPLINE! CLEANLINESS!

Then Bo sighed. 'Jian, these anti-corruption people... You should see them. They're like scary monks. It's all sunglasses, satellite phones, bottles of water. I've asked them out to dinner, they won't have it. Won't even take a cigarette. Everyone's on edge, trying to stay out of their way.' He lowered his voice. 'They've found the flat, Jian.'

'What flat?'

'You know. A three-bedroom luxury penthouse apartment with underfloor heating. In a new development called LIBERATION.'

'It's not luxury. They cut corners everywhere. And the building is called LISBON.'

'They changed the names, not patriotic enough.'

'So I have a flat. It's not a crime.'

'They had the developer in. Said you brought the idea to him. You helped run the peasants off the land. He put up his development, and you got free lease on a penthouse.'

'I see.'

'And they've been talking to the girl.'

'What girl?'

'The little honey you had shacked up in there. They interrogated her. They did it here. Two days she was parked with us.'

'Well. She wouldn't snitch. She's loyal. She loves me.'

'I've got her statement. Hang on. Here. It's fifteen pages.'

'Like what?'

He heard turning pages. 'Ah... you'd pick her up in an official car... you told her that you only drink the best whisky because the government is paying... when you took her skiing you told her you were investigating an assault, someone got stabbed with a ski-pole, so the whole trip was expenses... You made disparaging remarks about the Party representative... disparaging remarks about the Central Committee... disparaging remarks about your superiors... there's about five pages of the disparaging remarks. Do you want to hear some of it? The party chairman is a pig's head. The Chief Inspector is a rotten egg who got back trouble from all the fat whores he gets to sit on him. Very nice. Then there's unpatriotic voicings... Inspector Ma Jian said he had a trick of sleeping with his eyes open and that was useful in political strategy meetings... he said the New Year gala got worse every year...'

'The New Year gala? On television? How is that relevant to anything?'

'It's all part of the story. They want to show you're unreliable, disloyal, ill-disciplined...' a cough, then he carried on. 'Selfish, venal, individualistic. Character faults lead to economic crimes. They're painting a picture.'

'Fifteen pages.'

'And the whole report is nearly sixty.'

Jian imagined hearing fingers tapping a keyboard, a printer buzz, a photocopier hum. He seemed to hear the creak as seats were settled into and the clink of tea-jars being uncapped.

Then he heard pages turning, over and over, all through the building, in every office, on every storey, more and more pages, the little rustles gathering, coming together, growing into a great crackling storm. Everyone would have read it, or be reading it now.

He would like to have ended the call there, with a flurry of curses. But he couldn't afford to burn any bridges so he made rote inquiries about the health of colleagues, chuckled at a dirty story, then mumbled platitudes until he could get off the line.

His disgrace, it seemed, was thorough and exhaustive and likely irreparable. He was still brooding on the capriciousness of human nature and the operations of power, when a black SUV pulled up alongside and stopped. They were blocking a taxi driver in. The man waddled over to remonstrate. The SUV passenger door opened suddenly, smacking his midriff. Words were exchanged, then the taxi driver thought better of his complaint, and retreated, holding his balls.

The driver's window hummed down, revealing two Asian men looking at Jian.

Jian glared back. The driver was stocky with protruding ears, a shaved head. He dressed like a teenage hood, in a Hawaiian shirt with gold and jade glittering on wrist and neck. He held up a smartphone. The screen showed a map. He pointed at a pulsing dot. 'That's you,' he said in Mandarin. Jian had worked out how they had found him earlier: a car tracking device on the Manager's phone. No doubt he was looking at the device now.

The bald man swept the phone around like a kid playing with a toy car. 'You've been tootling round. Back and forth, up and down. Here and there. Left and right.' He tossed the phone into the passenger's lap. 'Looks to us like you're driving round in a panic.'

'Then you're obviously not familiar with police work. Except perhaps from the business end. What's your name? I haven't had the pleasure of an introduction.'

'You don't need to know my name.'

'Then I'll call you Baldie.'

Baldie jerked a thumb at the club. The place was shutting and a stream of revellers was pouring out and milling around. Many looked unsteady on their feet. Some blinked and shook their heads or buttoned up coats. There was a lot of shouting and laughter. Bouncers in suits called and gesticulated to get them moving. The taxi drivers waved and whistled. People got into cabs and the cabs moved away and others took their place.

'He in there is he?'

'Could be. Could be one of my sources.'

'Come on Inspector, don't get coy on us.'

'I'm not at liberty to reveal my methods. Plus I worry you wouldn't understand them.'

'Might want to hurry it up a bit. Make your move. The clock is ticking.'

The headlights of a passing car swept them, and Jian saw the wear in the man's face, the lines across his forehead and around his hooded eyes. HIs passenger was tall and lean, with sallow cheeks. Never mind their dress and manner, these guys were as old as he was.

Jian grinned. 'You're too senior to be red poles. And those hands look soft, from easy living. You know what I think? You're management, who've been given dogsbody work cause of the earlier embarrassment. Was the same back home. After a high-profile fuck-up the desk boys are sent to pound the streets. Have to relearn some old lessons, yes?' He chuckled. 'You must be loving every moment of this.'

There was his daughter, hurrying away, snuggling with a guy. He had his hand on her waist and she was leaning into his shoulder. One of the youths she went in with: slim, heavily styled hair, a loose gait. They swayed drunkenly, moving together, then were lost in the crowd. Jian didn't want to lose them, but he didn't want these guys to see him watching them either.

Baldie snapped his fingers. 'Get it done, then we can all move on.'

The passenger craned across. 'Hey cop, let me ask...'

Jian didn't hear the rest. The jockeying of the cabs had given him an opening. He reversed behind the SUV, then braked, sped and swerved. He slipped into the tight space between that bullish vehicle and a taxi and barely scraped either. Drivers shouted and horns blared as he left them behind. In the rear view he watched the trapped SUV manoeuvring fussily, thuggish driver and passenger arguing. It would take them a minute to get out and by then he would be gone. Of course it was no real victory: they had the phone to trace him at their leisure. But at least he could keep them from breathing down his neck.

He spotted WeiWei and her wolf in the back seat of a bowler hat taxi. The cab veered from the kerb and he tucked in behind. He watched the back of their heads in the dim glass, and sensed conviviality, intimacy, maybe drunkenness, from the way they swayed and tilted. They were in there on their own. When the heads came together and formed a single shape he had to look away.

14)

WeiWei woke. In the bedsit she would groggily come to in a miasma of stale odours, and hear strangers talking through thin walls, her father coughing and clumping about. Now she breathed fresh, cool air in silence, was supported by a firm mattress, caressed by silky sheets. She rose to her elbows and looked around a dim interior, pristine, luxurious and rather bare. The furniture, bedding and curtains were all white. The blotchy abstract art on the walls was in shades of grey. The only sharp colours were the red digits of a clock. They said 9.43.

HuaGua slept beside her. She shifted to one elbow and considered him with an analytical, morning-after gaze, braced for disappointment.

At least he was not snoring or dribbling. Sharp cheekbones, jutting jaw, soft lips. His hair tousled attractively, invitingly. She peeked beneath the sheets, approved of slim frame, flat stomach, the tone on the arms. Perhaps a few too many moles on the shoulders. Overall not too bad, and there was no need to look for a reason why this one didn't count.

Memories of last night came, lurid and fragmentary. Hip-hop blaring. Laser lines slicing darkness. Shots slamming. Laughing mouths and pumping limbs, swaying bodies pressing close. She remembered teaching some of those modest east coast girls how to size guys up – spender, loser, alpha, bruiser – and get them to come to you. She remembered – oh dear – doing that dance where she put a finger on her lips.

And then this HuaGua guy… ignoring him, teasing him, scolding him, hitting him, snogging him. Fumbling in a taxi, furtling in a lift... she considered her clothes scattered on the floor and a condom wrapper. Sex had been fine. They had both been drunk but after initial awkwardness events had proceeded smoothly. She rubbed a soreness on her neck. Oh yeah, he had squeezed there, a couple of times. Feeling her out, it seemed, as, after, he'd opened a drawer in the bedside cabinet, revealing scarves, toys and cuffs. She'd put a stop to that. These guys wanted it like porn. She just wanted it nice.

Such encounters evoked mixed feelings. On the one hand, it was another step on the road away from an ideal of feminine purity. On the other, it was an affirmation of independence, it was taking ownership of her body and putting her powers to use. There was no single angle to consider it from. She was going home soon, wasn't about to get into anything long distance, so this should be considered a one-off, to be dealt with by brisk forward motion. She got out of bed, gathered her clothes, and shuffled to the en suite. A scalding shower then she'd leave.

Nice bathroom, all marble and frosted glass. Bottles, sprays and creams were arrayed around the sink, all high-end Japanese and Korean brands. Make-up too: That 'little fresh meat' pretty-boy look had to be carefully cultivated. The shower jets sprayed from all sides. It was glorious, after the tepid dribble of the bedsit stall. Thinking about that brought her father to mind. She had kept him waiting for hours, had not bothered to ring, and still had not completed the mission he had given her. Was she really that shallow that the prospect of a good time put everything else out of mind? Maybe she was.

Out of the shower, briskly dressed, she found her phone and turned it on. Around twenty nonsense texts arrived. They got shorter, the last few were single letters. They were spaced throughout the night. Why, he must have not slept at all. He was going to be livid. She assembled excuses – one of the girls seemed to know something about this – Tod? Tom? Tim? – so they went to a café together, then she was invited back to watch a film, but she fell asleep on a sofa: something like that. Or, no, she could tell the truth. She should tell the truth. In fact, it was the least she should do. Not entirely the truth though.

There'd be a number for this T- something guy in HuaGua's phone. But that was charging on his bedside, and anyway it had a fingerprint scanner to unlock it. Perhaps he had an address book?

She padded into the living room. She must have been very drunk last night, or perhaps hadn't spent more than a moment here in the dark, because she couldn't recall this space at all, and it was very memorable. It was the kind of interior she'd been reading about, and phrases she'd frowned over seemed vividly brought to life: five-star splendour, first-class lifestyle, boutique duplex. A property designed for twenty-first-century elite living, with bold contemporary styling, high-end furnishings, and floor-to-ceiling windows giving jaw-dropping views of the fashionable district of … wherever the hell she was.

Almost everything was white and what wasn't was black. Even the art on the walls – which was baffling and ugly, so presumably very expensive and on trend – had no colour in it. The flat was gorgeous yes, but also, in her view, rather severe and empty. It could do with some cheery cushions or throws or ornaments, to add vitality and homeliness.

Her phone buzzed. She answered it quickly.

Her father barked 'Are you okay?'

'Hang on,' she whispered.

She stepped out onto a balcony to talk. She was on the top floor of a high rise. Landscaped grounds spread prettily below. Beyond were more blocks identical to this one, then a light rail station, an angular jumble of new builds, a river. There was nothing foreign in the scene, she could be in some new development back home.

'I'm fine,' she said, leaning on the wall. 'I've been working on the case.'

'I'm downstairs,' he snapped. 'Come right now.'

'You're what? Downstairs? How did you…'

He ended the call. Oh what the… fuck. She craned out over the balcony wall, half expecting to see him below, glaring up at her. If he was here then… that meant he must have followed her from All-Stars Karaoke to that club – Attic or Fragment or Fab or whatever – then waited outside for hours. Somehow he'd seen her leave… followed a taxi in his car… all the way here. It made her wince to think of him seeing her drunk, rowdy, kissing in public. No possibility now of lying about what had happened.

Completing this mission would make amends. She'd wake HuaGua and ask him directly if she had to. She went back to her search with more urgency. A chrome coffee table had a discreet recessed drawer. It opened to reveal the only clutter she'd seen. Mostly keys, each with a fob and address tag. She sifted and found lighters, putty, gum, bracelets, and then a leather book. A namecard collection. Her father had something similar. There were hundreds of cards in transparent sleeves, arranged alphabetically by pinyin or English name. Many of the Chinese ones looked important: CEOs, company directors, army officers, councillors, cadres, diplomats and the like. They were almost all white with black lettering and a restrained, monochrome graphic. The more diverse and colourful English cards were for less elite personages – tutors, tailors, tennis coaches, masseuses. She found a Tom Xiang. That would be the guy. An image on the card showed a lad in a blue wig wearing a silver costume and toting a futuristic silver rifle. Cartoony script read COSPLAYER EXTRAORDINAIRE. How cute. She slid the card out. Number one prize: a phone number and an address on the reverse, a district called Sutton.

She heard swishing and looked up. HuaGua was in the doorway, naked but for boxers, scratching and yawning. She held the card behind her back.

He considered the open drawer. 'You robbing me?'

'I'm just naturally nosy. You've got more keys than a luggage room.'

He shlepped to the kitchen, poured a glass of water, dropped in a tablet. 'My father's. He owns places all over. All the flats in this building, for example.'

Trying to discreetly tuck the namecard into her leggings, she fumbled and dropped it. She supposed it had fallen into the shaggy rug beside the table. She went down on her knees to search. 'So you're a landlord?'

'He leaves them empty. Thinks if he gets tenants they'll mess the places up, refuse to leave. They're investments. Flats in London are like gold bricks. So he says.'

'What kind of places?'

'He likes new builds. Doesn't even come to see them before he buys, just looks at floorplans, measures on a map how close to a station.'

'You look after them?' Being, or sounding, interested lent cover to her probings in the hairy pile.

'Exactly. I'm a caretaker. Sitting on his bricks. What are you doing now, checking the value of the rug?'

'Lost the back of an earring.' Not bad, for spur of the moment, as long as he didn't remember she hadn't been wearing any.

'You'll not find it now, I've lost shoes in there. So what does your father do?'

Morning-after conversation, even when you knew and liked the other person, always seemed a strain. This seemed the kind of stilted talk that always ended up happening in these situations, when it was clear that what was best for both parties was the swift exit of the visiting one. Where was the card? Keep talking.

'Why are you interested in him?'

'We share a birthday, remember. I already feel he's like an uncle.'

'Oh. Well, you know. He does this and that.'

'You don't want to talk about it. That's interesting.'

'Why?'

'I saw him, remember? He's clearly not an official or a business guy. He doesn't dress money, but he must have it, he sends his girl to England to be educated. Now you're refusing to tell me what he is. So it's quite clear that...' He made gun hands. 'He's a gangster.'

Why not let him think that, if he wanted to? It could add to her allure, and give a valid reason for further vagueness on her part. 'I wouldn't say he was black... A bit grey maybe.'

He was watching her with an appraising gaze that she didn't much care for. Perhaps kneading the rug like this made her look a bit deranged. Finally he said, 'I wasn't sure last night. But I know now.'

'Know what?'

'You're one of us. Another poor little rich kid. Only people like us would think of going out looking that cheap. An ordinary girl would be dressed up.'

'You put me to some kind of test and I should be glad I've passed?'

'More proof, that attitude. I have to be wary of gold diggers.'

'You can only relax around your own kind, can't you?' He padded over, and she worried he was going to try to help her, but instead he picked up his namecard book, pulled a blank from the back and found a pen. 'Give me your number.'

She wasn't getting her phone out. 'No. Give me yours.'

He gave her a card. Black and white, of course: thick, with a first name and a mobile number in raised type. She took it and spotted the one she was really interested in, nestled side-on in a dense thicket of rug. He was back in the kitchen area, adding more tablets to his drink, so it was easy to snatch it up and pair the two. With his facing outwards there was now no need to tuck anything away. She would be out of here in seconds, mission accomplished, soaking in her father's guarded, reluctant praise.

He came back and said 'Oh, by the way, you'd better tell your father he's taking a bit of a risk.'

'Huh?'

'The tigers and flies anti-corruption campaign is kicking hard. Grey people are under scrutiny. Especially anyone with a kid abroad. Your dad came here to see you? That might be enough to start an investigation by itself.'

'What do you mean?'

The static hissing sound of tablets dissolving in his glass seemed suddenly to have increased in volume. She did not bother trying to hide her interest. 'Why would coming here spark an investigation?'

'Think about it. The high-ups see he's gone abroad. They'll worry he's been funnelling money through you, and is now absconding with ill-gotten gains. Happens all the time, they're up on it. Anyone going abroad is asking to be probed.'

'Huh. So… if they found something amiss… What would they do?'

'Get a berth ready in a camp. Freeze bank accounts, confiscate assets. Bang, all gone. You okay? You look worried.

I've worried you. I don't mean... it's just idle talk, I'm sure your father is fine.'

'You mean all his assets? They can do that? Just take everything?'

'There's nothing they can't do. You look concerned. Didn't mean to frighten you. I'm sure he's fine.'

'Oh of course he is. Still, it's good to be aware of these things. Well, this was fun.' She barely heard the lad talking unconvincingly about maybe having brunch later, something about getting the right exit on the way out, and her own rote phrases that got her to the door. She did not feel the hug.

Then she was alone, and breathing shakily. Suspicions were hardening into certainties. The grimmest possibility regarding their plight was the actual and horrible truth of it. She told herself that she had always known, she just hadn't wanted to see. She glared at a foolish girl looking small in the mirror in the lift.

The doors opened and she stepped out, mental voice raging. How could she be so – oh. It was dark. This could not be right. She shuffled to a halt. She was in an empty underground car park. It was not where she needed to be, even if it's dungeony look did fit her state of mind. She rushed back into the lift before the doors closed and jabbed the button for the floor above. They opened on more gloom, on doors labelled HEALTH SUITE locked with a chain. She caught a fetid stench: perhaps a pool needed draining. She couldn't find her way out of the building and she couldn't see the obvious. 'G' for 'ground', silly girl, and she jabbed the button so hard it cracked a nail.

She came out in a gleaming lobby with a deserted concierge desk, a plastic plant. Complex reflections on glass walls and marble floor seemed to enhance the emptiness. Again she took the wrong door, as if going astray was instinct or destiny, and found herself in the grounds. The door closed behind her and wouldn't open again. More proof of idiocy, not that it was needed.

Paths zig-zagged through a Minecraft-style landscape of precise lawns, bushes trimmed into oblongs. She couldn't see road, shop or hoarding, could barely hear cars. In the windows of the other blocks she could see hints of occupation, like vases or books on a sill, shifting light from a TV. On his block every window below the penthouse had its blinds down. Eight storeys, three flats on each one: his lonely eyrie sat atop twenty-one empties.

Trying to get out, she was once more presented with ridiculous and infuriating difficulties. What she took for an exit ended in a blank wall, and she had to traipse around before she found an underpass with a gate at the end, then it was a frustrating few moments before she discovered it was opened by an unmarked button on the wall.

Here she was, finally, back in public, and here her father was too, looking, as so often these days, haggard and out of place.

She said, 'You didn't have to stay up. You could have just gone home. You look tired. So. You think I'm a tramp, yes?'

'Never mind about that. Did you get the...?'

It was not at all the expected response. But she had worked on her script and was sticking to it. 'Well, I'm glad I'm a tramp. Better that than a criminal.'

He was abruptly defensive. 'What?'

She aimed an accusing finger. 'You're a criminal. That's what you are! That's all you are! And a liar. It's all bullshit, isn't it? There's no bank mistakes. You've been investigated, they found corruption, and if you go home they'll throw you in prison. Your bank accounts are frozen. You're a criminal and a fugitive and a liar.'

To her disappointment, he did not contradict her, or match her outrage. He just held her gaze and said quietly, 'I was going to tell you... It just never seeemed the right... Yes.'

Her indignation melted. Her hands dropped, then her shoulders, then her voice. 'Fuck.'

She had so wanted to be wrong. He sounded as weary as he looked as he said, 'A warrant is out for my arrest for economic crime. All assets have been confiscated. If I go home I will be put on trial, found guilty, and sent to a labour camp. I have, as people say, fallen off my horse.'

'Fuck. Dad. Oh fuck. Oh Dad. Oh fuck.' Her distress made her turn away, and she kept on turning until she had gone all the way round, and was facing him again, hot fingers pressed to her cheeks. 'Why didn't you say? Why – oh... What are we going to do?' Another silence stretched, this one deep and hopeless, and she repeated herself just to stop it carrying on. 'What are we going to do?'

15)

'Mum? I've got something I have to do. I… it's going to be fine. But I can't talk about it right now. Don't call me. I'll see you in a couple of days… Monday, I think. I'll see you on Monday.' Something I have to do. That could mean just about anything. How could he not know that such calculated vagueness would just inspire frantic speculation?

Shan lay rigid in bed, mentally replaying events of the previous weeks in as granular detail as she could muster, searching for anything that might shed light on Tom's present predicament. A conclusive sign eluded her but she believed she'd spotted trends that might be meaningful – he'd been staying out more than usual, communicating less than usual, giving even more cursory descriptions of his movements, feelings and doings than usual. Could this be more than typical teenishness, evidence of some new concern or brewing crisis?

Her treacherous imagination conjured dreadful scenarios. He had gone mad, got into hard drugs, joined a gang or cult. How? Why? Was it her fault? She dropped into fitful sleep towards dawn, was oppressed by vile dreams, and woke unrested some hours later. Immediately she ran to his room to see if he had slipped home while she was asleep. He hadn't, of course, and the sight of his bed, its emptiness just going on and on, brought a stab of dismay.

Might there be a clue to his whereabouts in here? He did not like her coming in, and usually she respected his privacy. But these were not normal circumstances. She could have a quick poke around, then tidy afterwards and he would never know.

She started her search bashfully, opening desk drawers and sifting contents with a finger. Passport, those daft namecards, college stuff – headphones, keys, old phones, USB sticks. She grew bolder, and rifled through comics and notebooks, looked under his figurines, shook out his textbooks and folders. Doodles and jottings were scrutinised, pencil cases and bags ransacked. She had momentum now: she re-opened drawers and rummaged shamelessly. He arranged his T-shirts by colour, kept his pants folded and his socks balled. She used to tell her colleagues how neat he was, and listen with secret satisfaction to tales of the grossness of their children. Oh, my Tom is no trouble, he's never been a problem. In fact, he's almost too tidy. Well, she was not smug any more.

She pulled out drawers, unpacked costumes, and took down posters to see if anything was written on the back. She deconstructed a home-made sword, stripping silver tape to reveal foam and balsa wood. It was blameless of course, and now ruined, and contemplating her pointless destruction brought her fever to an end. She sat glumly, dispirited. She was a wild woman in a nightdress who had invaded her son's privacy and broken his trust, ruined costumes and props he'd spent months on, worked herself up to a new pitch of unhappiness, and all for nothing.

Plus she had given herself a tiresome task for her day: putting his room back in order. She set to work with much tutting and sighing. As she was slotting the top drawer back into the desk her fingers registered a change of texture on the underside. Checking, she found a sheet of paper fixed there with masking tape. It was a handwritten list of his logins and passwords.

A mental voice advised caution. It was that of her mother, the practical old owl, and it remarked that after the drama, whatever it was, was over, this particular trespass, were it discovered, would not be easily forgiven. If Tom didn't want to tell her what he was up to then she should accept that. Probably off on a dirty weekend. He's a man now, and men follow their little brother wherever it leads. He'd come back sheepish on Monday morning. Her mother with her folksy ways was, annoyingly, often right: for instance about that charming gambler she'd married. Yes okay, she snapped back, but stop now and what? Go back to not sleeping? No, she had to know.

She opened his Mac using the first password on the list, TOMTOTEM2. Folders on the desktop were labelled COSPLAY, COLLEGE, CVs, PHOTOS, MISCELLANEOUS. She opened a browser and, with the help of the list, got into his online bank account. She thought this was rather cunning of her. Any recent card purchase, even just a coffee in a café, might provide the means to track him down. What she saw made her gasp and bite a knuckle. His account was empty. On Thursday morning, at a branch in Hoxton, he had withdrawn nearly five thousand pounds: all the money he owned, down to the last penny.

All her worst fears seemed confirmed. This was genuine trouble. She closed her eyes and waited for her breathing to settle. Then logged into his email account. She considered a string of unopened missives: from college, friends, her. He hadn't looked at his email for four days. And this was a lad who once demanded they cut short a trip to the Tate because his phone had run out of battery and he couldn't check his messages.

The last opened email was from thecostumedbutterfly@sina. com. Shan clicked and scanned a long chain of correspondence. *Attack on Titan? Way too BASIC. Tokyo Ghouls – who would be Keneki Ken? No no no shinagami, you look like a Kiss groupie. Marios? Super ke-ai, double Luigi.* It meant little to her, but she got the gist: they were planning to go to the Comecon festival, where all the dress-up enthusiasts got together, and to coordinate outfits.

Tom's correspondent always signed off 'love love love Butterfly' and a long string of Xs. They both wrote in English but judging from the stilted grammar and wayward spelling it was not Butterfly's first language. A Chinese girl, she supposed, someone in this new, rather fast group of mainland rich kids he had started hanging out with.

Then, oh: a late-night email from Tom to her, which began with how much he missed the smoothness of Butterfly's lips and thighs which were like honey on his starved tongue. She did not read on, and tactfully lowered the screen. She had found out what she needed, anything more was the lowest form of snooping.

She recalled walking into the bathroom after he'd finished one of his epic showers and finding a butterfly doodle drawn with a finger on the steamed-up mirror. A proper girlfriend. First love: a tempest of intense emotions, enough to make even the smartest, neatest and quietest of lads lose his mind. This girl, she was convinced, was the key to the mystery.

Another file on the computer held a list of contacts. Nothing under B for Butterfly, but she found a number under H for HuDie, the name in pinyin Chinese. There was a phone number and an address, a flat in Hoxton. Which was where he'd withdrawn his money. She would find out what this Butterfly had to say for herself; clearing up could wait.

16)

Jian led his daughter along prosperous streets, becalmed with Sunday morning sleepiness. The few other pedestrians were deliverymen, joggers, mothers pushing prams, who all seemed to be leading enviously dull lives. WeiWei's unanswered questions shrouded him. To her credit she had only asked them once. When finally he spoke, he picked his words carefully, as if they were being recorded.

'At first I didn't want to tell you because I was confident the situation could be harmoniously resolved. Perhaps some kind of deal... Or maybe it would blow over. I attempted to negotiate, call in favours... but I came to realise there is nothing I can do... I knew I had to tell you. But I found I could not say. I kept finding reasons not to. Putting it off.'

'What sort of sentence are you looking at?'

'Who can say? Ten years in jail perhaps. Longer.'

'This is all my fault. If you hadn't rushed over to save me you wouldn't have been investigated.'

That was true, but he wasn't about to say it. He winced now as he remembered the calamitous day he had found out. They were at a vast buzzing airport, busy with babbling people and full of signs he couldn't understand. He was shouting at Inspector Bo on the phone, asking why his cards had been stopped, how he was supposed to come home. He had listened aghast to his superior talking about the Central Discipline Inspection Committee visiting from Beijing, how irresponsible and stupid he had been to rush off abroad to a country without an extradition treaty, about what the Discipline Committee had found, and how any funds he might have at home could be considered lost. How it might be better to stay where he was.

After that phone call Jian had made many more. Colleagues and acquaintances were sympathetic but, regretfully, unable to wire funds due to temporary financial difficulties. Others were distant or embarrassed, one put the phone down straight away. He could not blame them. You didn't want to be observed lending a sympathetic ear to a man being investigated by the Central Discipline Inspection Committee, let alone helping him.

'They've taken everything?' said WeiWei. 'What about the house? You've got investments, shares. That gold bull.'

'If I go home and hand myself in, maybe I would get something back. A deal perhaps could be made. But while I'm here, nothing.'

'But if you are… a bit… well, grey. Then… you'll have money hidden away in secret foreign bank accounts. Won't you?'

If he really had absconded with state funds, he wouldn't have any problems: he'd be relaxing in a steam room right now, planning a mellow retirement in the sun. It would be amusing if it was happening to someone else.

'Everyone thinks that. They just assume. But I don't have money hidden away. The only money I ever moved abroad was what I put into your account, and we have emptied that.'

'So… if you'd really been properly corrupt, we'd be fine. The problem was you weren't black enough.' She looked about her suddenly. 'What about the Foxcatchers? Are they after you?' She meant the Chinese police who specialised in snatching criminals who had fled abroad. She would know them from TV, where they were presented as remorseless trackers. He knew what they were really like: cadres near retirement, dumb loyalists and boffins, who did most of their searching on the internet. He dismissed them with a wave. 'They don't operate here.'

'Could the police here catch you and send you home?'

'Not at China's behest. But I am an illegal here, so perhaps I could be deported. I don't know what the rules are. I wouldn't like to end up in the hands of the British authorities and find out. I have to keep my head down.'

'I see.' He was pleased to hear her level tone. She was taking it far better than he had dared hope. She was working it through, asking the right questions. 'These so-called emergency loans we've been living on, where did you really get the money?'

'Gambling Mahjong.'

'Well, that's a future. We could be Mahjong hustlers together.'

'Absolutely not.'

'We will have to do something, though, won't we? Cause… we're stuck here.'

'No we're not. I'm stuck here. You are free to go home.'

This was the crux of the matter, an unresolvable dilemma that was the real reason he had kept her so long in the dark. He did not want her to go. He did not want to be left alone. And he did not want her living on her own in China: a young woman without connections, with the dark cloud of family disgrace over her head: her prospects there were bleak. But… to keep her here with him was cruel. It was condemning a young woman at the start of her life to scrabble for survival as a penniless illegal immigrant in a harsh alien world. So what then? What to do? He had wrestled with this over and over, while lying on his lumpy mattress in the dark, or walking the unknowable streets.

In the end, the matter was over in a moment. She said quickly and firmly, 'How could I leave you here? To live on gambling winnings, ducking across the road when you see a policeman?' Her voice grew strident. 'What kind of daughter do you think I am? Out of the question. This is our problem. We are together. We'll eat bitterness, and we'll survive.'

'No money. No visa. No future.'

She seemed angry. 'Come on, Dad, I'm a Ma. Tough sons of Dongbei bitches. Remember Gran telling us how she had to eat insects? What's this to that? Fuck this! Oil up!'

Her doughty optimism had brought relief and pride, but her next statements inspired a jab of reproach. 'This is us managing now, isn't it? You're working as a private detective, and I'm your assistant. This job will lead to others, before you know it we'll be set up.' She had believed his lies. How mixed she could be, smart and knowing, yet immature and guileless. 'I did find something out anyway, I did the job you asked.' She gave him a namecard. The To-Mu in the photo, smiling and posing, looked camp, pretty and ridiculous.

'And that's his address on the back.'

'Good work. The car is just down here.'

'Why so far away? Why didn't you park outside the flat and sit in the car?'

It was because of the tracking device. It left a trail and he didn't want that trail ever leading to her. He couldn't explain this without revealing too much, so he fell back on giving orders. 'Keep yourself amused for a few hours. I'll ring you when this is finished, and we'll go out for that big meal.'

'I want to come.'

'The next bit might be dangerous. If something happened to you, I'd never forgive myself.'

'Bit late for that, isn't it?'

'Yes, it is. Still...'

'Alright, alright, don't give me that hangdog expression. I'll go twiddle my thumbs.'

The Treasure Horse was parked some distance up ahead and there was a figure in the front seat. With the driver's window broken, anyone could get in. A tramp might have decided to sleep there. But Jian suspected this wasn't just anyone. He tugged his daughter into an alley and out of view, and got out his map book.

'I need the lad's address marked.' Once she had done that he walked her to a café, and after he had waved her safely inside he walked to the car. He opened the passenger seat and got in. Baldie, in the driver's seat, said, 'You want to get that window fixed. Anyone could get in here.'

'Where's your boyfriend? Let me guess, sleeping in your car. You cranky? I would be, if I'd spent all night traipsing after a dot on a screen.'

'Boss wants to talk to you. Give me the keys, I'll drive.'

'Thanks. I like being chauffeured.'

He wasn't going to give the man the satisfaction of asking where they were headed. 'I need to catch up on my sleep. Warning you, I snore.' Jian reclined the seat. He had a talent for rest, an ability honed in noisy canteens, bumping trucks, political meetings. He put his hood up and tugged the rim down, settled his hands over his stomach and closed his eyes.

WeiWei hadn't eaten since yesterday's popcorn. But the only food in the café counter display was cakes and pastries, and she knew they would upset her stomach. She had only ordered tea. In the traditional manner, she brought cup to lip, and blew across the surface to cool it. She considered her hand. No shakiness. Good.

She refused to let herself panic or grow sad. She knew she could get flustered over trivial things, but was capable of equanimity in the face of disaster. This was not as big as her mother dying or her ex trying to kill her. Look at it rationally. Her father was in a terrible mess and was not dealing well with his misfortunes. By pretending it wasn't happening, by becoming secretive and evasive, and now, this scramble for cash: Mahjong gambling and private detection, what nonsense. Such desperate schemes could not end well.

She had no faith in his ability to look after them. He was a baffled dinosaur. She, on the other hand, understood the modern world, was resourceful, energetic and smart, and could speak the lingo. It was her duty to step up and sort it out.

A shabby, abject man came into the store and began asking customers for money. She and her father, if they failed, would be joining his club, alarmingly soon. The barista chased the beggar out, and she addressed him as he was returning to his station. 'Do you need any staff?'

'You'll have to ask the boss.'

'How much do you earn?'

'Eight pounds an hour. Plus tips,' he added, glancing at a jar of change on the counter. Unfortunately the man seemed to take her inquiry as indicative of another kind of interest, and started telling her about his band. WeiWei tuned out as she did mental arithmetic. Just to pay the rent on some shitty room she'd have to work four days a week. She interrupted him. 'That rate is pretty standard, would you say?'

'I've worked for less.'

'Do you take workers without a visa?'

'Of course not. They'd close us down.'

'Do you know anywhere you can work without a visa?'

'There isn't anywhere. Far as I know. They fine businesses that take workers like that, so employers won't hire them...'

She felt a flash of anger. People like you can get hired despite the tattoos and the attitude, but decent, hard-working, presentable her had no hope – and just because of a piece of paper, or rather lack of it.

'Places that would hire you... they'd exploit you. You'd probably get paid half that.'

Living here as a poor person was rubbish, she'd had enough of it already. It was eating rice with spam from a cracked bowl, sticking tissue in her ears to keep ranting alcoholics from waking her at night, washing in the tepid dribble from a rusty showerhead, avoiding the reflection of her unmade-up face, finding flecks of the windowsill's peeling paint under her fingernails, stepping on a damp blot in the corridor and knowing it was spit, trying not to hear the remarks of skulking youths as she passed them – it was all this and a million other petty inconveniences, humiliations and distresses, and she had had enough of it.

She thought of the elite existence she'd tasted last night. How glorious, how intoxicating. Her life should be that gorgeous whirl. Like those girls, she should be treating the city as an exotic playground, being constantly pleased at all the beauty, wit and good taste around, creating her best and most enjoyable self. She should be keeping a street fashion portfolio, curating her social media presence, planning to renovate a courtyard house in a *hutong*. And, what was especially vexing, she'd be so good at it! If that was her group, she'd rise to be the queen. She had the class and the smarts and the taste and the looks, the right level of exuberance and extroversion, she was exceptional at singing, dancing, joking around, and all forms of social calibration. All she lacked was money.

The barista intruded on her ruminations, gauchely giving her his number. Easiest just to take it. Western guys were so forward, it could be annoying. Pity there wasn't a way to charge them for the privilege of her attention. Well, obviously there was, but that was not a road she was going down, however shit things got.

She considered last night's lover. Specifically, his wit, elegance and indifference; his slim waist, squishy lips and thickly textured hair; his designer clothes, penthouse apartment and drawer full of keys to empty flats. Might he not be her entry to that world – and the solution to all their problems?

A fantasy blossomed, playing out like the fairy tale of Ye Xian, or the American film *Cinderella*. In both stories, a poor girl is helped by a magical intermediary – a granny in the Western story, a carp in the Chinese one – to masquerade briefly as a lady of status. She enjoys the company of a rich and powerful man. After the spell wears off, she flees, and he tracks her down. She is now back in rags, and admits to having deceived him. But that's not an issue, as now he's smitten. He's just happy she's still around. They get married in the next scene, and shack up in the palace.

Could she play the same tale out? It was a pity they had already shagged, it meant her best card had been played, early and cheaply; how advantageous it would be to any campaign, if she could still dangle that prospect. Plus those disparaging remarks he'd made about gold diggers suggested he'd be less tractable than the fairy-tale dupe. Developing the situation from here would be a challenge. Well, she liked those. A mission then. Hadn't he mentioned brunch?

She took out his card and her shameful phone. She forced a smile, to cultivate a positive mindset, which would be detected in her voice, and called.

太子党 **PRINCELINGS**

18)

Jian felt a poke and jerked into consciousness. He was instantly alert and defensive, like a sentry caught napping. He was in the passenger seat of a parked car. Why was the steering wheel on the wrong side? Then it all came back, a wave of concerns smacking him in the face, which was pretty much how he always woke up these days.

Baldie was jabbing him with a stun gun, his finger resting on the trigger.

Jian yawned. 'Back home only whores use those. They keep them in their handbags.'

'I have to escort you in. Or they'll think you're a tramp and throw you out.'

They were in an underground car park. On the way to the lift Jian checked out Bentleys and Rolls-Royces – how insolently wide they were, back home you'd need a HGV licence to drive one. They ascended and came out in a hotel reception with the look of a country house from a subtitled drama. At last Jian saw men dressed with the panache and style he expected of the English, in suits, waistcoats and hats. They were the staff. The guests – sitting on luggage, schlepping around in sandals – lowered the tone. They took a carpeted lift to the eighth floor and Baldie led him to suite 8, and into a reception room with dark wood furnishings. He said, 'Wait here,' and hurried away.

'See you soon,' called Jian.

He sat and stretched his arms out along the back of a deep red leather sofa. Of course he would be made to wait. It was just what he would do, back home. But after only a couple of minutes, a door opened. It was not Uncle Seven though. To his surprise, it was the young gambler from last night, the high roller from the Dragon table. He came in quickly, saw Jian and stopped dead. He looked as surprised as Jian.

He wore jeans that were too big, without a belt. They sat low on his hips and rucked up at his big red trainers. His baggy sweatshirt had a design like the graffitti that infested the streets. He slid his headphones down past his cap and Jian heard his music faintly, an angry man shouting over a martial beat. They glared at one another. The lad said, 'You look like you've been sleeping in a doorway.'

'Does your big brother ever ask for his clothes back?'

'You've got a big mouth, for a man who's looking at a murder charge if he doesn't please his masters. The police here are good. They'll catch you very fast. If they want to. If you fail us. Oh yes, I heard about it.'

He tugged at the skin under his chin. Jian had seen that gesture before. Now it made sense, what the lad was doing here, how he knew.

He pointed, 'I get it. You're his son.' The lad had a book tucked under his shoulder. A big paperback with a bright cover, it must be a textbook. Jian chuckled. 'You don't want to be here. This is your punishment, right, for gambling? Dad's keeping his eye on you, making you study.'

The lines that briefly furrowed the lad's wide brow told Jian he had guessed right. 'I bet you miss being called sir, don't you? Taking backhanders. Beating up Falun Gong. Bossing dissidents around.'

'Are you always this annoyed? Or is it a bad weekend for you, what with being robbed by guys with fake guns, dressed up like cartoon characters? Then getting a smack on the wrist from Daddy, like a naughty little boy?'

'It'll be worth it when you catch the robbers. They'll pay.'

'You could play them your music, that's punishment enough.'

Their sparring was cut short when Uncle Seven opened another door. He was once more wearing a dressing gown, of the same design, though this one was cleaner. Without his glasses his eyes looked small and bright. He said to the boy. 'Where are you going?'

'Lunch.'

'Come back in one hour.'

'How long I got to do this?'

'Till it's done.'

'I've studied till numbers are coming out of my ears. I want to go out tonight.'

'Gambling? Whoring?'

'It's a business thing. I'm studying business, it's business, let me go and do my business.'

'You can go out if you finish. Not before.'

The lad put his headphones back on and sloped off. His gait was a loping roll, so different from his father's. Was it teenage affectation, or the effect of the trainers? It looked easy-going at a glance, but Jian noted tense fists, tight jaw: he was angry. Being told off was bad enough, far worse to have it happen in front of the help. Jian wondered if that was his purpose in being here.

When his son was gone, Uncle Seven said, 'At every age, a different trouble. Shitting everywhere when they're little. Watching too much TV when they're medium-sized. Not listening to their betters when they're older. When I was his age I was living on the streets, selling drugs, fighting rivals. This lot? They think the hard life is not having wi-fi.'

The inability of modern youth to graft, listen or withstand privation was one of Jian's own pet subjects, and in normal circumstances he would have joined in with hearty agreement, adding examples from his own experience. But doing so now would hint at family connections he did not want broadcast, so he repeated an oft-heard mollifying truism: 'Every generation is a disappointment to its elders.'

'I have been told it improves, if they learn their lessons.' He led Jian into a larger room, again without a bed – how big was this suite? A small round table was laid for two, and crowded with bamboo baskets holding steaming dumplings, plump rolls, glistening buns and tarts. Jian smelled the feast, realised he was very hungry, and calculated that he had not eaten for two days.

'I don't like to eat alone. And as you saw, my son refuses to join me. My companion excels at horizontal pleasures but her conversation is limited. So… Eat, eat.'

There was no purpose in refusing. Uncle Seven used the wide end of his chopsticks to put a dumpling on Jian's plate, then twirled them the right way round. He clacked chopsticks. 'Using these stimulates the pressure point at the base of the thumb, which is connected to the brain. So when we eat, our minds get nourished as well as our stomachs. I don't want you going hungry, Inspector. I want that formidable investigator's brain working at full capacity.'

Jian was not, as a rule, a fan of Cantonese dim sum, regarding it as fiddly, effete, over-elaborate. But he had to admit that, done properly like this, it was very satisfying. The succulence of the meat in the pork dumplings was complemented by the light dough. The crispy crust of the turnip cakes broke with ease to reveal an interior that was spongy without gooiness. When his hunger had dimmed, Jian savoured each morsel, and began to construct a lively taste medley, following a sweet egg custard tart with a meaty bun, popping a chewy sesame ball after a crunchy dumpling of shrimp and peanut. He'd have liked a beer to wash it down with but this tea – a delicate Longjin – was most refreshing.

'Try the *lor mai gai*,' said Uncle Seven, 'it has a salty duck egg inside. I'm a mainlander at heart. But my time in Hong Kong turned my mouth Cantonese.'

'You were a refugee?'

'Our father was accused of being a rightist. You know what that meant for the family, in the struggle years. So me and my two brothers swam to Hong Kong. They both drowned. Some tough times after that. The locals hated refugees. The lowest kind of scum. We banded together. No choice. Rose from nothing to rule the streets. How is the hunt going?'

'Almost done.'

'I want you to understand that we are not animals. Of course there will be punishment. But I am not in favour of torture. In case you had concerns.'

Jian shrugged. 'Doesn't bother me. Won't be the first armed robbers I've sent for execution. I just want you to hold up your end of the bargain.'

'Ask anyone who's worked for me. Ask if I am a man of honour, who keeps his word.'

As if to emphasise his civilised credentials, he put his chopsticks down precisely on the ceramic stand, and refilled Jian's teacup.

'I looked you up. You'd think maybe a local newspaper article or two, some official reports, court documents. But no. News, blogs, cop fan sites. Iron Man Jian. The scourge of the hoodlum. A tough cop who gets things done. Notorious for his unorthodox methods. Who likes to attend every arrest, at least the significant ones. Something of a showman. With his big coat and a bullhorn. There was talk of a TV show. What was it going to be called? The Fox from the North?'

'The show wasn't about me. I was just consulted.'

It was all exaggeration, of course, designed for flattery. What small public profile Jian had was the result of a few notorious cases and a drive he had helmed to break up some gangs. That led to the meetings with TV people. He was never paid, the promises of the slick media folk were lies, and that, he vowed, was the last time he would have any dealings with those types.

'A profile on a blog here...' His host began reading off a phone. 'Iron Man Jian says he visits the condemned before execution, to take their mind off things. It's the least we can do, says the public defender, they deserve company. Then... Oh, this is interesting. Iron Man Jian believes there's a danger in relying on forensic science, such as fingerprinting, as it makes the forces of law lose their practical skills. They become reactive, not active. The best policework is about stopping crime before it happens... Interesting, that bit about fingerprints. Considering.'

He wiped his lips with a napkin, then fiddled in his mouth with a toothpick, politely covering his work with his free hand.

'Then the way you were let go. A man of such great worth and experience, loyal public servant, thrown aside for nothing. Betrayed by the system you were dedicated to supporting. It must make you so angry.'

'I would not go that far.' Jian was full, for the first time in what felt like months. He put his chopsticks on the stand.

'No, really, look at what they did to you. Living on gambling money, dressing like a kitchen hand. A sad story. Even a tragic one. But it does not have to have a sad ending. I like helping people. I like helping people who help me.'

He went to a cupboard and took out a suit in a plastic wrapping, shoes, shirt. 'I had to guess the size. I can't have you walking around like that, not while you work for me. You can get dressed in there. There's a shower, if you'd like to freshen up.'

He called, 'A friend is coming through,' and opened the door to a bedroom. A naked girl lounged on a huge, unmade bed, playing on her phone. She did not glance up as he passed. Jian showered in the en suite and changed into the suit. It was single-breasted, with slimmer lapels than he was used to, but the material was fine and silky and the fit snug. There were notes in the inside pocket, at least two hundred pounds. He could hardly recognise himself in the steamed up mirror. He unwrapped and used hotel comb and toothbrush. The shoes, surprisingly, were a good fit. He left his old clothes on the bathroom floor. This time when he came out the girl watched him pass.

Uncle Seven said, 'Like a new man. You know what, Jian? I don't think this will be the last time we work together.' He held up a hand. 'Before you protest, hear me out. Now I can see how, for someone like you, it might seem a big step to make common cause with me. It isn't really. You won't have to be initiated, or get a tattoo. What do you think we do? Say a prayer in a holy circle, thrust a hand in a bag of rice, swear to restore the Ming dynasty – then go out and chop a labour organiser? No one does that shit, if they ever did, it's ancient history. I know how we sound – our reputation can be useful – but all we really are is a loose conglomeration of multinational business concerns. You would simply be an affiliate, with a freelance role that suits your skills, and in many important respects, resembles your previous position.'

He went to the window, opened the drapes.

'I know what you are thinking. You think you are a servant of the law, it's too big a step. But you are a servant of Chinese law. Here, the rules are different. Look.'

He gestured at the view. Buildings with iron balconies and shuttered windows looked like they had stood for centuries, as did the huge trees. 'What do you see? Your people? No. Your government, your rules? No. A strange world that has no place for you. I'm not sure what you are now. Are you?

111

Certainly not a policeman. So. Adapt. The way I did all those years ago.'

He stepped away from the window. 'Well, that's for the future. Let's sort the business in hand first. You'll make the deadline?'

'I'm confident.'

'Excellent. So am I. You always get your man. That's what it says.'

19

WeiWei considered herself in a dressing-room mirror. She reckoned she looked about the worst she ever had, with tangled hair, dull eyes, furry unbrushed teeth, and no makeup. She was in last night's rumpled clothes, which smelled of booze and cigarettes. Simply to be seen in public like this was bad enough, but she had a date. A transformation was required. With no fairy grandmother or magic carpet to effect it, she was resorting to desperate measures: she was trying her hand at shoplifting.

She had taken a couple of random items into the fitting room. The strappy top and jeans she intended to steal were secreted in a plastic bag. Now she just had to get them wrapped in silver foil. This trick was learned from her father: she'd once heard him mention a shoplifting gang using foil-lined bags to block the signals from RFID markers. She had assumed the wrapping to be the easy part of the operation, but the foil was so noisy. After a particularly loud crackle, the fittings girl knocked on the door. 'Everything okay there Miss?'

'Yes, fine. Just… fine.'

Her phone rang, and she was glad of the interruption.

It was HuaGua. 'Just wanted to check you were still coming. Where are you?'

Her go-to response formed: *wo zai wai mian* – 'I'm out!' It was repeated as often as a catchphrase, to guys on the phone pestering to know where she was. She liked to make a game out of seeing how vague she could be. 'I'm out!' 'Out where?' 'Not at home!' 'Yes but where are you?' 'I just felt like getting out, there was nothing on TV, where are you?' – and so on. Never tell a boy where you are, if you could avoid it: a basic rule, like never be on time, never pay, and *sajiao* – throw a pouty sulk – on date three.

She faltered. She no longer possessed the ease and indifference that came from being a girl with options. For once she was heavily invested in the outcome, and that tied her tongue. Debating what might be the smartest thing to say robbed her of the ability to say anything smart at all. She blustered 'I'm picking my outfit. I won't be late,' and ended the call. What a stupid remark. Now she was committed to turning up well-dressed. She should have said she was riding or boating or some similar elite time-waster. Then she could turn up in any old clothes, with the excuse that she had been so engrossed she had not seen the time and had to rush.

She sneezed to cover the ripping and wrapping. All of this was justified, she reminded herself, by extreme circumstances. The usual rules could be discreetly set aside until normal conditions resumed. She had used most of the foil, so she stashed the tube under the chair. When she walked out the girl glared at her, and WeiWei gave another fake sneeze as she handed over the items she had entered with.

Back on the shop floor, instinct told her to skulk and scoot but she forced herself to walk slowly, keep head and gaze level, notice but not look at staff, and resist the temptation to check behind her. The illicit goods in her bag seemed to radiate heat and light: how could they not be seen? Coming to the electronic sentry posts at the door, she held her breath and braced for a siren blast. But she passed in silence, normal life persisted, and then she was, gloriously, just another roving shopper in a crowd. She felt a giddy rush.

She was in an underground mall in a smart part of the city called Canary Wharf. She could see why the Red Scholars and their ilk gravitated towards it, as it was quite like home, more so than that chintzy Chinatown *hutong* in Soho. The restaurant couldn't be more than a five-minute walk, so she had at least an hour to get ready. She hit more shops, taking pumps, cosmetics, scrunchie, comb. All easily concealable and tag-free.

She began to almost enjoy herself, or at least to find something to relish, in this new role. She felt herself a predatory animal moving sleek and unnoticed in a herd, privy to a dangerous and powerful secret: after all, it was possible to live outside the law.

On a rising escalator she stood behind a middle-aged lady with a handbag dangling off her arm. A plump purse was almost falling out. It would be the simplest matter to pluck it, like reaching into a tree for a ripe apricot. If stealing from shops was justifiable, then why not from people? A purse like that would complete her outfit, plus there would likely be cash in there, which meant she could pay her way later. The woman was expensively dressed, no doubt rich: for her, the loss would be only a momentary inconvenience. She was ugly and had bad taste: her many resources would only be spent on more pricey clothes that did not suit her or make her more attractive, you could say it would be wasted. WeiWei would find far better ways to spend the money, and her need was greater.

If it were to happen, it must be now, before the escalator reached its apex. WeiWei's fingers stole forward. Just as nail touched leather, she caught her reflection in glass at the side. She saw someone just like her, but sly and underhand. She was abruptly unhappy and ashamed, and wanted an end to this sport. She shrank back, and flicked her fingers as if to shake them dry.

Then she saw at the top, a security guard, a portly black man, watching her, waiting for her, and holding the tube of foil. He pointed it at her. 'Excuse me, madam...'

She ran away, and he hurried after her. She turned aside in front of a slow-moving group of shoppers, and as they advanced they blocked his way, allowing her to extend her lead. She heard him saying, 'Excuse me, excuse me,' then he was out of sight and hearing. She sprinted down some stairs, took random turns, hurried upstairs again. Momentum and panic kept her going for more than a minute, long after she had seen any sign of the guard. She stopped and panted, hands on knees, and realised people were looking at her.

She followed signs to the ladies loos, where she locked herself in a cubicle. It took her several minutes to calm down. She had come shockingly close to being arrested, perhaps sent to prison, even deported. She did not want to risk walking around out there any more. She would stay shut in here till it was time to go to the restaurant. These risks had better be worth it. When her hands were steady she lined stolen cosmetics on the cistern and began making herself nice.

20

Jian had his map book flattened against the Treasure Horse steering wheel. He navigated by counting turn-offs, from landmarks such as roundabouts, parks and churches, and by following railway lines. He reckoned he was growing more adept at finding his way around, and now rarely had to brake to check the map, reverse back the way he had come, or do a U-turn in busy traffic. He was getting used to the road system and was, for the most part, staying out of the lane reserved for buses and bowler hat taxis, and not speeding or going the wrong way down one-way streets. He was getting shouted and honked at much less frequently.

Heading out of the city centre, he passed through a genteel residential area, with no graffiti or billboards and more whites. He supposed that the grand residences here were inhabited by three generations of the same family, with servants in the basement and a patriarch in the penthouse: a practical and elegant style of living. Perhaps he would finally see those figures so disappointingly absent in his travels thus far: those elegant imperialists with their hats and umbrellas, the English gentlemen.

Further out and it was all low houses with gardens. Such wasteful use of land, within commuting distance of the city centre, seemed selfish and impractical. Why couldn't they live in flats in tall multistoreys the way people had learned to live in cities everywhere else? No wonder rents were so high. To-Mu's road was a long quiet strip of semi-detached houses. Annoyingly, householders were allowed to put their number up anywhere they felt like, and he only found 34 on his second pass. A low wall did nothing to screen neat little lawn, shrubbery, gravel path to front door. Through a downstairs window he could see shelves of books and ornaments and framed pictures on walls. A dwelling very respectable in appearance, and if this was the lair of a gang of desperate armed robbers, they were good at hiding it.

He drove on, came to a high street, and double-parked. In an Indian shop, he tried to make himself understood, using the phrase his daughter had taught him, *Po-ku ska-ching*. No one had yet understood him, and today was no different, he got the usual frowns and head shakes. Never mind: he found the delicious salty pork bits by himself. At the counter, he considered his reflection in the mirror door that screened the cigarettes. It was the first time in weeks he could bear holding his own gaze. Finally he had some face. The suit was not his style though: too sharp, too fashionable.

Just before he left home there had been a move to encourage officials into Zhongshans. Every right-thinking cadre should be following the example set by the Central Committee. Each detail on a Zhongshan suit was designed to represent a virtue suitable for a public official. The three buttons near the end of the sleeve stood for propriety, justice and integrity. The back of a Zhongshan was one piece to symbolise the unity of the country. And so on. The way things were going – well, he bet everyone back at the office was wearing one of those boxy numbers now. He checked his suit's sleeve. No buttons at all. His reflections, and his reflection, were interrupted when the counter boy slid the door open, revealing a gallery of grim medical pictures. He pointed and was given a packet with a diseased organ on the cover. He was reminded of similar grotesques pasted up outside the station back home, designed to shock citizens out of walking on train lines, drinking bleach or driving drunk, and felt a jab of homesickness. Funny what brought it on.

At a second-hand shop he bought leather gloves and a cap, and at a hardware store he bought crowbar, scissors, rope, duct tape, and a bag for it all. The car was distinctive, so he drove it to a side street, left it and walked back. He hoped that To-Mu lived alone, and could be easily subdued, but it looked like he might be living with his parents. He could hardly bop the lad on the head and drag him out before hysterical mother, enraged father. Backup might be useful. But he was not asking Uncle Seven for help, tong thugs would likely start shooting the place up and endangering civilians. They might extend their revenge to a blameless family.

Outside the house, Jian crouched to tie his shoelaces. No lights on inside, and he did not see an alarm system. A flimsy wooden fence round the side blocked access to the back. That would be a wall back home, with glass shards on top. It swayed and cracked as he went over. Just beyond it he found a window. He was preparing to smash it when he realised it was only resting on the sill. He levered it open with the crowbar and clambered into a washroom.

No one was in. The homely dwelling was entirely lacking evidence of vice, poverty or madness. There were crocheted antimacassars on the armchairs in the living room, and coasters stacked on an occasional table. He examined family photos in gilt frames. To-Mu, from gurning toddler to gauche adolescent, and his mother, a compact Asian woman with a taste for colourful, flowing dresses. She had the same toothy grin in every shot. She was pretty striking in the older pictures, must have been a handful in her day. No evidence of a father anywhere. If he had died there'd be photos. He must have taken off.

In the mother's bedroom he found yoga mat, incense burner, discovered that her taste in clothes had not changed. A double bed but only one bedside table. A little study next door held filing cabinets and a desktop computer. To-Mu's bedroom had been ransacked. Drawers hung open, and clothes, books and papers were scattered. A burglar would surely have made off with that camera and laptop. The lad himself then, the nosy mother or an intruder hunting something specific? All the papers and books were in English but he owned a few well-thumbed Chinese-language textbooks. Presumably the lad couldn't read or write well – a common deficiency among Chinese who had the misfortune to grow up in foreign lands – and was trying to improve. His passion was for making and dressing up in outlandish outfits copied from his comics: there were swatches of material, a sewing machine, fake weapons and armour, masks, and costumes. A preponderance of improbably muscular and underdressed cartoon men on the wall posters hinted at homosexual tendencies.

Jian found a document with a cover design of whimsical beasts holding up a shield. Not more fantasy nonsense, despite initial appearance: it was a British passport. If the lad had done a runner, he'd surely have taken that. It seemed a good guess that he would be coming home soon.

After checking that he wouldn't be seen from the window, Jian made himself comfortable on the sofa in the lounge and munched pork bits. He craved a cigarette but that was out of the question, anyone arriving would smell it.

Only a desperate man would raid a tong gambling den with a fake gun. Perhaps illicit homosexual pleasures had got the lad into trouble: 'comrades' were prone to being blackmailed. Or he might have embraced a sordid life of criminality, which was so often the case when a father was not around to provide discipline and a good example. But most likely it was gambling debts. The lad had racked up substantial losses, and if he didn't pay them off would suffer dire consequences. A depressingly common eventuality, in Jian's experience.

Grab a skinny arm, control the elbow, twist it, force him down. Probably have to hit him on the head. Knee on his back. Gag him, tape him, hood him. What a hassle if the mother came home too, she'd also have to be silenced and restrained. Then drive the car up, risk a hernia in folding captive into capacious boot.

There was nothing like sitting in the semi-dark in a stranger's house with a weapon on your lap for prompting gloomy intro-spection. WeiWei had reacted far better than he had a right to expect. But in admitting the situation to her he was also finally acknowledging to himself that this was not a temporary embarrassment but a new way of life. This was him, then, for the foreseeable future: a man without wealth, employment or status, adrift in a baffling world, trying against the odds and the run of play, to make the best of a bad hand.

21)

Shan stood outside a modern residential block in Hoxton. Earlier, she had rung Butterfly's phone, and having received no reply, gone to visit. No answer at the intercom panel downstairs, and after she got in, no reply at Butterfly's front door on the third floor either. Blank door, silence, no answer, nothing, on and on: enraging. Then she had remembered spotting an unfamiliar Yale key in a drawer of Tom's desk, and wondered if just possibly Butterfly had given her lover the spare. So she had driven home for the key and here she was, for a second time.

Again she waited for someone exiting the block to leave the door open for her, which they did without question. One advantage of being a little middle-aged Asian lady, no one saw you as a threat, or even took much notice of you at all: you could go anywhere. As suspected, the Yale fitted Butterfly's door. She was pleased with herself, then apprehensive. What if someone was in, or came home now? She had no good explanation for being here. At best, she would be accused of prying and at worst, burglary. If confronted she would bluster some nonsense, maybe pretend not to speak English.

She turned the key, which made, as feared, a heavy clunk, and pushed the door slowly open, onto a hallway. A picture had fallen down. The frame was smashed, and broken glass glimmered among an untidy gathering of shoes. Something had happened here.

She fumbled her pepper spray out of her bag. Home-made, from pure capsaicin apparently, and in the unlikely vessel of a perfume bottle shaped like a busty chest. It had been given to her by an admin woman at a women's refuge, back when she was volunteering: the lady had sworn by its formidable stopping power. It was reassuring to have a weapon to raise before her as she trespassed.

She called, 'Hello?' and received no answer. 'Excuse me, hello? I'm looking for Butterfly.' Still nothing. She crept forward. It was a studio flat with wooden floors and white walls, crisp and compact, with bathroom, bedroom and a living-room-cum-kitchen, and it did not take long to discover that no one was here. She put the spray away, went back and closed the front door, opened the curtains in the main room. A spear and swords were propped against a bookshelf cluttered with comics and figurines. More shelves held fabrics, armour, sewing machine – the same model as Tom's. Another cosplayer: what a sweet couple they must make dressed in matching outfits. Her books were exhibition catalogues, tattoo collections and the like, in English and Chinese. She guessed Butterfly was studying art and she formed an impression of a girl who was flighty, creative, geeky. Too rich to have had any serious problems or life experience, perhaps a little spoiled.

She found photo albums. She had assumed the younger generations didn't go for those any more, but perhaps there was something retro cool about having it, like owning vinyl. Here were neatly labelled and dated images of Butterfly jumping at European beauty spots, striking cutesy poses in Japan, sitting cross-legged in India. A babyish face, dyed hair cut asymmetrically, statement glasses coordinated with outlandish outfits. Delicate features and wide, sensual lips. A couple of beach shots revealed butterfly tattoos over arms and chest. The images, she felt, confirmed her impressions. She was quite wrong on one account though: Butterfly was a boy.

Normally that would be an earthquake: but it wasn't something to bother with now, and did not occupy her for more than a quarter of second, just enough time to dismiss it as something to be processed another time. Another album held pictures of Butterfly posing in cosplay. She'd learned about the hobby from her son and recognised some outfits. That big hair and white face was 'L' from Deathnote, the freaky mask was a Tokyo Ghoul, that colourful pirate was maybe One Piece. An image labelled Resident Evil showed the lad in fatigues, toting a shotgun with a cut-down barrel. She found a set of Butterfly and Tom posing as the Mario brothers, in colourful overalls, caps, fake moustaches.

The last and oldest album showed a younger Butterfly. All the pictures had been taken in China – she recognised the Bund, Tian'anmen Gate, Lijiang's water wheel. There was a middle-aged man in a couple of pictures, standing stiff and unsmiling. The father was chubby and balding but he had the same full lips. So the kid used to go on holiday with his dad. She imagined their story. Back in China: a shy, awkward little emperor who never feels quite right. He leaves for a foreign country, escaping the clutches of culture and family, and starts exploring his sexuality, constructing a new identity. Believing he has reached his final flamboyant form, he renames himself Butterfly, dyes his hair and gets tattooed. Daddy would be in for a shock when his boy came home.

She continued investigating in the bedroom. The bed was unmade. The duvet and pillows were on the floor, as if thrown aside in a hurry. A lamp and a clock radio lay beside them, knocked off the bedside cabinet. When she switched the light on, she saw an arc of dark blobs on the wall at about head height. She spat on a tissue and rubbed one into a red smear. It was blood.

A bolt of panic shot through her. She sat on the bed to recover senses and breath. A few days' old, she guessed. As if someone had been smacked hard, quite high – in the face say, the mouth – and blood had spattered as their head snapped back.

Someone dragged out of bed maybe, then a fight... What if Butterfly had come to harm, at the hand of intruders say, and loyal Tom was now fretting by a hospital bed? Possible, but how would they have got in? There were no signs of forced entry. Not intruders then... say a party had got out of hand, punches had been thrown... Or how about... Butterfly had attacked someone, who had fallen and hit their head and had a cerebral haematoma and died – which after all happened all the time – and her son was off in wood or lake or quarry, helping Butterfly hide the corpse? Or – what a traitor her imagination was – Tom and Butterfly had a lover's tiff, and fists had flown, and Butterfly had hit his head and died, and poor petrified Tom was off hiding the body in one of the aforementioned dismal locales. That appalling scenario fitted the facts as well as anything else.

A missing boy, maybe two, a scene of disarray, and a spatter of blood: one thing was certain, the police needed to know. She would give him one last chance. She called Tom and, once more, got his voicemail.

She said, enunciating carefully, 'Tom? If you're getting my messages I wish you'd pick up. You definitely need to listen to this one. I found out about Butterfly. I went to his flat. Don't ask me how I... well, I used your key. I'm in the flat now. I'm in the bedroom, and – and I'm looking at a bloodstain, on the wall.' Saying it upset her over again, and her voice cracked. 'So you can understand... why I'm so worried. Something has happened here. I'm...'

The phone beeped. She had run out of time. She had more to say, so she phoned again, and carried on, talking faster this time, breathless and urgent. 'I don't care what it is, what kind of trouble you think you are in, I don't care what you've done.'

She was pacing. 'Call me and let's deal with it together. Call me right now. If you don't call right now I'm going to go to the police.'

She ended the call and closed her eyes and tried to calm her ragged breathing. She was still wondering how many minutes to give him when her phone rang. She answered it.

'Tom?'

'Mum.'

Oh, he sounded just the same. She pressed the hot phone hard against her face. It was damp from the sweat of her hands. 'What is going on? You need to tell me what is going on.'

'I told you, just wait, I'm dealing with it.'

'Dealing with what? Tom...'

'Don't call the police. Whatever you do, don't do that. Just... go home. On Monday everything will be okay.'

'I don't care about it, just tell me.'

'Go home. Please Mum. No police.'

'Tom...'

The line went dead.

'Oh bloody...bloody... fuckings.' She swore rarely, and only in English, though knew she never quite got it right.

She wanted to hurl something, so she threw the phone, though only at the bed, as she couldn't risk it breaking. It bounced off and hit the wall and dropped. She scrambled after it. The screen had cracked.

On her knees, she called him back. There was no reply.

)

WeiWei had cut the tag off the sparkly top, trimmed stolen jeans to thigh length, talked a bookshop cashier into giving her a cotton bag. With a touch of make-up she looked acceptable: she could pass as a dressed-down average rich girl, albeit one who didn't care all that much what others thought of her.

The restaurant was on the other side of the mall. She didn't want to go through it again and risk meeting the security guard so she traipsed around the outside. The buildings in this zone looked like harmonious parts of a grand design. Groomed parks and pedestrian areas made it feel more for people than traffic. She approved, it was pleasing to see the ramshackle city catching up with the modern world. It was, however, rather confusing to get around, and she arrived later than intended.

The restaurant had bare brick walls, pale wood furnishings and waifish, black-suited staff. HuaGua beckoned. He was on a quayside patio with a group of Asians, at least eight of them. She recognised some from the night before. Why, this wasn't a date at all. Had she got the wrong idea, had he just not told her, or could he be getting her back for the quick exit in the morning?

She opened glass doors and went out. They were all dressed in conservative smart casual, she was showing more skin and less class than any of the girls. Feeling out of place and under scrutiny, her cheeks burned. She blustered her hellos. It had felt so much easier last night. It was so bright out here, and the glimmer and sparkle on water and tableware was so distracting. She had forgotten who was who, and introduced herself to a boy she had met before, assumed a prior introduction to one she hadn't. Space was made for her on the opposite side of the table from HuaGua.

To her surprise – there was no clue in the decor – the food was Japanese. She thought Japanese cuisine suspect, even unpatriotic. Raw fish struck her as slimy and unhealthy, and bad for a lady's delicate stomach, especially at certain times of the month.

The menu was on handmade paper with ragged edges. She was only vaguely aware of what terms like sushi, sashimi and tempura meant, but clearly understood the prices: eighty quid for the brunch buffet, which they were all doing, and that didn't include drinks. This group was large, progressive in inclination, with no obvious leader. It would certainly be one of those occasions where everyone was expected to contribute equally to the bill, Western-style. How was she going to get out of this? She could not, for the second day in a row, plead that she had left her wallet at home.

HuaGua was ignoring her. Should she just get up and leave? But then she would never be able to face these people again. While she was deliberating, some girl poured her a glass of wine and started telling her about a ball she would be attending, how she was to be presented to a duke, would be wearing a tiara like an actual duchess. Lost for a reply, WeiWei slugged the drink, and swilled it round her mouth in a pretence of appreciation. It was just sour grape juice, but its rich red colour was lovely, and so was the glass, and the plates, and the well-groomed staff and the fashionable fittings. Abandon this and do what? Go back and look at the mould on the wall? She needed beauty in her life, without it she withered. She would stay, take things as they come and find a way to make it work out.

23)

Jian heard the front door open, and listened to a solitary new arrival take off shoes and pad into the kitchen. A cupboard door opened, a tap ran, a chair scraped as it was pulled out. He rose and stepped into the hallway. The mother sat at the kitchen table with her back to him, hunched over, head in her hands, shoulders juddering as she sobbed.

She was wrapped up in her own emotions and not attentive. She was small and weak. One hand over her mouth. Pull her hand behind her back. Pick her up, force her to the floor. Get tape over her mouth. A simple job. But an unpleasant one. There was another way to play it. He backed away with measured steps. He eased the latch on the front door and slipped out, then closed it softly.

He stood on the front step and smoked a cigarette. Tom came out here to smoke too, judging by the butts in a can on the wall. He considered the damaged organ on his packet. He'd be fucked if he got ill. He reminded himself to eat garlic and ginger, stretch every morning, do circuits in a park. When he finished smoking he cleared his lungs, hawking up goo. He examined it for blood flecks then smeared it with his heel, put the butt in the can.

He took off his gloves and rang the doorbell. She took a long time to answer. You wouldn't know she'd been weeping, just a little redness under the eyes. She was trim and short, the wrong side of forty but not so you'd care too much, dressed in jeans and slippers and a baggy cardigan. Her only jewellery, a hint at the flamboyance he'd seen in the photos, was a big ornate butterfly clip in her hair.

He said, in Mandarin, 'Hello. Is To-Mu there?'

'No.'

'Do you know when he might be back?'

'No.'

'Do you know where he is?'

She was crushing tissue in her hand. 'How do you know my son?'

'We hang out.' Jian added a camp lilt. 'He's a very nice boy.'

Her foggy gaze cleared. He had her full attention now.

'What's your name?'

'I'm Jian.'

'I'm Shan. What kind of relationship did you have with him?'

'I gave him advice.'

'He never mentioned you.'

'Well. That's me.' He let a silence stretch. He'd conducted enough interviews to know the power of not speaking. People hated silence, and would blurt their secrets to fill it. Finally she said, 'Well, he certainly doesn't tell me everything. I'm sure you're… Look… what it is…' She sighed. 'I'm worried about him. I haven't seen him for a while. Well actually, to be honest, I'm at my wits end.' Her voice grew strained. 'I have this idea… that he may be in trouble.'

'You know what? That's what I think, too.'

'You'd better come in.'

24)

This Jian was tall, rather stern-looking, with deep lines etched on a wide face. Well dressed, with a tone and accent that showed education and authority. A father figure: Tom was a sucker for those, his own having proved somewhat lacking. A mentor for Tom perhaps, an older gay man who was bringing her son into that world.

The intrusion of a figure from her son's secret world reignited an issue. So her boy was gay. She wondered how long he had known, how many men – no, it didn't matter. Who cared what bodies he liked. She just wanted him back.

She led her visitor into the kitchen. He said, 'What's wrong?'

'He hasn't come home for days. I don't know what to think. He's such a good, quiet boy, he's never been any trouble, and now…' It was a relief to unburden herself, but she realised she should not say too much. She shouldn't mention the empty flat with the bloodstains, for example. 'I keep thinking, has he run away, is he tracking down his father, what?'

'It must be so awful for you.'

'It is. That's why I'm sitting here going out of my mind.'

She brought herself back. 'But sorry, I'm so rude, my manners have all gone. Would you like a drink?'

'Water, please.'

'So… What made you worried enough to come here?'

'Oh, he didn't turn up for a lunch date. That's all.'

'Yes, and he's normally so conscientious. And you know this address because?'

'Well, he gave it to me. I'm sure we would have met some time. When do you think he'll come home?'

'I found out about his boyfriend. And now here you are. Are there any more secret friends I should know about?'

'Oh I don't think so.' His fingers tapped his lip. 'Oh, well there might be one. I did see him recently with a rather rough type who drives a dirty yellow van. Do you know who that might be?'

'No idea. He doesn't know any rough people. His friends are like him. Shy and nerdy. They do role playing, archery, they go to comic conventions… Describe this rough type.'

'I only caught a glimpse. Tattooed arms. White, tall, skinny. Walks with a kind of shuffle. Loud.'

'He's experimenting, finding out who he is. He must be consorting with new people. Who knows what kind of new person he…' Feeling in danger of insulting her guest she ground to a halt.

But he did not appear to be listening. He was staring out of the window and his glass was frozen on its way to his mouth. He put it down, said, 'It was nice talking to you. I hope he turns up soon. I have to go.'

She showed him out then returned to the kitchen. What an odd man. The fluttering voice and camp gestures did not fit the flinty tough-guy looks. Had he been putting her on? The way he hurried off. He'd been looking at the garden when he decided to go: he couldn't have seen something, could he? No, an absurd idea, there was nothing out there, just plant pots on the patio, shrubs along the wall, then at the back of the sloping lawn a shed, a fence and beyond, a glimpse of the railway line, down in a cutting. Graffiti was sprayed on the wall on the far side of the line, one of those childish anarchy symbols again. Another time, she'd get annoyed about that.

25

WeiWei was full and slightly tipsy. It was time for her plan. It wasn't great but it was the best she could come up with. She had been inspired by recent events: she would pretend to have been pickpocketed. A few minutes of acting flustered and annoyed, then she'd shrug it off, and come the end of the meal be absolved of paying her share of the bill. First a little theatre was necessary. She patted her pockets, frowned, looked in her book bag. 'That's funny,' then, as if to search it more thoroughly, she emptied the bag out onto the table. She was about to start wondering aloud where on earth her purse could have got to when she realised her mistake. Everyone was silent and looking at her phone. She may as well have dumped a six-inch cockroach.

Someone poked it. 'What is that?'

'WeiWei? Is that... That's never yours?'

She cringed and snatched up the ignoble thing. But it was too late. What a catastrophic loss of face. Maybe she should stand and shout, 'Yes, yes it's mine. Because I'm poor! I'm poor and my father is a fugitive and in disgrace.'

She might have done just that a week ago, or grabbed the phone and ran. But she decided – fuck it – to front it. After all, she had nothing to lose. She fought back the instinct to get the heinous thing out of sight and did the opposite: she brandished her shame like a trophy.

'Yes it's mine. And it is... amazing. It does calls and text and that is all. And that is freedom.' She banged it down. 'I want to connect with the real world. Not get lost in a screen. That's the problem with our generation. These things,' – she gestured at their phones on the table – 'they take as much as they give. I'm so sick of screens and internet and social media! It's a constant distraction.'

They looked dubious. But at least she had their attention. She surged recklessly on.

'All that, it's so… deadening and distracting and it's not real. I have so much time now, for reading, and talking face to face with actual people, and… just…' she gestured at the scene, 'looking at the world. Really looking. When did you last really look at something? Not to take a picture, not to post about it, just to… see.' For a finale she set her mobile spinning on the table. 'It's really improved my life. I call it… descreening.' She sat down, where she added, for the benefit of the sceptical, 'Lots of celebrities are doing it.'

'I don't see how it's possible to live without WeChat.'

'Without my phone I feel utterly alone.'

'How do you know what your friends are doing?'

'I wouldn't have the discipline.'

'I want to try.'

'We should all give it a go. Just for a week, say.'

'But it's so ugly-looking… maybe if it came in gold…'

She was not listening. It didn't matter if they agreed or not, she had got away with it.

'It is a bold choice,' said HuaGua. The first proper sentence he'd spoken to her since she'd arrived. 'Maybe we're all addicts, we're sick and we just don't know it.'

'Exactly.'

'But that phone doesn't even do characters. How do people IM you?'

'My real friends know to write to me in pinyin.'

'I know that now, does that make me a real friend?'

'There's a possibility.'

Content with the progress she was making, WeiWei went back to the buffet. Fortunately it wasn't all raw fish and seaweed. Back at the table, she revised her opinion of Japanese cuisine upwards. She would try these battered prawns again, if she ever got the chance, and resolved to learn their name. HuaGua changed places to be near her. He clinked his glass with hers, and a fine ringing note was struck.

She said, 'I thought this was a date.'

'Everyone wants to see you again. Not just me.'

'I don't believe you.'

'Let me take you shopping after, to apologise for the mix-up.'

'Certainly not. You can get my share of the bill though.'

'Sure.'

Six six six – how easy it could be sometimes.

26)

Two slanted uprights meeting at the top, slashed by a horizontal line halfway down – like the character *da* – 'big' – all inside a circle. Jian had seen the symbol flicker by yesterday: written with a finger on the grimy bodywork of a yellow van. He'd seen it again, sloppily sprayed on a wall beside the railway line, from the kitchen window of Tom's house. Now he was trudging the line and finding more examples. Assume the second robber, owner of the van, was the artist in question, leaving his sign everywhere he went like a dog – he had left a trail to be followed. Each symbol he found was a little neater than its predecessor. Presumably the vandal would have grown more slapdash as he repeated his sigil, so Jian was confident he was moving towards some manner of starting point.

He had walked over a kilometre, and passed more than thirty signs, and stepped up the slope into the bushes for two passing trains, when he found a trail of pale trampled greenery veering away from the line. He followed it, up through a screen of more bushes, and came to a chicken-wire fence. Beyond it lay a forlorn strip of scrub and a boxy, single-storey building, not much bigger than a shipping container. He could see a door and a window on the long side and on the short side he could see the familiar big white symbol: the neatest and largest so far.

The wire had been cut to make a discreet entrance. Jian peeled the sheet back and slipped through into spiky waist-high foliage peppered with rubbish. That gave way to knee-high clumps, then grass. The building seemed a temporary structure, rather grimly utilitarian, its windows blinded with wooden boards and the door secured with a padlock. A pallid strip showed where a vehicle parked up. Jian followed wheel ruts to a corrugated iron fence and found a loose sheet. He shifted it to reveal a track into a misty wood. At the edge of the sheet he found flecks of yellow paint, scraped from a passing vehicle.

As much by luck as design, he had found the den of the second robber, the Butcher. Likely the man was out now spending ill-gotten gains, celebrating success, fencing or pawning the jewellery. Hopefully, he would return soon, bleary and hungover, to rest. Jian could take him then. Much easier than going after To-Mu.

He stamped down a lookout post in the bushes and settled in to wait. He called his daughter. She had taken his news far better than expected, but she might have since fallen into despondency, and need bucking up. She sounded remarkably breezy, however, as she asked about the case. There was a buzz of conversation in the background, peels of laughter.

'Nearly there. I'll get paid when this is done, and take you out for that big dinner, have you thought about what you want to eat?'

She told him she wouldn't be hungry, as she was eating now: she was in a fancy restaurant with her new friends. He knew what that meant. She was dallying with last night's wolf. Lectures came to mind concerning care of reputation and name, the necessity of responsibility, how pleasure was fleeting and had long-term consequences, and what a certain kind of man was really like. But he paused. Now was not the time. Maybe it would never be the time again. All he said was, 'Don't eat anything too spicy, you know how it upsets your stomach.'

When he ended the call it was he who felt despondent. He had let her down in the most appalling way, consigned her to a grim and difficult future. And, it seemed, she had not even begun to take that in. To go out with meat-and-drink friends: of all the ridiculous and irresponsible things to do in a crisis. She was a pet rabbit thrown into a forest, hopping around, telling the bears how pretty their teeth looked. Well, it was his duty to keep the rabbit safe. His wait here could be a long one. He twitched and flexed to keep his circulation going and to jolt his mind from this track.

HuaGua was knocking back the sour grape juices. WeiWei didn't think she'd seen him sober. He asked her who she had been talking to.

'My dad.'

'He must be feeling pretty contrite after yesterday's display. You should use that. Ask him to bump up your allowance. That's what I'd do. Does he visit often?'

'This is his first trip.'

'So, what? Big Ben, London Eye, Bicester Village? Fish and chips that makes him ill? Inspect the stolen goods in the British Museum. Then on to Paris.'

She diverted the conversation. 'Have you shown your parents round?'

'They're too busy and important to bother. I'm left gloriously to myself. So why do you carry scissors? Self-defence?'

'Never know when you need to give the fringe a trim.'

'Your hair grows that fast?'

'I once mistook a bottle of fertilizer for shampoo, and it's never been the same.'

'I should tell my father to try it. You should see him fussing over his bald patch.'

'You want to know the real reason? So I can cut the labels off my clothes. I don't want people knowing where I bought them.'

'That fits. Goes with the whole "woman of mystery" shtick you've got going. What's she really doing here? Where does she live? She never tells.'

This was nice, but keeping it light and flirty while subtly deflecting inquiries required concentration. She was pleased to hear those disparaging remarks concerning his parents. It hinted that, if they did develop a more meaningful bond, family disapproval might not be an issue. In fact, it could be a factor in her favour. He could use their relationship to piss them off, if that was what he wanted: and how often, in her experience, was that just what was wanted. He was drawn into conversation with a boy opposite, and she relaxed into fantasy. Properly together, they'd be such a power couple, too cute for words. Any room graced with their presence would be elevated by their combined looks, wit and panache. And she knew she'd be good for him, helping him get a handle on his drinking, blunting his cynicism and encouraging him to experiment with colour.

Someone said, 'Let's go to that gambling den after. You know the one?'

'OMG,' said someone else, in English. 'It is bare retro.'

'And dirty! It's too ghetto. I don't like it. How could you want to go there? I must also be drunk.'

'You don't like it because you lose! Your game sucks! I am a god, I'll show you how it's done.'

'Didn't you hear? They got robbed! Last night!'

'No!'

'Robbed?'

'Yes, I saw it on WeChat! A gang turned the place over! They had machine guns.'

'People were getting hit! They took all the money!'

'I heard it was just two guys, Chinese and English.'

'Imagine if we were there!'

'Did anyone get killed?'

Hadn't her father talked about gambling Mahjong? And been beaten up for his troubles. Was he caught up in this? It would be typical. Just as WeiWei began to speculate whether there might be more than coincidence at play here, she was thrown into alarm by the sight, through a window and across the dining room, of a familiar uniform. The security guard had come in and was standing at the entrance, scanning the patrons. And he was accompanied by a second figure, a cop.

Acting without thinking much about it, she let her napkin drop, then got down under the table as if to retrieve it. She could see her hunter's trousered legs through a glass wall, striding towards the patio. Had she been seen coming in? The man, tenacious as a hawk, clearly knew, or at least suspected, she was here. Every other security guard she had ever encountered had been apathetic at best, what bad luck to encounter one with drive and determination. She was going to be arrested. To be humiliated in front of her new friends, dragged away, interrogated and thrown into a cell.

She ducked and scuttled past the table, then between other tables, and into the main dining area. Just at that moment, two waiters emerged from swing doors bearing with some ceremony a model bamboo boat full of raw fish and ice. A group of diners ahh-ed and clapped in response, drawing attention. Under cover of the distraction, WeiWei slipped through the doors, and found herself in a kitchen. Staff shouted and shooed. She strode past them, banged through an exit, hurried along a dim corridor, and barged through a fire door into brightness. She was back in the mall. She would get out of here as fast as she could and never return. She brought HuaGua's number up on her phone, and texted in pinyin 'YOU SHI! ZAI JIAN!!!' – 'I have something to do, lol, see you soon' – as she hurried away.

28)

Jian heard a vehicle growling through the wood. It stopped, then the loose corrugated sheet in the wall was shifted aside. The yellow snub-nosed minibus was parked with the engine running. The driver got back in and tooled it forward and parked in his habitual place.

Jian peeked and saw the Butcher get out and swig from a bottle. He still wore the clothes from the robbery and now a glut of jewellery sparkled round his neck and arms. Jian stalked forward, hands on his crowbar, observing with a predatory gaze: how drunk, how quick, how strong. He would not pull any strikes. Killing this man would be a mercy. He would make it quick, which the tong would not. Elbows, knees, fingers, were protuberances that could be used to subdue and control. The face was a meat slab, nothing important there but eyes which betrayed intention.

The Butcher ambled back to his improvised gate. He tried pulling it shut with one hand, realised that wasn't going to work, and put the bottle down so he could do it with two. Then he abruptly dropped the sheet, jerked upright and raised his hands in the air. He was responding to a second figure, who now stepped up from crackling undergrowth. A tall, ponytailed youth in oversize overalls: To-Mu. Aiming a compound bow. He pulled it back to full draw.

Jian sank back. So the melodrama of this hapless pair of villains was still playing out, before its inevitable unhappy ending. The Butcher had taken all the spoils, and gone out to celebrate: now here was the other thief to reclaim his rightful share. The lad must have been staking the place out from the other side, this whole time he had been within a hundred metres. The bow was presumably the best weapon he could come up with at short notice; the mother had mentioned friends who did archery. Not a terrible idea, an arrow could hit as hard as a bullet at short range, but there were obvious disadvantages: he only had one shot, could easily fumble the arrow off the riser, and would not have the strength to hold the bow taut for more than a few seconds at a time.

The Butcher flailed and stumbled, exaggerating his drunkenness. After more talk, he lay down on his front. Tom sidled round him and up to the vehicle. His arm began to quiver from the strain of keeping the bowstring tense.

The lad was such an amateur it was painful to watch. He put the bow down and fumbled the passenger door open, then reached into the minibus and snatched out the racing car pillowcase. It was laden still and awkward to hold. He seemed uncertain how to carry both it and the bow, and dithered, first picking up the bow and dropping the pillowcase, then holding the pillowcase and dropping the bow, finally trying to hold the bag with his teeth while fiddling to get the wavering arrow nocked.

There was a sense of the inevitable to the next move, the Butcher jumping up and running at him. Jian was only surprised he had waited this long. In a moment the Butcher was across the space with arms outstretched and they went down together, out of sight in the long grass. Jian listened to thumps and smacks. After some time the Butcher stood up and rested with his hands on his knees. To-Mu was prone at his feet. The Butcher went to his bottle and swigged it, rubbed his mouth with the back of his hand, then grabbed Tom by his ankles. The lad seemed insensible as the Butcher dragged him noisily and effortfully away. He hauled Tom through the hole in the fence, and started yanking and rolling him down the slope towards the railway line.

In a couple of minutes he came clumping back. The man should be easy to take down now, and Jian readied himself. But he did not get his chance. The man hurried to the minibus and drove it rapidly away, he didn't even stop to close his gate.

Jian thrashed down to the line. He found Tom sprawled on the tracks, unconscious. Now the Butcher's speedy exit made sense, he didn't want to be anywhere nearby when a train squished the lad into offal. He was presumably off establishing an alibi.

He heard a train approaching. Jian pulled the lad aside and it roared past. It whipped up dust which settled all over his new suit.

Jian unzipped his bag, found his duct tape and scratched with a nail for the edge. The next part of the operation looked exhausting and inconvenient. He'd have to truss the kid and leave him. Then jog to get the car, bring it round, park as close as possible. With luck he would find some quiet access road not too far away, perhaps in the wood. Maybe there were trails in there he could get the car down. Then he'd have to lug his captive to it. All without being seen.

The lad was coming round. His face was bruised and one eye was swelling shut. He considered Jian with the other, blinking rapidly. He bore a striking facial resemblance to the mother. That woman, soon enough, would have something to cry about. Well, he was used to that. Wailing mothers had spat and slapped him. The lowliest criminal had a mother to weep for him and declare his persecutors monstrous. You didn't last long as a cop if you were swayed by such.

The lad opened his mouth and blood trickled from a split lip. He coughed and swallowed. Finally he got it out. He said 'You… you saved me…'

Jian found the edge and tape screeched as he pulled it out. 'Not really.'

恶劣环境 **HOSTILE ENVIRONMENT**

After a second brush with elite living, the bedsit seemed to WeiWei even smaller and shabbier. That mould patch could not really have grown in such a brief absence, could it? As at every arrival, she first propped the window open with an empty bottle then spent long fiddly moments on her knees, jamming her phone upright under the plug to keep the capricious cable at a right angle for it to charge. HuaGua had still not contacted her. Had he dismissed her from his mind? How tempting just to ring him. She could make up an excuse, say her father had called her away for instance, or something more glamorous – her yacht was sinking, her horse escaped. Get an explanation out and move quickly on, ask about his lunch, make a date for another time. What a lovely chat they would have.

But she mustn't call! The only way to make her sudden exit work for her – just like in the story! – was to play intriguing woman of mystery, and for that she had to be aloof. However their conversation went it would telegraph her as available, ordinary, explicable, all of which would lower her value and decrease his interest. She would become just another face on his no doubt considerable roster. But what if he didn't call, what then?

To keep herself occupied she swept the floor, made beds, had another try at fixing the broken window catch. She scrubbed to little effect at mottled grouting in the shower. She washed clothes in the sink and hung them round the room. Her wrists hurt from all the wringing and the chemicals in the washing powder made her palms sting. How much of this before she ruined her hands with gnarled knuckles and hard yellow callouses? A year, two? Careworn hands were an immediate low status giveaway: there would be no possibility of snagging a HuaGua then.

The phone rang. She rushed to it. It was him. With every trill her spirits rose. She did not answer it, of course, and presently he rang off. She waited, glaring intently at the device, willing it to life. Finally, the hoped for text arrived, a message written in pinyin. NI ZAI NAR? – 'Where are you, pretty girl?'

She should take her time. She dried her hands, then, on her knees again by the plug, wrote back. ZAI WAI MIAN! – 'I'm out!' She deleted the exclamation mark, added it, deleted it, counted to a hundred, sent it. Then remembered she had left the water running. She ran to the bathroom and found the sink overflowing and a puddle below. She turned off the taps and started mopping before being interrupted by a new message arriving, this one partially in English.

POOR LIL PLJJ

The acronym was short for *piaoliang jiejie*, pretty girl. Why 'poor', what was he driving at? She would text twice more, say something intriguing and sexy, then ghost. Copying his style she wrote: EXACTLY PLGG

Pretty boy – that risked being seen as a little effeminising. This kind of banter was much easier in person, or when you could use emojis to help clarify tone.

The reply came, in English: U STEALING AGAIN?

She jerked as if the phone had nipped her. She was busted. How? She texted: ?

The reply was unusually long: COP CAME TO THE TABLE. V EXCITING. WE DIDNT GIVE U UP THO!!!! SHOPLIFTER!!!

Her fingers jabbing in a frenzy, she typed I ACIDENTLY TOOK A TJING FROM SHOP THEN RAN WEN THEY CALL ME BACK!!! MISNDERSTNDING!!!!

She stopped. She was protesting too much, it just made her look guilty. She wiped all but the last word, added '88' to say goodbye. Then deleted the whole message and sat glumly slumped. She had nothing to say. Or rather too many possible things to say and no way of telling which might be right, which amounted to the same thing, paralysis and silence. And he was not going to be adding anything now, the secret rules of text conversation did not allow it – it would be a form of losing, and people like him did not lose. So the dialogue was over and perhaps that was the last she would ever hear from him. It seemed likely. A shoplifter was hardly girlfriend material.

She keeled over until she was lying down, and never mind the gritty air down here, the cloying dust, the rasping carpet tile. She was numb, immobilised, beached. This was going to go on, there was to be no progress, only a banality that spread like the mould.

30)

Shan poured boiled water from the kettle into a pot of instant noodles. She was not hungry but knew she had to eat to keep her strength up. She folded the foil top back around the lid to keep heat in while the noodles stewed. She recapped. Tom was on a mission, and did not want her, or the police, involved. He had a boyfriend called Butterfly, who might or might not be relevant. There had been recent violence in Butterfly's flat, and he might also be missing. A second strand: Tom had a mentor called Jian: an imposing figure with a brutish edge, camp affectations, and recent bruises. And he knew this address, which was quite odd come to think of it, as was the abrupt manner of his leaving. Reviewing their conversation, she wondered if it hadn't been an interrogation. He had asked about a yellow van. Was that the true focus of his inquiry?

She took the lid off the pot and felt the steam on her face. Maybe they were all part of the same story, it was one long twisted noodle. She began stirring with a fork. *Huoche*, he had said. She had assumed van but the term had a wide definition, it could mean truck or minibus or… as she raised fork to mouth an image came to mind, a grainy photo of a grubby yellow camper. Something on the residents' internet forum.

She got out her phone, loaded the website, trawled the archive. Potholes, proposals, parking restrictions – none of this interested her usually and it seemed even more petty now. Ah, here it was. A VW van parked before a corrugated iron fence. SQUATTER SCANDAL: COUNCIL MUST ACT. The post concerned a man who was squatting in a portacabin near the railway line, and asking the rhetorical question, why hadn't the council evicted him yet? A commenter explained that the cabin had been installed by an over-ambitious developer, who had gone bankrupt and vanished before putting his development plans into action, that now the land ownership was contested and not much could be done till that issue was resolved. Another, barely literate post concerned the squatter's anti-social behaviour, how he asked for money at bus stops and frightened dog walkers. A comment wondered if he might be behind a recent spate of break-ins, another declared that if the council would not just BLOODY SORT IT OUT perhaps residents should GET UP A PETITION.

It was hard to believe that Tom might have anything to do with such a person. But, she was learning, her boy had secrets. Anyway, there was no harm in nosing around. The place was a couple of kilometres south down the line, a few minutes in the car. She binned her noodles.

31)

To-Mu was jammed into the boot, folded up and trussed. The tape bindings had already come loose in places, or bunched up and scrunched. A smell of sweat and earth came up off him. The overalls were streaked with dirt and one of the clownish buttons had come off the front and the shoulder strap limply flapped. He had lost a shoe, revealing a dirty sock with a cartoon character on it.

One bloodshot eye moved and focused, then gave a slow blink and a tear tracked his cheek and dissipated where it hit the gag. Jian slammed the lid on him then stood wincing and cursing. He hoped he hadn't slipped a disc. He was not supposed to do heavy lifting at his age. He'd ask WeiWei to walk on it later, might pop something back into place. He had not sprained his back hauling the lad up from the railway line, shoving him through the fence, running to fetch the car, picking him up again, dragging him – all that, remarkably, had gone without a hitch. He hadn't been seen: the obstacles had proved arduous but not impassable, the weight awkward but luggable. No, ironically, or just annoyingly, what had tweaked his back was the last move of the endeavour: hauling the body up into the boot. He had turned awkwardly with his burden, and something was sprained.

At least his task was straightforward now: all he had to do was drive, deliver, and not think about any of it too hard. Not think about any of it at all, ideally. He did not have the luxury of choice, so any brooding was pointless. And there was the image of his daughter to hammer away any pangs of disquiet.

Pity the lad had lost his shoe. A man should not die without his shoes, or his ghost would wander the earth looking for them. It was just a stupid superstition, but now the thought was stuck, niggling like a splinter. The lad was shoeless by the time Jian dragged him off the track, so it must be lying in the grass at the Butcher's compound. Wouldn't take a moment to fetch it. It was the least he could do, was it not?

Jian drove till he found a road into the wood. He followed a rutted track to the fence at the side of the compound. The loose corrugated sheet lay in the grass. Jian parked and trudged in and quickly found the shoe, a black trainer with a tick design. Small feet for a tall lad.

He returned to the Treasure Horse and opened the boot and grabbed his captive's ankle. He fixed the unlaced shoe on the dirty foot. It was an uncomfortably intimate gesture and he slammed the boot as soon as it was done. He wiped his hands on his thighs. There was a briskness to his gestures, and to the mental voice telling him to get on with it then.

He straightened and turned, and saw the lad's mother stepping towards him.

32)

Shan had left her car at the edge of the wood and was following muddy tyre tracks on foot. Through the trees ahead she saw a fence made of sheets of corrugated metal. She recognised it from the online photo. A sheet lay on the ground. A blue Mercedes was parked nearby. And here was that strange man. What was his name, Jia or Jian? Leaning against the car, holding his lower back as if in pain. He straightened, nodded.

She said, 'Fancy seeing you again.'

The man stepped stiffly from his car. 'I went for a walk.'

'Did you see a yellow van?'

'No.' He winced. He looked uncomfortable.

'Are you hurting?'

'Yes a bit. My back.'

'I have painkillers.' She gave him a blister pack from her bag. 'Take two. Another two this evening if it persists.'

'Thanks.'

'Keep them. That's so Chinese. Pretending you're not in pain.'

'You sound like a doctor.'

'I am a doctor. I get the Chinese patients, the ones that don't speak English. They're always very ill. Because they don't think to come in until they can barely stand. And all they can think about is how soon they can get back to work.' She sighed. 'It can be upsetting. Sometimes they're so desperate. They worry they'll end up a burden to their families. That's what they fear the most.'

'I see.'

'You haven't been in this country long?'

'No.'

'I can tell. You speak English?'

'No.'

'You should learn. I learned by starting with animals. That bird over there is called a "magpie". The locals believe that if you see one on its own, you must greet it, for luck.' She held up a finger. 'You hear that? It's the song of a bird called a 'wren'. A tiny bird that makes a big sound. When I first got here I felt alone. So I learned what things are called, the names of the flowers and the birds and the trees, and that helped.' She was prattling, she realised. Her habit when uneasy. She stopped her flow with a sigh, said, 'Come on, why are you here? Tell the truth. Are you chasing after the man with the dirty yellow van?'

'Yes.' He pointed at the fence. 'He's not in though.'

'Oh, pity. So tell me how you knew to come here.'

'No.'

'No? You can't talk or you won't?'

'I won't. Excuse me, I have to get going.'

'You should help me.'

He did not reply. He opened the passenger door and clambered across into the driver's seat. Clearly he was suppressing his aches, looking stiffly ahead because it hurt to look aside. He fumbled the seat belt.

'Let me help you.' She got in, knee on creaking passenger seat, before he had time to complain or close the door. It was all rather unexpectedly close and personal. Well, if he felt awkward that would serve him right, for keeping her in the dark. 'Even if you won't help me.'

She caught an odd mix of scents – pungent sauces and earth, as if he had eaten a banquet then worked an allotment. His smart new clothes had collected grass stains and earthy patches. Another oddity: broken glass glimmering in the driver's door gulley – the window had been smashed. She diagnosed his immediate problem: a Mah Jian tile blocking the buckle slot. She swept the tile onto the passenger seat, got him secured and backed out.

He said, 'Would you do anything for your son?'

'Anything.'

He nodded. 'I understand.'

She watched the car tilt first one way then the next as it rumbled away over uneven ground. What a strange man. The camp mannerisms from their first meeting had been absent second time around, suggesting they had been put on. He knew something. She had gabbled rather than interrogated. She should have confronted, challenged, demanded – refused to get out of the car until he coughed up what he knew. Curse her agreeableness, the strength of social convention, and her timidity. A chance to get closer to her son had been lost. She bit her lip in frustration.

Think! Think. She couldn't allow this setback to stop her. She must persevere, and start being much more assertive. She turned her attention to the squatter's compound. The fence was made from corrugated metal sheets roughly riveted together. One sheet was detached and lay on the ground. Shan stepped through the opening into the squatter's territory, reminding herself that actually she was not really trespassing, or not any more than he was, not really. There were no lights on in the boxy portacabin and his van was absent. It seemed he wasn't home: emboldened, she came forward, and spotted, lying on the litter-strewn grass, something metal and complicated. One of those futuristic-looking bows, reminiscent of a bicycle, with the string wound around what looked like cogs. Surely not something you would leave lying about. Hadn't she seen one just like it on Tom's Facebook? Her son and his mates, dressed like superheroes, larking about at an archery range.

The cabin door was padlocked, the windows blinded with boards. Her son wasn't inside unless he was being held prisoner. She called his name and got no reply. She wondered if she should break in. Perhaps too extreme an action for someone without evidence, who really was just chasing shadows, and anyway how would she manage it? There was more for her here though, she was convinced of it. She began scouring the ground for clues.

33)

'Hello? WayWay? I saw you come in.'

The Captain was cooing and knocking. She couldn't even be allowed to mope alone. WeiWei closed her eyes and counted to ten. Would he go if she just wanted that to happen very much? Of course not. These days, it seemed, the opposite was true. 'Way WayWayWay? Are you alright?' The concern, feigned or not, annoyed her as much as his previous veiled threats. 'I'm fine thank you,' she shouted. 'I'm resting.'

'Can we have a chat?'

'I'm afraid it's not convenient.'

'I haven't seen your father since yesterday.'

'He's busy.'

He unlocked the door, opened it, and came in. He saw the damp floor by the bathroom and frowned. 'You were instructed not to let water get on the tiles. They'll have to be replaced. Seepage. It won't do. And this other, dodging and ducking around, it won't do either. I won't be dodged or ducked.' Fingers backslapped an open palm. 'Time is up.'

'My father is on his way home, with the money, he will be here very soon. You said we had till this afternoon. It's not time yet.'

'Won't do, no it won't.'

'No it won't.' That was another male voice, from the corridor, and it was followed by a chuckle from yet another, and WeiWei realised with unease that he had brought backup. He came forward and she shuffled back, till there was nowhere left to go and she was stuck in the corner by the bed. He breathed apple beer into her face. His teeth were the colour of old bamboo. He was drunk. He said, 'Don't be a silly. Come on. Do you want to be living on the street?' His thin lips barely moved as he crooned and cajoled. 'You can't imagine how bad it is out there. The things that will happen to you on the street will be far worse than anything... I can help you. You just have to do... one... thing... for me.'

This brought chuckles and comments from the unseen chorus. 'He's getting to the point.' 'His point is the point.' 'Don't worry honey, you won't even feel it.' There were at least three of them out there. They must have been instructed to hang back, perhaps to give privacy to any negotiations.

He reached for her slowly. WeiWei brought up her phone and swatted the hand away. It barely qualified as a blow, but it set him off balance. He adjusted his feet, slithered, and plopped into the slot between the beds, with an arm slapping down on each mattress. He struggled upright, said with hurt dignity. 'I've given you a chance.'

Then he called to the men in the corridor and they began to shuffle in. She knew them, had seen the group laughing and drinking in the lobby, talking in a mix of English and another language that she did not recognise. Once the Captain had called her over when she was passing, invited her for a cheeky tipple. She'd made excuses and backed away, shaking her head. She hadn't liked the look of them then and liked them less now, slouching, grinning, hands in pockets or holding cans.

'What's up?'

'She's not very keen.'

'Not yet.'

Sharing the small space like this seemed unendurable. She dashed past them, ducked into the bathroom and fiddled the bolt home.

'Please leave me alone,' she shouted.

The door was of flimsy plastic, the bolt was thin as a pencil: the Captain could break through with ease. But it was his door: he'd have to repair or replace it himself, and he wouldn't want to do that. She hoped he would slink off to sober up. That pratfall might cool his ardour – you couldn't take a tumble like that and not think that maybe you were a bit drunker than you thought, and needed to go and have a lie down.

He called, 'You're making things worse for yourself.' Then there was nothing for a while, just the mumble of the men talking, a peal or two of sardonic laughter. Nothing: still nothing: then a thump on the door that made her flinch.

She could hear him breathing hard, just on the other side. 'You have a duty, as tenant, to pay your way, and you should fulfill those duties however you are able, and I am trying to help you with that. You want to continue living here, you pay. Otherwise, I'll just get someone new. There's a queue. For my rooms. They're in demand. Give you a couple of minutes to come to your senses then we're going to be looking at more drastic measures.'

'Going to get drastic on them titties,' said a gruff voice from the chorus.

There seemed to be something wrong with her breathing, as if the air had grown gritty and recalcitrant. She bullied her senses into, if not calm, at least a state where they might usefully function, and got out her phone.

34)

Jian sat in the stationary Treasure Horse, considering a park. Such spaces were the true gems of this city in his eyes, far more impressive than any of the stuffy old buildings. On cheery grass, in the dappled shadow of antique trees, children played and adults chatted. A man used a launcher to pick up a ball and throw it for a dog to chase. A crow flapped out of a tree. Jian said '*Nihao, lao niu.*' He was calling Chief Inspector Bo. It was early in the morning in China, but you never knew, his boss kept irregular hours and sometimes overnighted on a fold-up bed in his office.

As the phone rang on, Jian shifted his gaze. It surprised him to see, among the grand residences nearby, a church converted into flats, its steeple remaining as a decorative feature. It struck a jarring note in the bucolic scene. Astonishing that anyone could live there, and so wantonly disrespect their ancestors. In the Cultural Revolution, temples had been turned into factories and suchlike. He remembered as a teenager pissing against a spirit wall turned into a urinal. Perhaps a similar cataclysm was happening here.

Just as he was about to give up, the call was answered. That was surprising and good, and Bo didn't sound like he'd been woken up, which was better. Jian said, 'What are you doing at the office at this hour?'

'We've got a murder. Not gangs or drunks, not a domestic, the real thing. A sex murder.'

No doubt everyone was on extended shifts. The incident room would stink of feet and cigarettes, the whiteboards would be crammed with sheets and photos. Ah, he missed it, all of it, the focus and the grind.

'What happened?'

'Typical story. No money, no family, no connections. Naive as hell, thinks her looks are her passport, thinks she's better than everyone else – this is just what her friends say. She arrives in the city, gets a job in a factory. Gives it up after a week cause she can't handle the workload, so gets a sing and giggle job at a karaoke dive. Has to wear a uniform – there's even a headpiece – you should see it. Then she vanishes. A week later, today, her body pops up in a duck pond. Strangled with her silver tights.'

Jian said, 'Was she wrapped in plastic, weighted with stones?'

'What? How did you...'

'Because she wasn't found for days and duck ponds aren't deep. Like the Fading case.'

'What?'

'Four years ago. Tier three township, Jilin Province. Girl strangled with her own clothes, wrapped in sheet and stones, dumped in a body of water near a road.'

'We checked for similar cases. That one never came up. You must be mistaken.'

'The locals were anxious that their figures weren't looking good, it was filed under misadventure. Talk to the cops that worked that. Look for someone who's moved up from there.'

'Actually... oh... we have a suspect from Jilin – lorry driver – was just interviewed, then they let him go... I'd better...'

'One moment. I have a question.' Jian squeezed his free hand then released it. 'What if I came in?'

Bo said, 'You miss me?'

'I'm serious.'

A pause, then, 'It'll be bad, Jian.'

'I'd make a full confession. I'll write a self-criticism, I'll read it out on TV. I have betrayed the guiding principles of socialism. In my lust for material wealth my hallowed duties drifted from my mind. All that.' Jian had read, or begun to read, many such confessions, and was confident he could produce, without even trying, a fine example of the genre: full, frank, ideologically aware, with no hint of whining or special pleading. 'With all that, what might I be looking at? Because a couple of years of re-education camp then decades of house arrest on health grounds... I could live with that. It would be a good collar for you. You used your wiles and persuaded me to give myself up.'

'If they knew I'd kept channels of communication open, I'd have questions to answer. Maybe I'd be joining you in the camp.'

'Just ask around. Test the water for me.'

Jian heard scraping, a door shutting. Bo started whispering. 'Jian. I'm not going to bullshit.' His voice now had a hollow, echoey quality. He must have taken his phone into the document room off his office. He would be standing by dusty filing cabinets in the dark. 'Everyone's shit scared, and scrambling to cover their arse... You're not here to defend yourself so, well, some people may have gone overboard. Pinned you for things that might not have been entirely your fault. You're the sacrifice. You're a demon, you're the ox head. You're wearing a pointy hat, there's a placard round your neck, and a lot of fingers are being pointed. You turn up now, you'll have to eat all the shit that's being thrown. You're looking at worse than a camp.'

'Seriously?'

'Why are we even having this conversation? Stay out of things and everyone's happy. Enjoy your well-earned retirement. There are worse things than homesickness.'

'Forget it. I wasn't serious. A moment of weakness.'

'You'll get used to life over there. Learn the language is my advice. Your stomach will adjust, given time. I'm going to have to go.'

Jian said goodbye then called a number he had been given. He talked to Baldie, told him the latest. He was instructed to stay where he was, they would come meet him. He was to follow their car to a location of their choosing where they'd take custody of the package. It could have been any piece of minor business.

The weak sun was sinking beneath the frilly tops of the magnificent trees. Abandon this mission, and the tong would frame him for the Manager's murder, and the British police would start chasing him. The tong would chase him too, and if they caught him, they would torture him till he revealed what he knew about the robbers, then kill him. If the police caught him they would put him in prison: where the tong would be waiting, to torture him till he… and so on. So, if he did not do as asked he would wind up dead. On the other hand… doing as asked would not be the end of his troubles. The tong would no doubt keep him on the hook and he'd be given more jobs, probably equally distasteful. But there would be time, space to think and manoeuvre, a degree of comfort, the possibility of finding some way to take advantage of the situation: life would continue in some form.

Jian turned – wincing briefly at the pain that caused in his back – and shouted at the rear. 'You're an idiot, you know that?' Then turning back, quietly, to himself: 'A fucking idiot.'

He remembered the mother crying in her kitchen. He screwed up his face, his eyes, laid his forehead against the steering wheel. Fuck your grandfather. Fuck your fucking mother's fucker. Bright sparkles flashed in darkness. It would be nice to live there rather than here. Then – the major tile – he thought about his daughter, and how fragile she looked when she was asleep. She was all that mattered. Let him be in hell to give her a shot at a common life on earth. As if summoned by his preoccupations, here she was, calling on the phone. There was a ring in her voice, and a stumbling tone he'd hoped never to hear again. 'Dad? Got an issue here.'

35)

Shan shuffled around the squatter's compound, using her phone for light. Was that silver foil drug paraphernalia? The unpleasant squatter liked to drink German beers and eat burgers, though he tossed the gherkin. She found an empty packet of Wang Wang Snow Cookies. They were Tom's favourite snack, she picked them up for him whenever she was in Chinatown. You couldn't get them anywhere else. The red design on the transparent packet was still bright, so it hadn't been here long. If Tom had been here, what had he been doing: hanging out? Having sex – oh God, what a place for that to happen – buying drugs?

She uncovered blood flecks glimmering darkly on grass. Not even dry. Had her son been injured at Butterfly's house, then come here for refuge? Or maybe it was Butterfly's blood, or the squatter's? Studying the ground was making her neck sore, exacerbated, no doubt, by the tension caused by her frantic speculations. She stood and stretched. The idea that she had missed something niggled, then she realised it was perfectly obvious and she was looking at it: the gap in the fence. Why had he left it open? Anyone could come in, as she had done. The man would surely keep it locked, especially, as now, at night when he wasn't in. Had he run away then?

The notion was refuted only a moment later: she could hear a vehicle rumbling up the track. Headlights raked the fence. He was coming home. She had seen that the wire fence by the line was cut. Thinking to head through there and scuttle away along the line she high-stepped through the long greenery, feeling furtive, vulnerable and daft. The foliage was denser closer to the fence. Branches and leaves seemed to taunt or resist her, and her movements set off what seemed a tremendously loud rustling and crackling. She realised she wasn't going to make it in time, and crouched to hide, and for long scary seconds fiddled with the phone to get its light off.

The boxy yellow van drove in and parked up, then headlights switched off, then engine. A tall man came out and loped back to the metal fence. He lifted the loose sheet and secured it in place with a clanging length of chain. His movements were slovenly, as if he were drunk. He strolled to the cabin and unlocked the padlock on the door and went in. Now, how was she going to get out of this? Shan licked dry lips and started trying to calculate, how far, how long it would it take, what noise would be made.

She was winding herself up for her move, when here was the squatter, coming clunkily back out. Had he heard her? He held a spade in one hand, a sack and a torch in the other. He swept his torch. Shan ducked and laid herself on the prickly ground. The beam tracked across bushes, travelled right over her, continued and settled on a spot at the back corner of the compound, close to the wire. He set off for the spot, humming to himself. He passed close by and she heard his trousers swishing and jewellery tinkling. Jade bracelets glinted green on the arm holding the spade. It looked just like her spade, oddly enough. He stopped, then she heard digging. She wanted to get her spray from her bag but didn't dare move.

She'd never seen a white person wearing jade; it was, in her experience, an exclusively Asian custom: another oddity, perhaps a clue. The digging ended, was followed by rustling and patting, then the man trudged back to the cabin, dragging the spade. He shut the door, and a moment later a faint glow appeared round the edges of the boarded window. He had turned a light on.

Shan rose cautiously. She was still trapped. She could not go for the fence without making a racket, and he would hear it, and come to check. Maybe she could outrun him, and maybe he'd have difficulty finding her in the dark, but she had no desire to test that out.

She was furious with herself. What a position to get caught in. She glared at the cabin, willing the light off. Half an hour after that, he would surely be asleep. Then, and only then, she would risk the fence.

36

WeiWei sat on the toilet seat. She had been there an interminable time. In her anxiety she crumped the handwritten sign that said DONT THROW SANTARY IN TOYLET OR FINE!!! The men outside had, for the most part, grown bored of rapping on the door or making lewd comments through it, and were now, as far as she could tell, sitting around drinking and chatting, just as if the room was theirs and she wasn't present. She supposed they were waiting for her to 'come to her senses', as someone had put it earlier, and come out in meek acquiescence. She had told them that her father was on the way, and they had said that was fine. Presumably they thought he would agree to their disgusting proposal. One of the men gave her to understand that what was proposed was not an uncommon arrangement, one that parents came to see the sense of. Well, they did not know this parent.

A rap, then the Captain spoke. 'If we have to pull the door down, I'll be adding the cost of its replacement to what you owe.'

'My father will be here in a moment.'

'Then me and him are going to have a discussion. Either he pays the rent, plus a penalty for lateness and inconvenience, or he's going to give the nod on the alternative arrangement.'

One of the men said, 'He don't speak English, does he?'

'We'll explain with diagrams,' said another, which set all to laughing.

She heard what sounded like a new arrival, and tensed, ripping the sign in two.

'Oh, here he comes. Hello. It's the yellow peril.'

The Captain coughed, and said, slow and loud, 'Mister. There is going to be a discussion. The girl is fine, she's in there.'

Her father called – 'WeiWei? *Nihao ma*?'

She shouted through the door. '*Shi de.*'

'*Mei ren mo ni*?… no one has touched you?'

'*Bu*… No.'

Here was the Captain again. 'You owe big money. If no money, arrangement. We talk man to man now. Serious chat. Arrangement is, me and the girl, lovey love love, every week. Then rent, no problem.'

'He still doesn't understand. He's starting to get it, I think.'

'Why is it just you? We should all have a smash.'

'I don't think he understands.'

'He's fucking – shit.'

'We got a live one.'

Suddenly there was a flurry of rapid thumping and oofing sounds.

'Think you're tasty, yeah?'

'Hit him then.'

'Teach him a...'

'Fuck.'

'Ow.'

'Get him off me.'

'No please.'

'Let me go.'

'Leave me alone.'

Something heavy slammed the door, setting it to rattle, and WeiWei backed into the shower area. Stomps and screeches were followed by squelchy thunking then low sobs. Finally there was only heavy breathing.

Her father called, 'WeiWei?'

'*Baba*? Dad?'

'You can come out now.'

WeiWei tentatively opened the door on a tableau of suffering figures. Two, pale and moaning, slumped in the alley between the beds. A third lay flat out on his back. The Captain sat curled at the base of the kitchen unit with his hands tight between his legs, keening. He coughed, and a tooth plopped out on a dribble of blood. Her panting father stood rubbing his knuckles.

She said, 'Are you alright?'

'My knees have gone, my back hurts, I get this twinge if I turn too quickly. Come on, let's go.' He found their passports. 'Anything you want?'

Someone had been reading her book. It was open on the bed. She picked it up and skimmed it. At one end her language notes. To have a cake and eat it too. Stop having kittens. Bare jokes fam. And at the other, her research, pages of fastidious handwritten English. The principles that animate Scandinavian design. Curate your autumn wardrobe. The ten best modern coffee tables.

'Quickly.'

Ideas for her shop name, of course it was going to be in English – BOOBOO, REBEL REBEL, LOVE A DUCK. It was like a different girl had written it.

Her dreams and ambitions – a joke now. She dropped it and hurried after him. All along the corridor, heads poked out from doorways and watched them impassively. A curious child stepped forward, then an arm yanked it back and out of sight.

The Beamer was badly parked at the end of a dramatic curl of tyre burn, the passenger door open. As they approached a couple of lads, thieving types in her estimation, skulked away. WeiWei followed her father into the car. She said, 'They'll come after us. And bring more friends.'

'I know.'

He got the car away, driving too fast as usual. 'I'm going to take you a decent distance, then drop you off. I have something to do. You go wait in a bar for me. Okay? I'll be an hour at most.'

'He tried... they were going to...'

'All over now. Never go near there again.'

They travelled quiet streets lined with pokey semi-detached houses. She had strolled here once, found nothing of interest, and wondered if this maze wasn't as soul-crushing as the big block in its way. The gardens that hadn't been paved over were overgrown, the house fronts weary and neglected. Lights burned behind closed curtains but there were few people out. She realised he was taking turns at random.

'Why are you wearing that?' It looked an expensive suit: dark grey, single-breasted, narrow-lapelled, in, she guessed, a fine wool. Sharper and foxier than his usual taste. He looked dapper and imposing in it but she preferred his previous outfit. In his sweats he had looked in disguise. Now he looked like some weirdly distorted version of his old self.

He didn't answer. Seemed barely aware of her. He kept checking his mirrors. 'Are we being followed?' She craned to look back. The only other vehicle in view was a black SUV. Bulky and proud, it looked out of place on the cramped streets. Jian accelerated and took a quick turn, then another. She kept watching and soon enough the SUV nosed into view, turned after them. 'Is it that car? Is it following us?'

'I'm going to drive a while, then drop you off.'

She said, 'You said you were going to tell me what's going on.'

'It's work.'

Back home, his catch all excuse, the explanation for everything from not kissing her goodnight to forgetting her birthday. As if he was her keeper, she a pet to be cared for, indulged and patronised. Why would you explain anything to a pet?

Something hard and knobbly was caught in the seat crease, and whenever she shifted it dug into her thigh. She pulled it out. A Mahjong tile, a three of circles. There was a dark brown smear on it. It looked like dried blood.

This was the third time the game had come up that day. Could it all be connected? She mused aloud. 'I know you've been gambling Mahjong. And I heard about a Mahjong den being heisted. Was that you? No. No, I don't think so. Not your style.' She tapped the tile on the dash as she worked it through. 'But you're involved. You're working as a detective. So... of course, you're finding the thieves, aren't you? This Tom, he's one of the robbery gang, and now you're finding him for the people he robbed. And this car belongs to someone from the school. It was lent to you for this job. They dressed you too. That's it isn't it, that's how it all fits.' She was rather proud of herself. 'Well? Dad? I'm right aren't I?'

She banged the tile on the dash.

'You told me you'd start telling me the truth. Only this morning. You told me you'd be straight with me. You said that now that the only thing that we had in the world is each other, we have to join together, we have to be candid. And truthful.' He had said no such thing of course, but she felt the sentiment – a new era of openness and cooperation – had been heavily implied in their conversation. 'Well? You can't just sit there now and not say anything.'

'Yes. Alright? Yes.'

She fingered the ridges of the recessed design. 'But... Dad, Mahjong dens are tong places. You've been hired by a bunch of gangsters. If you find him... and give him to them... they'll... they'll kill him! Won't they?'

She closed her eyes, dug her finger hard into the tile. Once again, the truth was painful. How pleasant ignorance was. 'No wonder you didn't want to talk about it. I thought you had that look, like you had something to hide. Ever since yesterday, you've had this expression on your face like a… turtle in cold water. I thought it was odd. It's not a mission face. It's a guilty as hell look. And no wonder. You're working for a bunch of gangsters.'

'He shouldn't have done it.'

'He didn't kill anyone though, did he? I heard about it. No one died. He's just a student. A nerd who likes to dress up like computer game characters. A boy. A dumb boy who, it looks like, made one bad decision. And you're going to hand him to a bunch of thugs who are going to torture and kill him.'

'How do you know what he's like? He robbed people with threats of violence. He took life savings, family jewellery. He terrorised innocent people.'

'And you are their hope for justice? Bullshit! Dad, come on. I can see why you're doing it. You're doing the only thing you know how. You think you're catching a criminal. Like you're still on the force. You've had your whole life fall apart and now you think… you can keep doing what you know and somehow build it up again. But this isn't that. It's a… you're living in a lie. It's like you're… a parody of who you were. If you work for gangsters then you're just another gangster.'

'You think you know what life is like for us, down here, in the shit? We have no visa, no money, no housing permit. We are destitute, jobless, illegal. Insects. And like insects we can't afford to care about anyone or anything except ourselves. We do what we have to. I do what I have to do.'

'Listen to you. You can't do anything you want just cause you're poor. Ignore your conscience, and everything that makes you real. Is that what you're saying? That's what I'm hearing.'

She was banging the tile again, with a hot hand. The chunk of sweat-slick plastic slipped out and dropped to settle on a bag in the footwell. She had kicked it on getting in but not paid it heed since. Now she wondered what it was doing here. She unzipped, and considered duct tape, scissors, crowbar. 'Fuck. This is a… kit for kidnapping people. Isn't it? For hitting them, tying them up… Fuck, Dad.'

'Just let me sort us out.'

The scissor blade was sticky. A frayed edge showed the duct tape had been cut. 'You've used this.'

He pointed. 'There's a bar down there. That sign. The deer with a hat on? Go wait in there. I'll stop round the corner up there, I want you to get out quick.'

'No.'

'I just have to do something, I won't be long, then I'll come. We can have a proper drink in an English pub, we haven't done that yet.'

'I said, you've used this.'

He parked outside the pub. She did not get out. He stared fixedly at the rear-view mirror. Then grumbled and accelerated and turned sharply, onto a dim residential street. He took a speed bump too fast, and WeiWei lurched and gasped. A thump came from the boot. 'What was that?'

'What was what?'

They were approaching another bump. This time he braked to creep sluggishly over it. She studied his frozen face. 'I don't believe it. That's him, isn't it? He's in the boot. And you're delivering him. Yes?' She knew she was right. 'And that's them following, is that it, they're going to take him off you?'

Jian braked again. 'Get out. I'll catch you later.'

'Get out so you can go give him away and he can be murdered?' She crossed her arms. 'I don't think so. I'm not going anywhere.'

'I'm not going to argue with you. I want you to get out.'

'You're going to kill him.'

'I'm not going to kill him.'

'You're giving him to people who will, that's as bad as killing him. What happened, Dad?'

A car behind honked its horn and then overtook, and the driver glared across. She watched its rear lights retreat.

'Is this what you want now? You want to be a gangster? A kidnapper? A murderer?'

'Get out of the car.'

She took out her phone, unclipped the seat belt. 'Sure I'll get out. Then I'll call the police.'

'You'd do that? Why don't you just… Why are you like this? You're so wilful and pig-headed. Just do what I say.'

'You say you do everything for me, but you don't even care what I think. If you wanted to look after me, you'd care. Well this is what I think and you have to pay attention.' She enunciated carefully. 'I think it's wrong. Let the boy go. Or I'll call the police.'

He drove on. Looking out of the passenger-side window she saw her reflected face: dirty, tired, pinched. But with her jaw set tight. 'I know you. This isn't you. Stop pretending it is. Don't do this. Let him go or I'll call the cops.'

His hands kneaded the steering wheel. Finally he said, 'I want you to give me that phone.'

'Take my phone, I'll just use a phone box. I'll find someone to call the police for me. Say I need to report a murder. I want to be a good daughter. Of course I do. But I can't let this happen.'

They turned into a street lined on one side with fencing. Beyond it she could see trees, goalposts. Jian's tone grew careful as he said, 'I came here to help you. I need you to help now.'

'Well maybe I don't want to be helped, not like this. I'm going to call the police.'

'Please don't. Just don't… Or…'

'Or what? You tie me up too, throw me in the boot?'

'Don't tempt me.'

'Seriously?' WeiWei dialled 999. Jian reached for the phone. She held it away with an outstretched arm.

A voice said, 'Emergency which service?'

Abruptly she grew aware that they were in the wrong lane, that a car was bearing down on them, that a collision was moments away and that there wasn't anything she could do about it. Nothing happened for an odd, stretched second, then her father jerked away and yanked at the wheel. WeiWei lurched as the car slid back into its lane. The approaching car swept past, then they entered a new mode of movement, swinging from one side of the road to the other in smooth leaps. The swinging increased, and suddenly a slim fence post was bright in the headlights. Jian twirled the wheel, a delicate gesture in the face of disaster, and the big bonnet slipped past it and then was tearing at wire. It snapped then the car pitched off the road and down a slope.

A thunk was Jian's seat belt tightening. WeiWei was not wearing hers. She was thrown forward and her head smacked the dashboard.

The car slewed to a halt and she slumped back, dazed. She heard a buzzing that came from inside and a voice that didn't. 'WeiWei? WeiWei? Are you alright?' He was shaking her shoulders.

'I'm fine.' She rubbed her head. She saw distant white posts and realised they had come to rest at the side of a strip of football pitches.

'You sure you're alright? What's five plus nine?'

'I'm fine.'

'Five plus nine.'

'Dad. I said. Fourteen.'

'How many fingers am I holding up?'

'Really I'm fine.'

'Fingers?'

'Three.'

'If anything happened to you…'

She followed his gaze. Behind them, on the road, a car was approaching. The headlights swept the broken fence. A familiar black SUV, bullish and chunky and persistent as a shadow. It stopped.

She said, 'That's them. That's the gangsters.'

'Yes. I need you to get out. Run and hide.'

She leaned across. He smelled of earth and grass. She whispered in his ear. 'If you give him to those guys, I'll never talk to you again. I mean it a hundred per cent. I will. Never. Talk. To. You. Again.'

He breathed out slowly. Then his mouth was in her hair, and she felt his hot breath. '*Hao ba*… alright. You win. Okay? You win. But trust me now, I'll sort this out. Now get out, I can't let them see you.'

'Promise on a thousand gold?'

'I promise.'

'Promise on mum's grave?'

'Yes. I promise.'

'Okay.'

She opened the door.

37

Jian stood with his back to a tree and watched Lanky and Baldie get out of their car. They sidled sideways down the rough slope towards the Treasure Horse. He could hear them cursing the awkward and uneven ground.

When they had gone Jian walked to their chunky car. He had his crowbar, but he didn't need it, the driver's window was open. He reached in and plucked the Manager's phone from a windscreen mounted stand by the driver's door. Beside it lay a severed human thumb, looking like nothing so much as a slice of pig's tail, wrapped in bloody tissue. The Manager's, presumably, the fingerprint would unlock the phone.

Beyond the goalposts Jian could see another fence, trees, a road. He scanned for his daughter and spotted her almost immediately, crouched among the trees on the other side of the pitch. Perhaps she wanted to watch. He wished she had retreated further. He went back down the slope, following the tyre ruts, and approached the two men at the Treasure Horse.

Jian slid the chilly crowbar up his sleeve, then whistled, and they turned. Baldie called, 'Fuck you playing at?'

Lanky said, 'You want to play football?'

Jian said, 'What can I say. I wanted to think it over so I drove and thought it over.'

'Led us on a dance. Boss is going to hear. He won't be impressed. And now you've crashed the fucking car.'

'Yes, I'm a terrible driver.'

'You're an idiot.'

'He's still in the boot. I want him out. I want it done now. Go get your car, drive it over.'

'Why?'

'I can't move this one, it got fucked coming down the slope.'

'What's wrong with it?'

'I don't know, I'm not a mechanic. Just won't start. You can try if you like.'

'Boss is going to hear about this.'

'You wanted to take him off my hands somewhere quiet, this'll do, take him here. Maybe get on with it, before we're seen.'

The two hoodlums exchanged words then Baldie trudged back towards the road, swinging the car keys round on a finger.

'Not impressed, the way you mess around,' said Lanky. 'You're a moron. Why did you take off, really?'

'Honestly? I thought I'd make a run for it. Then I realised I had no choice. I changed my mind and came back.'

'Moron.'

The curved edge of the crowbar dug into Jian's fingers as he brought his arm up and around and whacked the side of Lanky's head. The man went straight down. Jian stalked to the front of the car, got in and drove off. He rumbled in first gear, bumping in darkness towards the spindly goals. In the mirror he watched Baldie run to his felled comrade. The man waved and shouted at him. 'Hey cop? Cop? You're dead now.' There was more but Jian didn't hear it. He drove on, turned, slowed, then WeiWei scooted over and in and closed the door behind her.

'Oh God, I saw you hit him. I heard what he said.'

'Don't worry about them.'

'How did they know where you were?'

He showed her the blood smeared phone. 'They were tracking the car, with this.'

'They can't find you again?'

'No.'

'And you'll have nothing more to do with those horrible people?'

'Not if I can help it.'

He took the car over a hump and into a car park. He turned on the lights and aimed at a road. When they were back in traffic, Jian opened his little map book, found the page, gave it to her. 'Navigate. That mark there.'

'Where are we going?'

'Take him home.'

38)

'I'm really happy that you listened to me on this.' She said, almost shyly, 'You're six six six.'

'What?'

'Means awesome. You know what? We've got no money and no home... and I don't mind. I think... I really think, you know, that we will be fine. Because we are working together.'

They passed the bar with the crowned deer sign. Through steamed windows Jian glimpsed merry drinkers. It was exactly the kind of snug locale where he could imagine spinning out his twilight years. For a little thrill, have a flutter in the betting shop next door, which – shockingly – openly advertised its business. Drink, bet, grow old: good enough.

But of course there was no possibility of a quiet retirement, of any kind of retirement. He had no doubt that the tong, furious at his betrayal, would make good on their promise to frame him for murder. Which would leave him dodging the British police. Eventually they would find him. He would be put in prison, and be found there by the long reach of the tong. There was only one way to avoid his fate. He'd have to be dead.

Never mind: all things considered, he'd had a good run. His own destiny should not be of much concern, not at his age. It was her he worried about now. He would be leaving her tremendously alone, without friends, family, money, visa. With, basically, nothing. Well, she had her looks of course, but beauty was a curse, all Chinese parents knew. He recalled Chief Inspector Bo's new case: a naive pretty thing, out on her own to seek her fortune, ends up strangled in a duck pond.

He said, 'What if we weren't together? What if I wasn't here? If I was… indisposed?' He tried to keep it light, as if these were merely offhand musings, to fill time on the journey. 'What would you do, do you think?'

'Indisposed how?'

'I'll say. Just an idea to discuss.'

She waved a hand, dismissing the notion. 'I'd be devastated, I would visit you every day. In hospital, I would bring you flowers and chocolates. No, not chocolates, pork bits.'

'Just imagine though. What would you do, for you?'

'I'd think of something.'

'Specifically?'

'You want to go left here. It's a long way but at least the roads are quiet. I think your driving might have improved.'

'My question.'

'I'd be a slash youth.'

'A what?'

'This slash that. Lots of part-time hustles. Everyone is at it these days. No steady work, any more, no iron rice bowls. In this country or any other.'

'Pick something.'

'Yoga teacher. Anyone can learn to do that, it only takes a couple of months. You can teach rich ladies in their houses. Cat, camel, dog…' She stretched. 'I imagine this client, she absolutely loves my lessons, so gives me a room. I spend more and more time with the family. One day, at a dinner party, I meet a dashing, rich friend of the family. An owner of property, recently divorced. He…'

'Yes, yes. But actually?' He abandoned the pretence of light-heartedness. 'What would you actually do?'

'Why are you talking like this? You're not leaving me, are you?'

'It pays to prepare for things. What about a real job? A normal office lady position?'

'Oh no, I can't do anything normal like that, I'd need a visa.'

'How would you go about getting a visa, if you had to?'

'There's no easy way. Except get married to a British guy. I guess that would work.'

'What's the process?'

'Bit of a rigamarole. I think it goes something like...' she ticked points off on raised fingers. 'First you get a fiancé visa, then you get a temporary residence permit, then when you're married you get a spouse visa, then you get permanent residence, and then you can work. And each step costs loads of money, takes ages, involves lawyers, and you have to prove to the government you're not trying to cheat the system. What a hassle! So, that's not happening.'

'I want to give you some advice. Please think a little harder. Before you act. You're not going to be able to behave like a girl any more. There won't be room in the future to be flighty and self-indulgent.'

'I know this, the good-girl speech.'

'I'm not going to tell you to be good. I'm going to tell you to be smart.' This lesson would mean nothing without examples, which he struggled to conjure. The sight of a gaggle of drunks provided inspiration. 'For example... I'm not going to tell you not to drink.'

'Makes a change.'

'Drink helps make friends. But always stop at two. Okay, that's trivial... When you meet someone, ask yourself what they want, and how they're trying to get it, and make them think you can help them...' That seemed more like it. Other principles that had served him in navigating the vast, capricious bureaucracies back home came to mind. 'Always agree with your superiors in their presence... Think what you want but in public always agree with the majority opinion... Your reputation is vital, you must guard it jealously, because it's not who you are that matters, it's who people think you are.'

'What is this, Old Ma's Rules for Life? You should write a book.'

'Never write anything down, one day it will be used against you.' He was aware of sounding absurd, the elder mouthing platitudes to a cocky youth who was destined to ignore them. But he had momentum now. 'Act with certainty, as prevarication ensures failure. Watch what people do, not what they say. Avoid the unlucky and hapless, as those qualities are infectious. And be wary of losers, they will change the game to one they can win.'

Yes, good. 'If you need to destroy someone, destroy them utterly. No mercy or half measures or they will regroup and come for you.' That one didn't seem too relevant, at least he hoped it never would be. Stopping for an ungainly woman on a zebra crossing, he said, 'Beware ugly people, they will find your beauty vexing and will try to bring you down to their level.'

'Is this really the time?'

'Don't believe a man with more houses than he needs, he'll have parked a mistress in the others.'

'Well you'd know.'

'I just want you to…' What? To be different. Smarter. Tougher. Be ruthless and hard and political because the world will conspire to fuck you, as it fucked me. He made more points: banal, vague, contradictory even to his own ears – then lost his thread as they navigated a fiddly set of turns. This city was a maze, with barely one straight road.

No longer bothering to hide her impatience, she changed the subject. 'So does the lad live on his own?'

'With his mother. She's a doctor, she can take care of him.'

'She'll get a big surprise. He'll have a lot of explaining to do. I wonder why he did it? He has everything. Family, college, friends. A home. The ability to live and work. Job prospects. A lover. So… it doesn't make sense.'

'I suppose not.' He realised that, to prepare for the role of agent of the lad's demise, he had been cultivating disinterest towards him. He had barely thought of him as anything but a target. Whereas if he were at work, and this a case, motive would have been his starting point. 'Very well – why?'

'Have you met this boyfriend?'

'Butterfly. No. I heard about him. They're inseparable, apparently.'

'Only heard about him? He wasn't there last night?'

'No. He was expected. They both were. Their absence was remarked on.'

A theory had formed. If it was right, it led somewhere interesting. Jian pulled the car in and parked. He was in the bus lane, not far from a stop, and a couple, made self-conscious by the headlight's glare, stopped kissing.

Jian turned to WeiWei and said, 'I'd like you to get out.'

'What?' Her voice was small and disappointed. She did not want another fight.

'It'll be fine, I haven't forgotten. Here's some money.' He found the notes in his inside pocket and pressed them on her. 'Go. I'll ring. I won't be long.'

'Why? Where are you going?'

'Go to a bar and wait for me to be in touch.'

'Again with this. You're suddenly very keen on me going to bars on my own.'

'No time to argue. Trust me. Please. I want to make this right. Can you believe me?'

'You're not going to give him to the tongs?'

'I am not.'

She stared at him, as if she could read his mind, and he looked straight back, as if he could open it for her.

'You are all I have. But if he's dead,' – Jian jerked a thumb towards the boot – 'then do as you threatened, and never talk to me again.'

He handed her the lad's namecard. 'You can call him tomorrow to check.'

Abruptly, she left the car. He watched her walk away, and be whittled by the general darkness to a slim silhouette. Nothing to read in her steady pace or the set of her shoulders. He supposed she intended to obey him to the letter, to walk till she found a bar. Who wouldn't need a drink after all this?

He drove sedately away. It seemed very quiet in the car now. He liked being alone in here again. Well, not quite alone of course. He drove till he found a car park etched with shadows and pulled into the darkest corner, turned off the lights. He got the scissors and went round to the back of the car and opened the boot. His captive shifted, and looked up at him with a bloodshot eye.

蝴蝶 BUTTERFLY

39

Four days earlier, on a balmy Thursday evening, Thomas Xiang had joined the Red Scholars at a noisy Xinjiang restaurant in Camberwell. The dishes cramming the table were oily, spicy and delicious: big plate chicken, lamb and fish skewers, grilled aubergine, plump dumplings. All washed down with chilly Tsingtaos that kept on coming – they weren't being added to the bill as a favour to HuaGua, who knew the owner, a terse Han whose ebullient Uighur wife ran the kitchen.

The Chinese folk Tom had met previously – his mother's friends and family – seemed kind but staid, twee, old-fashioned. This bunch were nothing like that. They were carefree, cool and casual; well-dressed, winsome, witty. They made him welcome despite his iffy Chinese and geek life. Best of all, he and Butterfly were accepted as a couple. It wasn't something that anyone made a thing about. It was a giddy joy to be truly himself, for the first time in his life.

They held hands on the table. They were celebrating four months of being together. It should have been a joyous occasion. But something was wrong. His lover was subdued: he picked at his food, and his smiles and jokes and the flights of fancy he was celebrated for seemed forced. His lips were clenched tight during toasts, he barely sipped. He said he was fine but Tom wasn't fooled. Could it be his, Tom's, fault? After the meal they trooped, to his surprise, to a dingy Mahjong school. HuaGua explained: you hit the skankiest dives, then the swankiest bar: it was all about shaking up a cocktail of contrasting delights, being a passionate connoisseur of urban experience, high and low. A few hands here then the loser gets the Manhattans in at the Savoy. The Red Scholars played for pennies on a cat table, with great enthusiasm. He felt daring and transgressive, and part of him wanted his mum to see, and be astonished – hark at me, sitting in a haze of smoke at an illegal gambling den with my dazzling new friends and glitzy gay lover. Some of the gamblers, though, made him uneasy: hollow men pinched thin by addiction, slab-faced hoods in cheap suits, tattooed toughs and their sharp little honeys.

After a couple of rounds Butterfly made his excuses, saying he had drunk too much and needed to lie down. He had barely been there twenty minutes. What was wrong? Was he having doubts about their relationship? Could it have been something he, Tom, had said? He couldn't concentrate on his tiles, didn't even notice when he had a chance at an 'Imperial Jade'. It was a great relief when, some minutes later, he received a message: Butterfly saying he needed to talk. He abandoned the game and rushed away, getting an Uber to Hoxton and never mind bailing on the night, failing to complete his experience cocktail, or the expense.

At his flat, Butterfly unburdened himself. His father had called earlier in the day. He had been placed under house arrest. He described having a guard stood at the gate, another by the front door and one sat smoking in the living room. They would not talk to him or meet his eye. His router and computer had been taken away. He was working on a self-criticism. Depending on how things went, he might be transferred to a jail. A camp was a possibility. His assets had been frozen and might be confiscated. All this, and he still had not been told what he was accused of beyond the vague label 'economic crime'. He had called from the toilet on a secret phone, whispering because if the guards discovered the phone, it too would be taken. He finished by apologising that there would be no more money coming into Butterfly's account.

Butterfly had described his father as a quiet dull man, whose only interest, outside his job in the Provincial Department of Transport, was his collection of ceramics. A man who had never been abroad or read a novel, whose reaction to his son revealing his homosexual tendencies was to pack him off to another country till he was over it. Tom knew the man took bribes – the suspect practices of their relations was a running joke in his new crowd – but he assumed that was normal in China, just the way things were done. This development seemed ruthless beyond comprehension. Someone had given an order, and in an hour this bland man had been ruined and everything he owned taken away. It was hard to imagine such a reversal of fortune. But that's China, said Butterfly. Happens all the time.

Nashi Zhongguo – that's China. He kept saying it, a different way each time, with a rueful head shake or a shrug. He was drinking Hennessy from the bottle. He was sure this wasn't the end of the story, that there would be trials and appeals, and changes at the top might cause an abrupt turnaround, even a full pardon and compensation. He swore Tom to secrecy. Finally Tom worked up the courage for the question he needed but dreaded to ask – was Butterfly going home? No, no, God no: he had enough money in his bank account to last months, and he had relatives who would help fund him further. He was just going to carry on as if nothing had happened. It hadn't worked today but maybe next week it would. Going home would only cause complications. He kept pacing, and at one point started laughing, strident and loud.

Tom didn't like that laugh. He suspected that his lover had not begun to come to terms with what had happened, that carrying on as normal would never work. He diluted the booze with tap water when Butterfly was in the loo. Of course he'd stay over, he said. Secretly he was relieved not to be the source of dissatisfaction. The trauma might even bring them closer. He could nurse his lover through the crisis and they would come out stronger together.

'I'm here for you,' he said. 'One thousand per cent. You are everything to me, you know that?' In bed he cradled Butterfly and stroked his hair till the pale, delicate youth fell into fitful, drunken sleep.

40

Tom woke to shrill pain followed by violent, lurching motion. In darkness, he thrashed, screamed, fell. A bruising impact, then he was still. He gasped and pushed through lancing pain to gather his senses. He was on the floor of Butterfly's bedroom, smothered in duvet. Something had happened to his insides, some kind of spasm, then he had launched himself, or been shoved, out of bed.

He struggled to his hands and knees. A patch of light boomeranged round the walls. He could hear humps and moans.

The moaning was Butterfly. Butterfly was being beaten with a torch. By an intruder. On his bed. The intruder had attacked him first, pushed him out of bed, and now was setting about Butterfly.

The light steadied, flickered, then went out. Tom heard pants, tears, then the bed creaking. Tom knew what it was like to be beaten – yellow batty boy, they had shouted, chink queer – he knew how to pull himself away from pain, and stand and sway and point, and spit, that all you got? He clambered groggily to his feet.

On the bed, Butterfly lay naked and wrapped. Thick tape snaked round his torso and legs and pinned his arms to his side. A hood was taped over his head. A shapeless figure in black took Butterfly's phone off the bedside cabinet. Then tugged Butterfly off the bed by his feet till he thumped to the floor. The figure began to drag the captive out of the room into the hallway, breathing heavily with the effort.

Tom had no thought beyond the desire to stop this nightmare. He lumbered forward, arms raised, and the intruder watched him come. He let go of Butterfly, stepped forward, and swung his club-like torch.

41

When Tom came groggily to, it was daytime. Light was filtering through the blinds, casting pale oblongs on the wall. A spattering of dark blobs broke the pattern. That was blood. He supposed it was his. His mouth felt raw and swollen. He tested with his tongue, pressing sore points. Dried blood crusted round his lips. It tasted bitter.

His phone, on the bedside cabinet, was ringing. He hauled himself up, leaned against the side of the bed, and watched it awhile. It stopped. He didn't move. He was a simple creature, he breathed and blinked and saw, and thought came sluggishly. A monster had come in the night to snatch his lover away. There was no logic or sense to it. The phone started up again. His weak fingers groped for the charging cable and pulled it to him. It was Butterfly's number. He lurched as if the thing had shocked him, and sharpened. He answered.

'Hello? Where… where are you? What happened?' It hurt to speak, and his voice sounded strange to him, thick and muddy.

Butterfly sobbed, in Mandarin, 'I've been kidnapped.'

'What? No. Why?'

'They want my dad to pay a ransom.'

'He can't.'

Butterfly was talking very fast. 'I know, I keep trying to explain, I try to call my dad but there's no answer. They don't believe me, this guy keeps, he's got a knife pressed on my neck, he's got a hood on my head, I can't even… I'm tied up, I can't feel my arms, he's holding the phone to my face. Oh

God, no... he's pressing the knife on me. Tom I'm so scared, Tom, help me, please. Tell him, tell him it's true, tell him my dad can't pay.'

Tom said, 'I love you and it's going to be okay. Let me talk to him.'

He switched to English, raised his voice, pushed away the pain. 'Hello? There is no money. It's true. His father's been arrested. All his money has gone. There's no money. He can't pay you a ransom, he has nothing. Please let him go.'

Tom was sitting against the bed, knees drawn up, cold phone pressed hard against his cheek. Someone was there, he could hear breathing. Then a clearing of the throat. Then a gravelly voice said in English: 'Okay. You pay it.'

'Me? But... I have nothing. I'm a student.'

Long heavy breaths, then silence, then a sudden wail from Butterfly followed by sobbing and incoherent pleas. Tom's fingers tightened on the device. The voice – so distressingly flat and nonchalant – returned. 'Did you hear that? That was the sound of me slicing his finger. I'll cut it off next. Then his balls. I want fifty thousand pounds.'

'Please stop, no.'

'Someone's paying for him. Or I'll kill him. In stages.'

'I can't, I haven't got... I haven't got it. I haven't got anything. I said, I'm just a student.'

'He's naked. He's shivering. He's all taped up. You should see. I've got the gag back on him now. I've got a knife. He's watching it with his eyes. Following it. Huge eyes. You like those eyes, I bet you do. And the tattoos, and all that. He's so scared. He's shaking. He's sweating. You should see.' There was relish there, and a sense of theatricality to the sudden changes of tone. Tom imagined a hulking sadist with gnarled hands, piggy eyes, wet lips. Looking at his knife in an almost erotic way – looking for an excuse to use it. 'I'm going to slice again. You want to listen? I'm just going to slice away. Maybe cut one of those gay tattoos off.'

A hollow pause, then Tom heard muffled sounds of distress. The voice came back, a little breathless, excited. 'There we go. A cut on his arm. Blood coming. He's in a state. I don't think you heard. I should do it again maybe. I'm worried though. I'm worried, if I get into it, I might go too far. I'm going in again.'

'I'll pay,' Tom shouted, 'Stop. Please. I'll pay.'

Suddenly the caller was brusque and businesslike. 'Good lad. A location will be texted. You be there on Sunday, at midnight, with fifty thousand pounds in notes. Fifty thousand pounds. Midnight. This Sunday. Or he dies.'

42)

Now it was Sunday evening, mere hours from the deadline, and Tom was a trussed prisoner in a car boot. The injuries he had collected that awful night had been overlaid with newer, spikier pains. Every ragged breath brought stabbing needles to his chest. Ribs, leg and shoulder ached when he was still and burned when he shifted. Blood from split lip and loose tooth dampened his lips. One eye was swollen shut.

But his hurts were trivial compared to the anguish that came from the knowledge of failure. Butterfly was about to die. Every moment was desolation. He wanted to be unconscious again.

A click, then metal scraped and creaked. The lid of the boot was rising and some grey light came in. He shifted and squinted with his good eye. The crazy gambler looked down at him, a boxy silhouette against a starless city night. One hand held a glinting blade. If this was the end, let it be quick.

The other hand came in. Tom tensed and shied. It grasped and shook him, poked ribs and probed thighs. All his sorest points were tested. Was this the preliminary move of some sick torture – his vulnerabilities leisurely explored, before being used to torment him? Fingers swept damp hair off his face, prodded puffy flesh above his cheek and wobbled his jaw.

Then the man spoke, a bored mechanic judging a wreck. 'Lot of superficial bruising and some cuts, bit of bleeding, nothing deep. No big breaks. Going to need to get that eye looked at, could be a scratched cornea. Jaw might need wiring. At least one fractured rib, and you might have broken your clavicle. Could be worse.'

He yanked the tape off Tom's mouth and Tom screamed as the skin of his lips tore.

He croaked and sobbed. 'Please… just leave me alone.'

'How many fingers am I holding up?'

'What? Three.'

The blade, he saw, was a big pair of scissors.

'Your boyfriend Butterfly's been kidnapped and you're raising the ransom. Yes?'

'Er… Yes.'

'You should have told me. How much?'

'Fifty thousand pounds.'

'When do you have to pay it?'

'Midnight.'

'Tonight?'

'Yes.'

'We got a couple of hours… Are you married?'

'They're going to kill him.'

'Answer me,' snapped the man, annoyed, 'are you married?'

'Please, just… oh God they're going to kill him. No, no, of course I'm not married.'

'Good. I'll get your boyfriend back.'

'What?'

Tom blinked out tears and concentrated till the man's shadowed face sharpened into focus. He did not look to be making a joke. He sounded quite matter of fact as he said, 'This is what happens in return. I have a daughter. You are going to marry her, and you and your mother will look after her. She will live in your spare room.' He pointed the scissors. 'Can you square this with your mum?'

'Marry her? What? But… I'm gay.'

'Yes, be a good cover for you. With a wife you will appear normal, very convenient for everyone involved. You can convince your mother? I've met her, she seems like a reasonable person, you can convince her to go along with it?'

'Yes.'

'Deal?'

'Uh… I…'

He continued: patient, insistent. 'You need to get this ransom paid. I need someone to look after my daughter. Pay attention, time is pressing. Answer me.'

'Yes.' Tom tried to nod but that set off a pain in his neck. 'Yes, please, yes. Help me. Yes. Please.'

'I need you in front, reading a map, I hope you can see alright.' He dived in with the scissors, started cutting tape. 'She's a lovely girl. You'll like her.'

43)

WeiWei sipped at a gin and tonic, and made a face at the tart taste. She had retreated to the pub's darkest corner, but still felt conspicuous: a woman on her own, drinking alcohol. She glared at her dumb phone so no one would try to talk to her. There was nothing on the screen to look at. Her earlier bullshit on how liberating it was to live without a smartphone had come back to taunt her. She played a lame maze game, tried to imagine what it was like to be pleased by such a thing.

It rang. Her father's number. She answered. A youth addressed her in English, his voice croaky and faltering. 'Uh... hello there? I was in the car. My name is Tom.'

'Hello.'

'I'm with your father. He told me I owe you my life, you convinced him to rethink. So... thanks.'

'No problem.'

She could hear engine hum. He was in the Beamer, presumably, getting the Jian driving experience. 'Your dad is helping me. My boyfriend has been kidnapped. We're going to pay a ransom to free him.'

'Oh. Okay... Did he tell you he's a policeman back home? He's very good at that kind of thing. I am sure it will work out.'

'You... you can live in my house.'

'What?'

'You can go and live in my house.'

'Huh. I see. In return for his help, yes?'

'Yes.'

'Is that from now?'

'Yes. I need to talk to my mum but… yes.'

'Your mum? That's a… Hello? Are you there?'

Now here was her father, barking at twice normal volume, as he always did on the phone. 'Hello? WeiWei? I'm sorting things out, and without being a bad egg. It's all going to be fine. Did he tell you, you can live in his house? It's a very nice house, very clean, two storeys with garden at front and back, lovely bathroom, no pets. It smells fantastic, like lavender, a proper home. I'll get him to text the address, you can go straight there. It'll be all worked out with his mum.'

'You haven't told her?'

'Details. It's being sorted out.'

'Do we get a room each?'

'No it's the spare room.'

'Do we get our own bathroom?'

'It's a lovely bathroom, hot running water, very clean. I don't think I can overemphasise how clean this place is, there's a fluffy cover on the toilet seat. But yes it is shared.'

'Right. So, what, both of us go live with his family, in the guest room. Won't that be weird and awkward?'

'Just him and his mum and no more wolf landlords, it's a lovely place, you need to see it. You'll like the mother, very sensible lady, very kind, loves nature. She'll teach you the names of all the animals. Got to go. Bye.'

The call ended. What was this scheme? It was commendable of her father to try to help the lad, and it certainly beat killing him, but… if he could get hold of enough ready cash to pay what was presumably quite a considerable ransom, why not just keep it? Use it to get a place of their own, with separate bedrooms. But then this boyfriend might be dead, of course. Well, it was very regrettable and clearly a terrible situation, but on the other hand it wasn't their problem unless they made it so, and if they did then that was risky, wasn't it, and a cramped room in someone else's house could be considered scant reward… she realised she had drained her drink. A text arrived. An address, in a district she hadn't heard of called Sutton.

Another dose of boozy lemon sourness? No, she was already a little tipsy, could feel her cheeks heating up. There was nothing else for it. How did she get to Sutton? Someone at the bar would know.

44)

Tom found that his ribs didn't hurt too much if he stayed very still. But that was almost impossible, with the way the crazy gambler slalomed through traffic. The car accelerated on a straight and his head snapped back, then it lurched into the bus lane to pass a lorry on the inside, and he smacked the door. They rode one red then screeched to a stop at the next, and Tom braced on the dash, which sent shooting pains through his shoulder. He took the opportunity to fumble his seat belt on. The twisting set off a pain in his neck, and he winced and cursed. Then they were tearing off again at speed, and he was thrown forward, and the belt tightened on his ribs, setting off an explosion in his chest.

To see the map he had to hold the book at arm's length. 'I can't hardly see. I can't barely breathe, it hurts so much.'

'Oil up,' said the crazy gambler. 'You didn't say anything about marrying?'

'No.'

'Good.'

'Going to have to work her round to that cause she can be stubborn. She won't see the need, not just yet.'

An absurd subject. But it seemed wise to humour the crazy man.

'I'm sure it will be fine. Keep straight then next left.' Tom wiped tears from his good eye.

The man ran speed bumps like they weren't there. The jarring thumps aggravated aches and made Tom feel he was about to be sick.

'Just treat her like a lodger. You don't have to sleep together, if that's what you're worried about. You can carry on with your unnatural acts. Your mum will be pleased, won't she? You'll look normal.'

Tom pointed. 'Here. This one.' He muttered, in English, 'You homophobic nutter.'

'Why are you raising the money? Why not his family?'

'His dad's been arrested. Swept up in some anti-corruption drive. Something about being dark and evil?'

'Ah. The tigers and flies campaign.'

'That's the one.'

'A ruthless and indiscriminate crackdown that sweeps the good as much as the bad. Oh yes, I could tell you all about that one. So Daddy's suddenly broke. There's a lot of that about. The kidnappers didn't know?'

'No.'

'You couldn't explain? Save a lot of aggravation, if you'd just explained.'

'Of course I explained. They didn't care. They just... I said I'd have to do it. What option did I have? They were cutting him. I was listening on the phone, and they were... We're going to get him back. Aren't we? We have to.'

In a nervous habit, Tom gnawed at the cuticle of his index finger. He tore skin, which stung, and he thought how daft it was to be adding to his pain. Considering his driver leavened his anxiety somewhat. The man's single-minded focus was something to admire. He was powerful, determined, competent in some spheres at least and very resourceful; perhaps it didn't matter that he was insane.

Quite soon they were on familiar suburban streets. By degrees the roads grew dimmer, emptier and bumpier, and finally, the car was rumbling down a muddy track. They were near home, headed into the wood by the railway line. The crazy gambler turned off the headlights and nosed the bonnet forward into darkness. Branches and leaves scraped the sides, then he stopped and cut the engine and said into a sudden ringing silence, 'That's close enough. Don't want him to hear.'

Tom said, 'He lives in a cabin. Down that track.'

'I know. Excuse me.' He reached down into a bag at Tom's feet, and pulled out a wicked two-foot crowbar.

'Jesus,' said Tom, in English.

'Stay here.'

'I want to help.'

'You'll only get in the way. Ring your mum. Sort that out.'

'You'll need a lookout. I could…'

'Ring your mum.'

Tom had to get out to let the gambler exit. 'At night he locks the loose sheet with a bike lock but on the sheet next to it there's a space, near the bottom, you can crawl under. He keeps a big torch by the door. You won't… you won't hurt him, will you?'

He held the crowbar upright and there was something faintly animal in its long curved neck and wide, flattened head. An evil swan maybe. The barbarous totem mocked his pathetic and insincere concerns.

The man stalked away into darkness leaving Tom standing in the breezy dark. Footsteps faded then there was just the incessant rustle of leaves, the odd animal call. There was less light pollution here, he could make out a few stars above.

Tom took out his phone, pulled up his mother's contact details. His thumb hovered over the call icon. Probably she was doing her evening meditation. Or trying to, she might be too worried. He had not done a good job of reassuring her. He wanted to talk to her – had wanted to talk to her for days – but he knew that as soon as he began to explain the situation she would start trying to convince him, with her sensible 'giving it to you straight' medical professional voice, that this simply wasn't his problem, that the unfortunate lad's family should pay the ransom. And besides which, if the money wasn't paid the kidnappers would in all likelihood let their captive go. She would insist that they go to the authorities. And, he knew, there was a danger that he might start to believe it.

The suburban banality he usually chafed at looked appealing now. He wanted jacket potatoes and tea in the cosy kitchen, to snuggle in bed reading graphic novels, to eat toast and watch anime. He wanted to go home and he wanted his mum. He called her.

She answered right away. 'What's going on?'

'Mum? Why are you whispering?'

'Tell me.'

'A girl is coming to the house.'

'What?'

'Let her stay, okay? I'll explain later.'

'Tom, you can't...'

'I'll see you soon.'

'Wait...'

He ended the call, and turned the phone off, so that he wouldn't hear it when she called straight back. Oddly, she had sounded like she was outside. In the garden perhaps? And why the low voice? He didn't feel better for having talked to her, just guilty for all the pain he'd caused.

There was a Mahjong tile on the ground. He picked it up. A three of circles. Dirty. He supposed he must have swept it off the dashboard when clambering out. The circles on the face were recessed. He felt the ridges with his thumb and realised the tile was smeared with dried blood, his blood, and suddenly he was back in the den, in that fear haze and smoke stink. He was waving the fake gun. Mesh prickling on his hot skin and squishing his nose. A gallery of sullen or frightened faces. Eyes cast down, looking at him sidelong, glaring: afraid, angry, disgusted. Hands shaking or rubbing or pulling off rings. Paulie's arm grabbing tiles, cash, gold, jade.

He had met Paulie on the high street, some six months ago. The man was cadging money for the train fare to visit his mother in hospital in Aberdeen. Tom gave a fiver. A few weeks later he met Paulie at a bus stop. He asked about the mother and Paulie told him he would level with him, his ma had been dead for years. Tom said in that case, can I have my money back and Paulie told him he was a funny wee lad. The next time he saw him, Paulie was hiding in the garden. Tom confronted him and Paulie told him he was running away from a gentleman who wanted money as a result of an unfortunate misunderstanding. Tom told him he had to be gone in an hour. When Tom checked later, he was gone, and so was a spade from the shed. Tom trudged to the cabin by the railway line and asked for it back. Paulie said sure, it was for self-defence and no hard feelings and would the big man like a beverage? The Scot was jokey and spirited, though some of his questions seemed to be attempts to establish what valuables were kept at home and when the place was empty. Paulie showed him a jar filled with jewellery, nicked from an antique store, and tried to sell him drugs. It was a memorable, disorienting encounter, and he was aware that he had touched a world that, while seedy and dangerous, seemed more vital than his own. Only when he was halfway home did he realise he'd left the spade. When, on Friday, Tom went to the cabin and told Paulie he was going to heist a gambling den and needed help, Paulie laughed. He smiled indulgently as Tom showed the fake guns and the tights and the overalls, shook his head ruefully when Tom talked about getting the doorman down before he could trigger the alarm, frowned intently when Tom told him how much cash lay on the tables.

Tom squeezed his phone to jolt his mind back to the present. It was nearly eleven. So little time left. Hurry up, get it done.

He imagined the rancid scene. The crazy gambler beating up Paulie, taking the money… would that be the end of it? Really? The man was ruthless. He wouldn't want witnesses, loose ends, people with grudges who could talk. Or come after his precious daughter or her newly betrothed. He was going to kill Paulie, wasn't he?

He supposed he should have worked that out earlier. He had failed to notice what he would rather not see: Paulie had faults. And had tried to kill him of course. Still… he couldn't let that happen, could he? Not if it could be avoided. He only needed the money, he didn't want anyone hurt. Could he stop it? Perhaps. He should try. Or at least he should see.

45

A girl? What girl? Lover, friend, fugitive? Stay in the house? With them? Why? How long? Oh, what a nonsense. Shan was cold, uncomfortable, and needed a wee. Her mother, in her head, was telling her that she'd got into rather a silly mess, hadn't she? As a child, she'd run away from home and hid in the fields till dark, fearing her father's punishment for a now forgotten infraction. She felt the same mix of fear and embarrassment now.

The cabin door opened and torchlight lanced out. He called, 'Who's that? I know you're there. I heard you talking.'

The beam tracked away, then swung suddenly back. It found her and pinned her in an acid glare. Shan stood up and raised a hand to shade her eyes.

He sounded honestly baffled as he said 'What are you doing?' She squinted between red-rimmed fingers at a bulky silhouette in shorts, T-shirt and unlaced boots, a duvet round his shoulders like a cloak. He came forward and the duvet shucked away, revealing a lanky stooped figure, knock-kneed, as sharp as his voice as he snapped, 'Well? What? How long have you been there?'

'I just…' She fought the instinct to shy away and apologise, and said in a voice that started too high and shrill, 'I want to know what you know about my son. Please. He's called Tom.'

'I don't know him.'

'Yes you do.' She said, loudly, working not to sound afraid. 'I think he was here… The bow.' She waved a hand. 'That's… well not his exactly. But…'

'You watching my comings and goings?'

'I just want to know about my son. You know him. Where is he, tell me.'

'Just trees out here.' He swept the torch to either side, and the light passed over leaves and branches. 'Dangerous place for a woman on her own. Could slip, fall. Could have a nasty accident.'

'My husband knows I'm here.'

He turned off the torch and the scene was obliterated, leaving a darker darkness than before. A regular slapping, like a slow sardonic clap, began. He was swinging the torch up and down, into his palm. She could see it in her imagination: black, metal, hefty. The hands veiny and gnarled.

'You after the money, yes? Little lad told you all about it did he?'

'I'll scream.'

'Scream all you want. You don't have a husband. No one knows you're here. And there's no one to hear you.'

He came forward. She told herself this wasn't panic as she lurched and thrashed in retreat. Branches lashed her, leaves batted. She could hear him clumping behind. It was lucky she had spent so much time pacing here, and knew the ground. She skipped a familiar patch of thistles, he did not. She heard him curse as he blundered into them.

She came to the slit in the fence, yanked it, and the cold wire jabbed and scraped till she was through, and slithering down bristling grass, slick earth. She bumped to level ground and picked herself up. She had lost bag, shoe, composure. The cutting was a streak of pooled darkness without exit. She blundered along the track, her clumsy steps making the metal ring. Still he was coming after her, cursing and mumbling.

He had a way for walking the line, a short-stepped geisha shuffle that took him tripping rapidly along the sleepers. He was gaining and there didn't seem to be anything she could do about it. She wasn't even running in the right direction; she was going away from the houses, into nothing. The torch came on and light flashed on leaves and line and cast her distended shadow before her. It grew longer and its flailings more desperate as he came up behind. Then she was hit in the back and sent sprawling. Gravel bit palm and cheek. She was on the line. He was standing over her, rasping 'Get rid of you like I got rid of him.' He knelt on her back driving her breath away. He took a hank of hair and picked her head up and she gave a low fearful moan. The rail was a smooth blade-like slither in the yellow torchlight, and she knew he was going to smash her face into it and there was nothing she could do to stop him.

She heard approaching footsteps, the clang of the rail. Some-one else had arrived. The grip on her head loosened, and she wriggled and rolled onto her back. The torch beam whipped, and she caught a flash of this new figure, flat and bright – dark suit, raised arm. The arm came down, there was a crunch and a grunt and the torch fell and light settled into a pool on the ground. Two dark figures came together noisily then sprang apart before a black line chopped the air and struck her tormentor. He staggered back, moving slowly now, rasping for breath. She kicked out and caught the back of his knee with her foot. His leg buckled and in trying to regain his balance he stumbled on the rail. The newcomer's arm swung again and his weapon, a metal bar, cracked on her attacker's head, firing him down to the line, where he was still.

Shan realised she was making a throaty whine, which seemed to be coming from somewhere far below her vocal chords. She snapped her mouth shut to still the noise. Shock had fractured her senses. Now they came back in pieces. A big, heavy-breathing man looked down at her. One hand pressed his lower back. She knew that suit, that pose. Jian helped her to her feet. She looked at the body spreadeagled across the line.

The clumpy shoes were clownish on the pale bare legs. Her professional instinct had her bend and feel his neck for a pulse.

'He's dead.'

'Come away.' Jian picked up the torch and turned it off.

'My son... Have you seen him?'

'He's here. Come.'

'He's here? Now?'

She did not look back as he led her away, even when a train came blasting past. It made a terrible clatter and a wind that whipped her matted, sweat-slick hair across her face. It didn't stop.

46)

Metal rattled as Tom crawled below the fence into the compound. Worried that he had been heard, he launched himself up, ready for a fight. But no one was there. The cabin door was open and a little flickering light spilled onto rubbish-strewn scrub. A duvet was scrunched in the doorway: worn, red, with that familiar design of cartoon racing cars. Tom crept across and peeked in.

No one was here. A bare bulb strung up on a wire from a car battery swung gently to and fro, and shadows bloomed then receded. The torch Paulie kept by the door was gone. Tom guessed he'd heard or seen the gambler, then jumped out of bed, in his haste disturbing the bulb, then they must have run off, chasing each other in the dark wood.

Whatever, it didn't matter, he just needed the money. Make his own way if necessary. He checked under the mattress, swatted clothes piles, upended magazine stacks. He kicked and scattered bottles, cans, empty bags. Nothing. He overturned the crate that served as a table to look underneath and the keys to the VW tinkled as they fell off.

Perhaps it was stashed in the van. Tom used the light from his phone to illuminate his search of its interior. Paulie had been on a spree: there was an empty bottle of champagne, a cuddly toy, a drone in a box. Clothes and more bottles in the back. No money though. He was groping under the passenger seat when he heard metallic scraping. He scrambled out and backed away. Someone was coming up from the line. Leaves rustled and twigs snapped. He shouted, in English, 'I've got a gun,' but his voice sounded small and uncertain.

The crazy gambler shouted, in Mandarin, 'I told you to stay in the car.'

'What happened to the guy?'

'He had an accident.'

Tom said, 'I can't find the money. It's not in the cabin or in the car.'

Another voice came: indignant, familiar. 'What money?'

Tom aimed his phone. His mother, looking dirty, bedraggled, older. She hurried forward and grabbed him with both hands. 'There you are. Oh God, look at you, you're hurt. I can't believe it. My poor boy.'

He stood stiffly. Her hands went over him, pressing, then they were on his arms.

She was holding him too tightly. He said, 'Mum? There's a thing I have to go and do.'

'I don't want you to go. No. I'm not going to let go.'

'I have to do it.'

'No,' she shook her head with vehemence.

He sighed. 'I have to pay a ransom by midnight. I need the money that this guy has.'

'It's just nonsense. All of this is. You are coming home.'

'I am going with that man and we're going to pay the ransom.'

'No. No, no. A man is dead. The police have to be called. Oh God. Just come home.'

'Don't call the police. I need the money. I need to get Butterfly back. Or they'll kill him. Don't call the police.'

'Oh no no. You are coming home.'

'I'm sorry about everything. I'm sorry I couldn't tell you. You won't believe what I've gone through already. I have to see it through.'

Tom saw, over her head, the crazy gambler approach, kneel. His hands delved in his bag then he was cutting something with his scissors. After that, he rose and stood behind her with a strip of tape taut, one hand at each end. Ready to bring it down over her mouth, Tom realised. To truss her up as he had been. The man's eyebrows were raised – he was asking Tom if this was necessary. To bind and capture his own mother. Could he?

Tom pulled his mum to him, pressed her head to his chest. He shook his head at Jian, a definitive no. Something other than that. Anything.

He could smell earth on her hair. He said, 'Mum listen. This is me doing what I have to do. Let me do that. It's nearly done. We need to find the money and deliver it, then someone I really care about, care about nearly as much as you, will be alive instead of dead. I'm sorting it out. Trust me.'

Still Jian loomed with the glimmering tape.

'The best thing for you to do now, to help me, is to go back. Wait for the girl to come to the house. Tomorrow it will be over. I give you my word. I don't know what else I can say. I know it's hard for you but I want you to just… go home. Will you do that for me?'

The pressure of her arms lessened. She sniffed. Sighed. Let go.

She brushed hair from her face and pointed, said stiffly. 'He buried the money over there.'

Tom said over her head, in Chinese, 'He buried the money, she'll show us the place.'

She turned to address the crazy gambler. 'Look after him.'

'Of course.' Jian was nodding, smiling politely, as he scrunched his tape.

The respectable streets of suburban Sutton all looked the same. WeiWei had to ask the way twice from late-night dog-walkers. Her destination turned out to be a detached house in a long parade, inconveniently far from the station.

A middle-aged Asian lady answered the door right away, as if she'd been waiting on the other side. Her hair was disarranged, her clothes shabby and streaked with grass stains. She had been interrupted while washing her face. She was drying it with a towel. Red-rimmed eyes fixed WeiWei with such an intense stare she took a step back.

WeiWei said, in Chinese, 'Ahh... I think... I'm supposed to stay here?'

'Why is Tom raising the money?' The voice was a rapid bark. 'Why him? Why not the family?'

'Oh... Er, I don't know. I really don't know very much about the whole... basically I know nothing, actually.' Let her father explain when he arrived.

The lady turned. WeiWei assumed she was supposed to follow her in, as she kept talking shrilly. 'I've read about this kind of thing. I bet it's one of these horrible gangs.' WeiWei took her shoes off. A rack held practical ladies footwear on one shelf and the one below, that would be the lad's, had gaudy trainers. There was no empty space so she tucked hers underneath.

'They target students from China. The students come here and they're all alone and so naive, and they've got such a lot of money. Oh yes, easy picks.'

The place was homely and clean, as her father had said, but it wasn't spacious. She said, trying to sound reassuring, 'I don't know much about it, but I do know my father is on the case, and he is very good at this kind of thing. You should relax and let him deal with it.'

But the lady only grew more agitated. 'I should relax? How can I relax? Why is my son involved, why? It should be the lad's family. Fifty thousand pounds. He's had to steal it – God knows how he – I left him digging up buried loot. And there's a man – on the line… It's just awful.' She stopped in mid flow, and rubbed vigorously at her face. 'This should have nothing to do with my son, nothing at all. Oh, it's too absurd.'

'Well, I think it will be all over soon.'

'He has to pay the ransom at midnight.'

WeiWei followed her gaze to a clock on the wall. It was decorated with cartoons of cats and the hands were fish. The time was just gone eleven. 'That stupid thing was a present from my cousin. She's the only relative who ever makes it over, so I had to put it up. I hate it. I can't believe it's right. It's so slow. I keep thinking it's stopped. I can't bear this. A man is dead. Is my son next?'

'It will all be over soon.'

Long seconds passed, with the faint tick of the clock the only sound. The lady said, 'What about you staying?'

'In return for his help, we're staying with you, that's the deal.'

'It is, is it. How long?'

The alcohol at the bar had dried her mouth. WeiWei would quite like to be offered a drink. She considered asking for one but didn't want to seem rude, or ruder.

'Um, I don't know. But we haven't got anywhere else to go. So, um, a while. I guess.'

'How can you not have anywhere to go?'

'We're illegal immigrants.'

'Right. Of course you are. It sounds to me like your father has found a vulnerable boy in a terrible situation, and is looking to take advantage.'

'It's your son who has made all the problems. My father is the best person to sort them out, he's lucky to have met him. He was a top policeman back home. My father is putting himself at great risk.'

'It's hardly out of the goodness of his heart, is it? It's for my spare room.'

'And that's why you know you can trust him. Could we just wait till it's over and discuss it then?'

Pans on hooks above the hob, lists and notes on the fridge, spices in a rack. In the hallway, shelves crammed with shells, figurines, family photos. Hard to insert herself and her father into a scene so already thoroughly inhabited. For a start, the kitchen table would have to be pulled out, so that more than two could get around it, and chairs acquired.

WeiWei said she had to go to the bathroom, and went up carpeted stairs. She found the spare room. A desk piled with papers half-filled the narrow space, and another quarter was taken up by shelves stuffed with files and textbooks. Even if all that was cleared out, you couldn't fit two mattresses. How could she share this with her father?

In the bathroom she poked around. The cabinet was full. Some collection of aftershaves the lad had. Presumably all those essential oils were the mother's. Where was their stuff going to go? They'd have to add more shelves, maybe throw away those candles and seashells to make space on the sill. There was, as her father had said, a fluffy detachable cover on the toilet seat, with a matching splash rug round the porcelain base. He'd meant it as a selling point but to her this flashed a warning. These people were fussy over little comforts, and such folk didn't like to share with strangers. She would be tiptoeing round the whole time, trying not to get in the way, feeling like an imposition. It might be quite as bad, in its way, as the bedsit.

She drank from the tap, splashed water on her face. It made no sense. Why was her father running around playing at cop, putting himself at risk for nothing but a poky room in someone else's house? Was that really all there was to it? She sensed not. He was scheming, she would bet on it. He intended this frumpy lady and her nerdy gay son to be useful in some other way, as guides perhaps, as allies or aides. Feeding the towel back into its big metal ring on the tiled wall, she suddenly knew what it was. He'd arranged an engagement with the lad, hadn't he? She had given him the idea, with her blather about spouse visas, and how that would open up the possibility of getting a job. That was it, wasn't it? Because that would sort them out. She was to get married to Tom, get legal, and find work: then look after them both. It was pretty smart, she had to concede that.

The nerve of it though. As if she were a token, to be disposed of for profit. It was like – it was exactly like – being sold into concubinage. It was the sort of thing you heard about all the time in history class, it was the side plot of every TV costume drama. What was this, the fucking Song Dynasty? And she some hobbling, uneducated, decorative, simpering dependent.

Indignation fortified her. She would show him. She would sort it out herself, and no one would be getting married against their will, least of all her. She stomped downstairs and put on her pumps.

The lady heard her and called from the kitchen. 'Hello? Come and wait with me. I'm not myself. I'm sorry. I'm sorry I was sharp. I'm making a drink. I don't even know your name. I'm Shan.'

'I'm going out.'

'What?' She shuffled forwards, holding a teapot. 'Why? What's going on? I thought you were supposed to stay.' The prospect of leaving seemed to distress her as much as that of staying had previously. 'Well... Where are you going? You have to tell me. What if your father rings?'

'Tell him I'm sorting this out. I have friends. HuaGua will help me.' Opening the door she added, 'And you can tell him this is not the Song dynasty.'

48)

They'd found the pillowcase inside a taped-up black bin bag, buried about a foot deep in cold soil. The jewellery, and the random oddments that had been swept up, had been taken out. The wads of cash smelled rich and earthy when Tom, in the passenger seat of the BMW, dumped them in his lap. Now he was trying to count fifty thousand pounds back into the bag, while directing the crazy gambler from a little A-Z, listening to him ramble, and trying not to think about his pains and the impending deadline. Loose notes swirled as the car swerved.

'That's thirty... Straight up here and left... Thirty point five.'

'What are the instructions?'

'There were no instructions. The kidnappers texted a time and GPS coordinates. That's all I know. It's a car park behind some flats. Second right. It's nearly midnight.'

The crazy gambler flicked stray notes away. 'Keep any leftovers. A wedding gift.'

He accelerated to snatch an amber, overtook a bus on the inside.

'You don't have to control your urges. Go do what you do. But you do have to share a bed. For the visa. Because the government check, apparently. They come sniff the sheets.'

'Left in a minute.'

'I warn you, my daughter can be vexing, she will test your patience. She gets ideas in her head. She's smart but she's not very practical.'

'Coming up here. That's thirty-one.'

The crazy gambler rode a red. He swung the car round a corner and a tyre scraped the curb. 'Set a curfew, she isn't to stay out after midnight. She will try and get around it, she's quite persuasive, so you will have to be firm...' He crunched gears, slalomed round traffic.

'About work. No flower girl jobs: bar-lady, fashion model, cigarette girl, promotions and marketing – all that is right out. Waitressing is okay. But only the right kind of place.'

His voice, belying the hectic movement of the car, was languid and distinct. 'Ideally, a quiet office job. Unfortunately she doesn't have any qualifications. Her English, though, is remarkable, really, I think it is as good as yours. I wonder if your mother is in a position to help her. Doctors need receptionists, clerks, that kind of thing. You'll have to ask. That would be ideal. Only when the visa has come through, obviously. Wouldn't want you getting into trouble.'

'Right.' Tom tried to laugh but the pain morphed it into a groan. He realised he had lost his place on the present fistful of notes and would have to start again. 'No trouble.'

49)

Jian parked on an empty strip of tarmac at the dead end of a cul-de-sac. A line of skinny trees partially obscured a block of flats to one side, there was a brick wall opposite that, and in front, railings; then a playground. He turned off the engine and headlights.

'Twelve o'clock,' said the lad, excited now. 'We're in time. We're on time, we've got the money. Thank heaven... What do we do now?'

'We wait. They're watching us, I expect. They'll make us wait a while. Don't expect it to be soon.'

'Oh.'

'I'd like you to introduce my daughter to your student friends, the good ones, the... people who will influence her in the right direction. Watch that she doesn't make lots of meat-and-drink friends. When she's got a visa, residence permit, job, all that, when she's settled, you can divorce. She can move out, make a normal life for herself. I don't know how long that will take, a couple of years I guess. Five at the most. You've got normal guy friends, yes? Ones that like girls? Steer her, in time, towards a sensible one with prospects.'

'You're talking like it's all on me. Like you won't be around.'

'No.'

'Wait. Hang on. This is... Are you sure you've thought this through? Aren't you worried about the tong? They still want me. So... it's a risk isn't it, me being married to your daughter? Cause they'll come after me. That puts her in danger.'

'It's worked out.'

'Are you sure?'

'There'll be nothing linking you to the robbery. No leads. Think about it. The other robber is dead. You left no evidence. You have no dealings with people like that. It'll be fine. Long as you never tell anyone.'

'But... no, there is a lead. There's you. They know who you are... and they must know that you know me. They know you caught me, they know I was in your car. They'll think you know where I am. So they'll go after you. Won't they? Of course they will. They'll find you and force you to tell them everything about where I am. You said they... you said they torture people. Skin them. Isn't that... shit, isn't that what they'll... Won't they? Well? Isn't that a worry?'

'I said, nothing will lead them to you. You can stop worrying about them. Worry about your upcoming marriage.'

'But that means... you have to be out of the way. Like, completely, out of...'

'Yes. Exactly.'

'So... How are you going to be completely out of the way? You're going back to China?'

'How is that out of the way?'

'So what then? You're going to disappear? You're going to what, turn into a ghost or something?'

Jian sighed. 'I am old, I am tired, I am used up, and I am not of any good purpose to anyone here. I'm no use to anyone back home either, before you ask.'

'Wait so... Seriously? You... you want to...' he lowered his voice. 'You want to... kill yourself?'

'It has to be public, the tong has to know I've gone. I would like it to be in the newspapers. Disgraced Chinese official, in exile far from home, takes the honourable course out. That kind of thing. I'll go back to the big river, jump off one of those old bridges. That should do it.'

'What? Fuck. I didn't think... I'm so... Fuck. Seriously?'

'We'll sort this out first. None of this should concern you.'

'But... I knew you were crazy but... You can't just... It's...'

'Make sure my daughter is provided for, then exit. It's not bad. You said you wanted to know what real Chinese life was like. This is it. Do what it takes for your kin. Odd-looking but practical arrangements. Five thousand years of that. That's us. You'll learn.'

It would be good to hear his daughter's voice a final time but he worried he might become maudlin. Their last conversation, brief as it was, had ended on a good note. Good enough to go out on? It would have to do.

Jian got out of the car and stretched. The lad joined him and said solemnly, 'I will look after your daughter very well. She will be taken care of.'

'Good. We will not talk about this any more, I think the matter is fully settled.'

'Okay.'

They fell silent, smoked. The trick, Jian figured, was not to think about it, to just walk the chosen path. The lad displayed no such aptitude for forebearance. As time passed he grew unable to contain his agitation, and began to pace around the car. After a good ten circuits, he said, 'There's nothing here. There's nobody. Is it a trick?' He had his hands tight around the neck of the laden pillowcase and was wringing it like he was killing a chicken. 'Maybe we should shout. Should we shout? I think we should shout.'

'Stand still. Be quiet. They're watching us.' Perhaps from the trees, behind the wall, through a crack in drawn curtains. It was a well chosen venue: dark, discreet, long sightlines. This was reassuring. Jian wanted to be dealing with hardened professional criminals who had done this many times. That made it far likelier to go as planned.

Tom said, 'Maybe… They might keep him and ask for more. Or take the money and kill him anyway.'

'Yes, it's possible. But not likely.'

'How can you be sure?'

'It's not good business. The Chinese community isn't big here, right? If you pay up, and still don't get your loved one back, then word will get around. Soon everyone will know that paying these kidnappers is pointless. That's their business model screwed. I would like to buy a packet of fried pig-skin rinds. Very delicious. I would like to practise the name, so that I can ask a shopkeeper if I cannot see them on the shelf. It's something like *po-ku sha-qing*.'

50

'Por-k scrat-chings. Por-k scr-at-chings. Say it again.'

Tom found it hard to concentrate on teaching and wasn't listening to the reply. Butterfly took his name from Master Zhuang's puzzle: how do I know I am not a butterfly's dream? He was so sensitive. So gentle, kind, smart. So delicate and willowy. Whenever Tom imagined the ordeal he was going through, which was often, he felt the pain too, and the blind terror of captivity, and he winced and trembled.

Abruptly, he heard weeping: a gulp, a sob, a juddering intake of breath. It was close – impossibly so. But no one was there. The sound came again, the same awful noises at the same volume. Gulp, sob, judder. 'That's him. That's Butterfly.' He was looking wildly round, turning so hard it made him dizzy. 'It's not just me, right? You hear it too?'

The gambler fished in a bin and picked out a burger box closed with a rubber band. He opened it and took out a cheap phone. Gulp, sob, judder. It was a ringtone.

'Give it to me,' said Tom. 'I have to be the one to talk to them.'

He took the phone and answered the call. He heard heavy breathing. He said 'Hello? Hello? Hello?'

A quivering voice, not loud, as if the phone was a foot from the mouth. 'Tom… Tom.' It was Butterfly.

'Love, it's going to be okay. I'm coming for you. I've got the money, you'll be home soon.'

A pause, then another voice, louder, rougher, speaking English. 'You hear that? He's in pain. I've been hurting him. He wants to get out very much. You've got the money, yes?'

'Yes. Here.' Tom held the pillowcase high and waved it. 'Here, it's all here. You can see me right? I'm waving.'

'I see you. There's someone else there. What are you thinking? This isn't going to work like that. You need to be on your own. I specifically instructed you, to be on your own.'

'No you didn't, I don't remember that. The guy with me is no one, he's helped me get the money together, he...'

The caller was suddenly furious. 'Don't doubt me, you lanky streak of piss, don't tell me I didn't do what I did. For that, for disobeying instructions, I'm going to give the package a poke. How about that. A little jab. Just enough to draw blood, make a scar. Add to his collection.'

'Don't do that, please, come on, it was hard to get the money. He's been helping me out.'

'Get rid of him.'

'I...'

Tom reminded himself that the crazy gambler did not understand, though he could not help lowering his voice and turning away as he said, 'He won't want to go.'

'Then run away. Lose him, right now, or the deal's off.'

'Okay.'

'There's a gate, corner of the little playground, by the trees. You see it? You run through it. Then there's a path, go down and after ten metres you come to a road. Turn left, and pelt it hard along that road. After two hundred metres you'll see a red sign on the right. You turn down the alley just after that, you'll see a fence on the left. Made of wire. I've cut a hole in it for you. Go through the hole. You got all that?'

'With the money?'

'Yes with the money, twat. Run fast. Lose your bodyguard. Or I start slashing and poking.'

Tom looked at his companion: solid, useful, experienced. The voice on the phone said, 'Now. Or I hurt him.'

'Wait. Gate to road, left, at red sign right. Hole in fence.'

'At speed. What are you waiting for?'

Tom ran. The gambler was calling, coming after him. But it didn't take long to leave him behind. Tom was quick, running was something he could do, something he excelled at, and soon he could no longer hear pursuit. He settled into his rhythm. With every stride the pillowcase thumped his side and pain throbbed inside his chest. He spotted the sign: DANGEROUS STRUCTURE KEEP OUT, passed it, turned into an alley. Wire curling outwards showed where the fence had been cut. He ducked through the wire, then a slashed plastic sheet, and stopped, panting. The fencing circled a derelict three-storey building. Doors and windows were blinded with metal sheets. CAVENDISH ARMS was written faintly on one wall, and metal jutted where a sign had hung. A disused pub.

He held up the phone. 'I'm here… I'm here. He's gone.'

'Follow the arrows.'

A chalk arrow on manky tarmac pointed round the side, where he found another chalk arrow pointing to a fire door wedged open with a brick.

Tom shuffled into darkness, holding up the pillowcase. The place smelled damp and fusty.

'I've got the money. I'm on my own. I promise. Please.'

'Walk forward.'

'Is he in here?'

'He's in the back.'

'It's too dark, I can't see.'

He flashed the phone and cast cold pale light on broken and upended chairs and tables. Cables looping down from ruined ceiling. He heard water drip forlornly. The space was busy with shadows and there were many places to hide. He was just where they wanted him. He was powerless. He should not have come. He should have tried to make an alternative arrangement. They had what he needed: but he had what they needed. Why had he not set some terms of his own? He missed the gambler now. He was not playing this right, he knew it, but having come this far he had to go on.

'How do I know he's here?'

As if in reply, a plaintive wail swelled from the darkness. 'Tom?' Butterfly's voice.

Tom shouted, 'I'm here, I'm here.'

The stranger on the phone said, 'There's a table in front of you. Put the money on it.'

It was the only upright piece of furniture in the room. Up-ended chairs hemmed him in. He went around them like a rat in a maze.

Butterfly called again. 'Tom? Tom?'

'I'm coming. I'm coming now.'

The voice on the phone said, 'What are you waiting for? Put the money on the table and go and get him.'

Tom put the pillowcase down.

'Step away from it. That's right. Another step. Good.'

Tom kept the phone trained on the pillowcase as he backed off. He was reluctant to let it out of sight. He had still not seen Butterfly. What would the crazy gambler do now?

Tom shouted, 'It's all there, it's all there.'

'One more step. Good. Now turn. Look.'

A door had opened to his left, behind the bar. A faint red blush was coming through the doorway from the room beyond. Butterfly called again. 'Tom. Tom.' Louder now. He was in there. So close.

The voice on the phone said, 'Go get him tiger'.

Tom weaved round tables and chairs, then clambered over the dusty bar, picking up splinters. He was calling 'It's okay, it's okay.' The same feeble cry, unvaried in pitch and tone, came back. 'Tom... Tom.'

He pushed at the door, but something was blocking it from opening more than a couple of inches. Behind him, he heard footsteps approach, halt, then rapidly recede. Someone was taking the money and slipping away. He did not care: he just wanted to get into that room. He put his shoulder into the door and shoved, grunting with the effort. The blockage shifted, the door gave suddenly, and Tom tumbled through the doorway, landing on his knees.

He flashed the phone, illuminating the barrel that had blocked the door, curlicues of peeling wallpaper, gulleys in the walls where electrics had been ripped out, a staircase leading up. A portable speaker sat on the fifth step. The dim red light was cast by the LED display: 12.46, and a bluetooth icon. The speaker said, 'Tom… Tom.'

Every 'Tom' had been the same. How had he not noticed? It was a recording.

'Tom… Tom.'

The bluetooth icon flickered, went dark. The source of the recording had moved out of range. His tormentors had run off with his money.

He had fallen for a stupid, simple trick. Tom wailed in anguish then kicked the speaker. It hit the wall and the battery cover fell off. Batteries spilled and the red glow ended. He retreated to the doorway and peered into the gloom. There were no footsteps any more, just that forlorn drip, the blackness, the musty stink. No pillowcase full of cash. He knew he was alone.

Perhaps Butterfly was dead. He might have been dead for days. Tom screamed into the phone. 'I did everything you wanted. I gave you the money. Please, be fair, give him back. Give him back!'

But the call had ended.

大圈子 BIG CIRCLES

51

WeiWei pressed the CALL button on the front door panel. Looked at in the harsh electric light of the humourless high rise, her plan seemed pretty unpromising. Likely he would be asleep, out, or uninterested in meeting a girl unmasked as a thief; and this, like most other spontaneous gestures she had ever gone in for, would prove a waste of time. To her surprise a perky response came almost immediately as if he'd been hanging out near the door, alert and ready.

'Wei?''

She waved at a lens, tried to sound girlish and carefree. '*Nihao, wo lai*... Hi. It's me. Your naughty friend.'

A statement calculated to acknowledge her transgression straight away, and make light of it.

A pause. Did she hear a quick intake of breath, or was that her imagination, or mike static?

'It's very late.'

'So who doesn't like a booty call?' She grinned, stuck out her tongue and cocked her head. Over the top for normal circumstances, but as he was watching on a screen the size of a playing card, she figured she had to dial it up.

He said, 'I might be busy.'

'And what might you be busy doing? Your homework? Entertaining?'

'No, nothing like that. I'm on my own.'

She wagged a finger. 'Then you really have no excuses.' She touched finger to lip. 'Don't you like what I do to you?'

'Come up.'

WeiWei did not consider herself in the lift mirror but looked fixedly forward, gathering her wiles for the coming encounter. The lift opened onto carpeted hallway and almost immediately after he opened his door. He was wearing an unfastened black silk dressing gown over Versace boxers, with his bare feet in Fendi sliders. He turned and shlepped away. Perhaps it was his lack of artifice, his air of not caring very much, or just the way his slim hips swivelled, but she felt a spark of desire: good.

She slipped off shoes, dumped bag on chair, and went straight into it. 'So you know what happened earlier? I'd wandered into this shop and on the way out – I'm such a ditz – I realised I was still holding this lipstick. And this guard was shouting at me. Like the ditz that I am, I got frightened and you know what I did? I just ran away. What a ditz.'

'Come on.' He gave her that tight, sardonic smile. 'Don't bullshit. You were on a crime spree. The guard told us all about it. Wrapping stuff in foil, good trick.'

Her plan was instantly in ruins. Fuck. Her shoulders dropped. What now? She had no contingency to fall back on. So… maybe there was nothing else for it. Just do it, say it. Tell the truth. It couldn't get any worse. 'Alright. Yes. I was stealing. I am a thief. But… I had a reason.'

She straightened, took a deep breath. She wanted to look fierce and direct, like Dad. What to say exactly? W*o shi qiongren* meant 'I am one of the poor'. But there was something banal about merely having no money. More dramatic would be *Wo pinkun*! – 'I am destitute'. Then the idea that she was throwing herself on his mercy could not be missed. The prospect of unburdening herself, and forcing the moment to its crisis, excited her. She opened her mouth to let her secret bloom – but before she could speak a syllable, he said, 'You were bored, I know. It's cool.'

She smacked her lips shut and frowned. 'What?'

'What a lark! We all thought it was very funny.'

'Funny?'

'The strawberry life is tedious. Anything you want is just there for you. So what's the only thing left? Thrills. Horse-riding and skiiing are so lame. Nicking's a new buzz, right?'

'Huh.'

'But you didn't let yourself get caught. You were out of there like a bandit. Tell me the details of your daring escape. It looked very cool.'

Why, her thievery had made her more interesting, as if it were an intriguing character trait. The brazen immorality of his attitude sparked a flash of outrage, then her own reaction surprised her. Despite everything, it seemed she was still the policeman's daughter. As she talked, reconstructing her sordid spree and post-discovery flight as some jolly escapade, he stroked her hand and looked at her fondly, leaning in to drink up every word. His characteristic amused detachment had been replaced with unabashed interest. In a way, it was their first tender moment. Project Ye Xian was back on track.

Afterwards he gave her a red plastic folder with a sheet inside, a pastiche of a graduation certificate. 'We voted you honorary member of the Red Scholars. Congratulations.' Six characters, in two columns: *Hong xuezh* – 'Red Scholar'. He told her where to write her name. He inked a chop and stamped it.

Secret societies: it seemed a bit childish to her. Maybe he picked up on her scepticism, for he said, 'It's just a folly. Don't worry, you don't have to get a tattoo or anything. You will need to add us on WeChat for the meet-ups.'

He poured Japanese whisky into shot glasses. 'Come here.' They interlinked drinking arms, so their faces almost touched when they raised their glasses. His dark eyes were looking deep into hers. He had lovely eyelashes, any girl would covet those. Not the dark rings underneath his eyes, though: she should encourage him to get more sleep, eat better, drink less. 'To kindred spirits. To taking risks, and the strange roads they lead us. To new friends. New beginnings.' All hard liqour tasted to her like petrol, and this was no exception, but she got it down and didn't cough, and afterwards he kissed her.

'You shoplift because you need that sense of danger. Just to feel... real. Come here.'

He led her outside onto the bracing cold of the balcony where, to her alarm, he stood on a chair then stepped up onto the waist-high wall. She put a hand on her mouth. What was he doing? Was he going to jump? He stood rigidly upright with his shoulders back and his feet together, like a soldier at attention. The dressing gown billowed. Was this cocky display, drunken bravado, psychotic episode? And what should she do about it? He raised a straight leg, slow and meticulous as a clock hand, held it a moment, then lowered it and raised the other in the same measured way.

Was she supposed to be impressed? She just wanted him to get down. She reached out then paused. Perhaps it was better not to touch him, it might propel him in the wrong direction.

She looked over and down, at distant paving and the tops of bushes. It would be quite a fall. He said. 'The wall here is more than twenty centimetres wide. The wind is not strong. There is, actually, no real danger.' He rotated, with precise little shuffling movements, till he was facing her. 'It is all in the mind.'

She realised she was holding her breath. She exhaled and understood. He had seen her thrill, or thought he had, and now was showing her his. He said, 'I think we're quite similar.'

She forced a smile. 'I do too.' Perhaps that was all that was required.

He jumped down. 'It's late. Let's go to bed.'

52)

Jian found Tom alone, down on his knees in the road with his forehead pressed to the pavement. As soon as he saw the lad run off he knew it would go badly for him.

'Well?'

'They took... they took the money.' He raked his palms along the ground, sat back on his heels. His eyes were wild and sweat glistened on his face. Jian put a hand in his armpit and hauled him to his feet. 'Butterfly wasn't here... he was never here.'

'It's not over.'

'Maybe they will let him go. What do you think? They've got the money, of course they'll let him go, why wouldn't they? What use is he to them now? Well? What do you think?'

'Maybe.'

'Or maybe he's dead. That's what you really think, isn't it? Don't you. You think he's dead.'

Dead – *si le* – every time the lad forced the word out he winced. Jian did not reply. He suspected exactly that. There were plenty of reasons to kill a hostage. He might know too much – have seen his captors' faces, for example, overheard their names. Or it might be slightly more convenient than letting him go.

The lad's gaze turned accusing. 'You said it would be fine. You told me they had a reputation to consider, that's what you said. A business model.'

'Have you tried calling back?'

'Of course I have.' He waved the phone angrily. 'What do you think I've been doing? There's no reply. So? What do we do? We can't just... this can't be it. It can't be.'

The starless sky had a hint of burnished orange. Leaves moved in the breeze and distant traffic hummed and from flats down the street came the faint reedy crying of a baby. It was a quiet, undistinguished place, ill-suited for high emotion. Jian rubbed his chin, 'Tell me again about the night he was snatched.'

'What? Why?'

'I want to hear about it.'

'There's nothing to say.'

'When was it, Wednesday?'

'Thursday.'

'Before the snatch, what were you doing?'

He spoke quickly. 'I went to a restaurant with my friends, then I went back to Butterfly's, and he was upset about his dad being arrested.'

'How was he?'

'Angry. Drunk.'

'And then?'

'In the middle of the night I woke up. I was hit with a… a stunner. Someone was… someone grabbed him, put… put tape round him. Dragged him off.'

His body twisted, his arms swung. He was back in that room, fighting the pain. 'Tried to… I tried to follow. They hit me. Knocked me out. I woke up, my phone was ringing. He said, fifty thousand, Sunday night. And here we are. And it was just lies.' He slumped. 'All lies.'

'They broke the front door down?'

'Huh? No.'

'House or flat?'

'Flat.'

'What floor?'

'Three.'

'Lift?'

'Yes.'

'Concierge in the lobby?'

'No.'

'I wonder how they got him out?' mused Jian. 'Along a corridor past other front doors, into a lift, out of a lobby, onto the street, along a pavement, into a vehicle. I wonder how they did it. They must have put him in a box or something.'

'It doesn't matter does it?' snarled Tom. 'Who fucking cares?'

'Who was buying the drinks?'

'What?'

'At the restaurant.'

'What has that got to do with anything? No one was buying the beers. HuaGua knew the owner, they were free.'

'Was it his idea for you all to go out? He ask for you two especially?'

'Of course, we're friends. Yes it was his idea... So what? You think he had something to do with it? Another stupid idea. You're just asking questions for the sake of it, yes?' He started shouting, pointing. 'You're useless. This hasn't worked and you're just messing about, talking round and round, cause you don't know what to do, do you? You failed, it's all fucked up. You stupid, fucking...'

He slapped and punched. Jian swatted his hands away.

'You said it would work. Fuck you.' Jian closed his arms around the boy and restrained him with a hug.

'I just want him back.' Snot and tears dampened Jian's shoulder.

53)

WeiWei lay snuggled into sleeping HuaGua's divertingly smooth and bony form. His legs felt warm and long, his hair smelled clean and lemony. She was feeling whole and self-possessed in that post-sex hush. Imagine if she were here every night. Warm and cosy like this. Full of fine food, with gorgeous clothes waiting for the morning, beautiful objects all around. With the peace of mind that came from knowing such circumstances would never change. How just incredibly nice that would be. Nicer things, she mused, were much nicer than not nice things. It seemed a profound and useful revelation. For instance, it answered the famous question of whether it was better to be crying in the back of your boyfriend's BMW or smiling behind him on his bike. Of course you had to say bike, you had to say that you just wanted to be happy, you didn't want to seem shallow, but the right answer was BMW. Because emotions were fleeting and unreliable, and nice things were so very nice.

Another argument in favour of nice things: they could make you into a nicer person. Being secure and relaxed, being surrounded by beauty and comfort, would elevate the soul, and lead to thoughtful choices, considerate action, and a kind and charitable disposition. A sound theory, although... that didn't seem true with this guy, did it? None of those adjectives, unfortunately, applied. Also, he didn't, on the whole, seem to be having quite as tremendous a time as by rights he should be. For instance he seemed generally moody and distracted, relentlessly cynical, and usually drunk. Plus he was mad or sad enough to want to stand on a wall over a long drop. Well, perhaps wealth was wasted on the wealthy, just as, she had heard, youth was wasted on the young and beauty on the beautiful.

He shifted in his sleep and she turned away to give him room. She should come clean about her true situation, she couldn't keep putting it off. The longer her admission of poverty and helplessness was delayed, the more of a calculating bitch she would look for not mentioning it earlier.

As soon as he woke then. I have something to say. I haven't been entirely honest… I wanted you to like me… I was afraid you wouldn't notice me… She resisted the temptation to put it together now, as she didn't want to be over-prepared: the phrases should not be pat or they would sound insincere. It needed to be, or at least seem, fresh, heartfelt, spontaneous. Whisper, hold his hand, cast her gaze demurely down. At just the right moment, look up, let him see limpid eyes and quivering lip. I have deceived you, I know, I feel terrible, but please understand that pride, affection and lust, made me quite set aside propriety. The archaic phrases she had reached for tripped her mind, now tottering on the edge of sleep, into staging the scene as a historical tableau, in television colours: she sported flowing robes and a complex hairdo, he was stern and powerful in the gown and pigtail of a Qing mandarin. They stood on a bridge over a stream in a peony garden: butterflies flitted, a zither played. After her confession, he turned away: she sobbed: the rhythm of the music intensified: then he came to her: a single tear tracked his cheek. He took her in his arms and whispered in her ear…

54)

Gulp, sob, judder: the phone was ringing. Tom wiped tears, caught his breath, and considered the screen. 'Fuck. It's him.' He mashed the hot, sweaty device against his cheek. 'Hello? Yes?'

'Hello,' that same growling voice. 'You want your Butterfly back?'

'Please…' His breath was coming in gulps. 'You promised. It's fair, it's right. You've got the money. It's all there.'

'You're a good runner. Need to run again.'

'Just let him go.'

'No. You need to lose the bodyguard again. Listen. Go back to the car park. Where your car is.'

'Why?'

'We're there, we're waiting.'

'How can I trust you?'

'I've got the money, you think I want to look after your friend? I want rid. I've had fun, now I'm making good.'

'No tricks this time?'

'You've come through with the money, I'm coming through with the package. I need you to come pick him up. Those are the terms. We're there. We're waiting for you. Not for long though. I'm getting nervous. I'll be taking him away in thirty seconds. I see the bodyguard, I drive. In thirty seconds I drive. You'd better hurry. What are you waiting for? Come on!'

The crazy gambler seemed to sense Tom's intention, for he lunged just as Tom lurched. Tom dodged then pelted head-long. His technique left him: his arms flapped and he felt in danger of falling at every stride. The breeze drove tears back from his face. Once more he heard the crazy gambler shouting as he left him behind. The man seemed an irrelevance now, with his niggling questions, all the tedious talk of his daughter. Tom stumbled to the car park and stopped, his chest heaving. His vision was smeared, spotted with sparkling lights: through that opaque screen he saw a white van parked beside the BMW, back door open, lights off. It was nosing forward. The driver called to him, incongruously chirpy: 'Get in, hurry.'

Tom blundered up and pitched himself through the doorway into blackness. He landed heavily on a metal floor, cold to cheek and hands. The space was empty. The pitch of the engine rose as the vehicle accelerated. He struggled upright and looking back saw the crazy gambler arrive in the car park, stop, wave his arms above his head. To signal what? He shrank and faded into the general darkness, then the van took a sharp turn, the wheels squealed, Tom sprawled, and the back door slammed shut.

At least he was moving, something was happening. Maybe it was working out. Professionals, he told himself, who wanted to protect their business model. What could they want him for? He hadn't thought this through. Get money, go here, go there. He was acting like a puppet.

The van stopped, and the engine cut out and in the silence Tom could hear his breathing, frayed from nerves and exhaustion, and the blood beating in his head. The back door opened. Tom considered a chubby figure with a hood up, a scarf over his face.

'Well? Where's Butterfly?'

No reply came. This was all wrong, he was certain now. They didn't need him, did they? His presence was only a complication for them, one that they could not profit from. He thought again about the gambler. The man had been warning him. Why had he not paid attention? His hope, his need for activity, had betrayed him. He braced, wary and alarmed, and demanded again, petulant, 'Where is he? Where's Butterfly? I've paid you. Come on.'

The figure was chuckling behind the scarf. 'You didn't even get a new bag. Racing cars. Unbelievable.'

His voice was high, excitable, with an Essex tinge. This was his natural tone, Tom realised: he'd been roughing it up on the phone. It was an innocuous and ordinary voice, the kind heard on the bus, in the canteen, over headphones in co-op play. The laugh was an immature chortle. His tormentor was nothing but a callow youth. Chubby, shorter than him, younger. Tom felt indignant, as if he had been conned.

The lad lunged, and Tom flinched. He was a fraction too slow: a handheld device brushed his side. A snap and a flash, and a spasm gripped him and sent him sprawling. The stunner, again. Tom tried to rise, against the cramping pain, but the device was applied once more, and giggles merged with the electric cackle.

Shan glared at her horrible clock. Every plink of the second hand was another tear to her nerves. Nothing and still nothing, and still? Nothing. What could be taking so long? Say the swap took ten minutes. Ten for a tearful reunion. Another ten for this Jian character to say, right, let's get you home. Ten more, at the most, for practical concerns like phoning your fretful mother to be remembered.

It wasn't just a delay, not now, after all these tortuous minutes: something had gone wrong. Perhaps a double-cross. The kidnappers had taken the money and run and Tom was chasing after them. Or Jian had stolen it. Or perhaps – how her imagination betrayed her – the kidnappers took the money then grabbed Tom, and at any moment would call and demand money from her.

She told herself the wait was addling her mind: it was an exhausting, infuriating slog to just sit around. She hated being a helpless spectator.

One o'clock. The hand going vertical seemed definitive, a call to action. This was officially unendurable and something must be done. She hurried to Tom's room, opened his laptop, entered his password. She was reflected in the screen: bleary eyes, jaw set hard, hair scarecrowing outwards. She looked like one of those patients you knew were going to have you calling security.

Jian was central to the catastrophe. That flighty bitch who had barged in then straight out again – she was her only link to him. And she had gone to see a friend called HuaGua. It might be that Tom knew this HuaGua too, and would have his address.

She found him on Tom's contact list. An address in Harbourside. No phone number, they probably talked over WeChat or Snap or whatever it was these days. She looked the place up. A flat in a new development on the Isle of Dogs. Another Butterfly type no doubt. Damn these rich, heedless young mainlanders. If Tom had not grown pally with them this would not be happening.

Never mind the late hour, or looking like a wild woman, or the likelihood that this was just more chasing of shadows. She was going to go round there and she was going to find this girl, drag her out of bed if necessary, and not let her go until she had revealed how to get in touch with her father.

56)

Jian was once more throwing the Treasure Horse round corners and clunking over speed bumps, though this time without destination or deadline. He was hunting the white van he had glimpsed in the car park, the one that took the dumb lad away. It was a residential area and the abundant streets were narrow and meandering and every moment the odds of spotting his quarry diminished. He came to a dead end and made an irritable three-point turn. Had they grabbed the lad to hold him hostage? Was it the mother's turn to pay a ransom, and start stealing in desperation, as her son had done?

He spotted a white van. Jian accelerated, caught up, swerved in front, came to a crunchy stop. The van swerved onto the pavement and halted. Jian got out and waved his crowbar at the wide-eyed driver, who put his hands up. This vehicle didn't look right – the back was the wrong shape – but now he was here he might as well check. He opened a door and considered stacked boxes. He stepped smartly aside and ignored the driver's shouting as the van reversed. It stopped, turned, screech away.

He was not going to get anywhere like this. He lit a cigarette. You couldn't keep staring directly at the thing, you had to stop, and come at it sidelong, mull it over as if you had all the time you needed. He took in the placid scene. Parked cars, neat hedges, a little roundabout, all cast over with an orange pall. The streetlights were the wrong colour: even at night you knew you were far from home.

The roundabout was marked by a white circle with three regular gaps. A broken circle: the shape snagged his attention, and he wondered why that might be, and then he knew: he understood what had happened, and how it all fitted together, and he cursed himself for not realising earlier. He returned to his car, turned on the interior light. He folded his mapbook against the steering wheel and started the engine.

57

Tom lay in the back of the moving van. His ankles and wrists were bound with tape. Rough material was wrapped round his head and secured with tape at the neck. More tape covered his mouth. He was trying to keep mental note on how long he'd been here, how fast they were going, how many turns. It helped suppress his agitation. But after some minutes this frantic record-keeping seemed pointless, his attention slipped and he lost track, and tipped over into panic, and his heart ran so hard he felt it might burst, and his breathing grew ragged, and he spasmed and thrashed and muffled shrieks came from his mouth.

The fit passed, despair gripped him, and he fell limp, exhausted, and passive. A fatalistic blankness enveloped him. Let what was to happen, happen. Sooner rather than later, please. This went on and on, he did not know for how long, then when the van stopped and the engine cut out he was drawn back out of himself. He listened for the clunk of the back door being opened. But it didn't come. He heard footsteps moving away. There was an echo to them, so he guessed the van was parked in a large interior space. When they faded he felt miserable and alone. Why didn't they just get on with it? The waiting was the worst.

58)

WeiWei woke to the hum of a phone vibrating. She felt HuaGua wake, shift and reach. Who would ring at nearly two in the morning? Either someone from China who didn't appreciate the time difference, or another girl with a similar idea to hers. He moved her arm off his chest, turned over and answered his phone. He mumbled, then the mattress dipped as he got out of bed. She sensed him looking at her. She pretended to be asleep, hoping to overhear a clue to who was calling. He listened a while and she could sense him watching her. She stayed completely still, breathing softly like a sleeper. He whispered in English, 'Brilliant. Come up.'

He slipped away, closing the door softly behind him, and she opened her eyes. It had to be a girl. An English one maybe. She heard scraping outside the room, then a soft thump against the door. She needed to move, to know. She slipped out of bed and pattered to the door. Pressing her cheek against it she could hear nothing so she tried to open it. It was jammed shut. She recalled a thin sculpture in the corridor. About a metre tall, vaguely figurative, likely expensive, definitely heavy, metal and ugly – a simple matter to drag it across, jam it under the handle, and shut her in.

She had been locked in before by men, and the memory made her shiver. What was he thinking? He hadn't imprisoned her exactly. She could still leave if she wanted to, from the balcony. Presumably he just wanted to be sure she wouldn't wake, wander sleepily out to find him, and discover him entertaining this new arrival.

She had to know. Plus, as a general principle, anyone who tried to control her had to be resisted. She went out on the balcony into the brisk night and padded past metal furniture and workout bench to the thick glass doors that led into the living room. Heavy curtains blocked her view but there was a slim chink of light where they had not been pulled together. Through that slit she glimpsed the room. He had put the lights on but kept them dim. She saw a flash of dressing gown then the front door closing. He was going out to greet his new arrival at the lift. Not a courtesy he had afforded her. That seemed telling, and very annoying, if, as she was now certain, this was another girlfriend.

But you never knew: perhaps he would admit to this girl that another was stealing his heart, and dump her. She would hear nothing out here, and see little. She opened the heavy door, stepped in, and closed the door behind her. She hid behind the curtains. If he discovered her, she could add her voice to any ensuing argument. She was not afraid of a scene, if it came to that.

She heard murmurs. Two voices. To her surprise the visitor was a guy. She peeked. They came in and sat with their backs to her, HuaGua on his leather and chrome sofa, the new arrival on a matching armchair. HuaGua had dressing gown and sliders on. The guest wore red trainers, red baseball cap and grey overalls. A drug dealer perhaps. They were leaning forward, considering something between them on the rather impractically low coffee table.

They started counting. The guest was taking money from a bag and dividing it into two piles. Maybe something to do with gambling? Money was business, possibly illicit and certainly private. No wonder he didn't want her witnessing this. She should have stayed in bed. Curse her wilfulness and curiosity.

'Twenty-five thousand each,' said Red Shoes, leaning back. 'Paid in full.'

'They're smelly,' said HuaGua bending in and sniffing deep. 'Like tea and earth. I wonder where they came from. He didn't get them from a bank.'

WeiWei gasped. Fifty thousand. In dirty notes. Was this – it couldn't be – could it? The money just paid to free Butterfly.

'So amazed it worked out,' said HuaGua. 'When I heard that his father had been arrested, I thought the whole thing was fucked.'

'You improvise. What does it matter who pays?'

HuaGua said, 'We should drink to success.' He poured his Japanese whisky. 'To easy money. To kidnap express.'

She did not want to hear any more. She yearned to be out of here. The balcony door handle was right beside her. But to open it was out of the question – the metal clunk, and the swish of the door, the movement of the curtain, would be certain to snag their attention. She should have gone when they were engrossed in the counting. Now they sat there like guard dogs. Never mind the sound of the door – even the squeak of a floorboard, an overloud breath, or a flutter of movement in the drapes could give her away now.

She was an unwitting witness to a serious crime. If they knew she was here, they might... what might they do? Well, that guest might want to kill her, actually kill her. HuaGua wouldn't let him do that, would he? Of course not. But maybe he wouldn't be able to stop him. And up to now it had been going so well. She realised a tear was tracking her cheek, but she didn't dare move to brush it away.

Red Shoes got up and WeiWei got another peek at him. A stocky Asian lad with headphones round his neck. His grey workmen's overalls didn't fit with the shoes and hat unless it was some new street fashion. She tensed – what if he came towards her – to taste night air on the balcony? But he went in the other direction, towards the kitchen. He went out of sight and she heard drawers opening. HuaGua just sat there, holding his glass, looking like a statue of someone who was listening out for something, until his guest came back. He had knife and plates and a white cardboard box. With a degree of ceremony he slid a cake out of the box and onto a plate.

'Celebrate. The tong way.'

'I thought you celebrated with a drink. Or a whore.'

'Well, there are many things you don't know. Big Circle Boys have cake. Proper patisserie shit, not Tesco own brand. Look at that, kiwi fruit, got strawberry there, meringue.' He handed HuaGua the knife. 'You cut it.'

HuaGua bent forward and cut the cake and Red Shoes clapped. 'Nice big slice for me, come on.'

They sat and ate cake. There was silence but for tinny scraping sounds as HuaGua ate his with a fork. Red Shoes wiped cream from the corner of his mouth with his little finger.

HuaGua said, 'It is good actually. We can't eat it all.'

'You can have it for breakfast.'

'So... You didn't hurt him?'

'No,' said Red Shoes. 'He was scared, of course.'

'Yeah well, fuck that guy. Arty queers are the worst. I guess he got a good lesson. How did the swap go? Describe it.'

'Nothing to say. I took delivery of the money then kicked the queer out of the van. With his blindfold on. Told him if he took it off, I'd kill him. I drove away. I looked back, he still hadn't taken it off.'

'I thought that would be tricky, the swap.'

'I told you, I'm a professional. My dad's been doing it for decades. It's easy, don't know why more people don't give it a go.'

'That was the part that worried me.' There was no problem hearing HuaGua, his voice was a little louder and harder than she was used to: he was roughing it up.

'You admit that I did the difficult bit? I should get more than half, you think?'

HuaGua settled back. 'Well...'

'Relax, I'm kidding. We're a good team. That was hungry work. Cut me another piece.'

There was silence for a while, as they ate. Then HuaGua said, 'I did do half the work. I got the key. That wasn't easy. Getting that impression in the putty. That was risky.'

'That's true. And you provided the very convenient jail. I'm just joking around. You did half. You were most thoroughly involved. At every stage. I agree. Okay?'

She was flattened against the cold wall with the curtain drawn across her body. She did not even want to look directly any more, in case they sensed a gaze upon them, the way animals did. This was bad enough, but she knew the riskiest moment would come for her at the end, when the guest left and she had to try to get back to the bedroom before he did. Whether she could get away with it would depend on how the encounter finished, if he showed his guest to the door or not. She wanted it brought to a head, the gamble made: the wait was appalling. They'd split the money, they'd eaten the stupid cake, surely they had no more business to discuss. Why did they have to be right there? Why was this still going on?

HuaGua started talking again. 'Actually... I might have got us another target. I'm working on her at the moment. She's perfect.'

Her stomach lurched. If she were not leaning against a wall she might have fallen down. Her heart was pumping so hard and her breath was so ragged it seemed impossible that they did not hear it. She put a hand to her open mouth, mashing her lips to her teeth.

'You want to go again?'

'You don't? It's a thrill. Let me tell you about her. Her father's rich and corrupt, so that's perfect for us. She's young, naive, foolish, doesn't seem to have many friends. Easy meat.'

'Where does she live?'

'Not sure at the moment, still working on it. But she lives on her own.'

'I hope not a flat again. Flat's are hard. I nearly did my back in last time. Just getting him into the box. Then wheeling that out. There was the lift. It was a big hassle.'

'You could do it though, right? This girl will be lighter. She's skinny.'

'I could do it. With a copy of her key.'

'I'll get one tonight.'

'How?'

HuaGua brushed crumbs and settled back in his chair. 'She's in my bed.'

'She's here now?' Red Shoes stood. 'Right now?'

For the first time WeiWei could see him properly. A smooth-faced, chubby teenager, rather short. He looked away, towards the corridor that led to the bedroom.

HuaGua said, 'Relax, she's sound asleep.'

'You sure?'

'Course I'm sure. Sit down. I wouldn't want her harmed ...'

'There's no point in torturing them. Where's the percentage in that? It's civilised, they're well looked after, it's not too bad.' His voice was lower, and WeiWei had to strain to catch the words. 'It does the packages good. They grow up a bit, it toughens them up. They need that. And the parents, sitting at home, have to ask themselves, how much is my kid worth to me? Cause they've forgotten, they've got wrapped up in their careers and making money and... whatever. And then this big smack of reality hits them in the face, and they realise that the kid is everything to them, and they'll do anything to get the brat back. It takes a crisis to make them realise. Everyone can hug and learn. It brings the family closer together.'

'We could ask for more money.'

'No, it's the right amount. Any more and they'll take too long to raise the cash. You wouldn't want to keep the prisoner more than a few days, that's when things can start going wrong. You want to keep it simple and quick.'

'So back to plan A for this. Get Daddy to pay from China in crypto.'

'Facetime after the snatch, use a VPN of course, Monero address for the payment. Simple, quick, easy. You're keen now. I thought you would be. It's fun, right? A kick.'

'This smell is growing on me. You could sell it as an aftershave. Risk. For men who grab life by the balls.'

Red Shoes laughed, said, 'I'm off now. Have fun. Don't catch anything.'

They were moving towards the front door. 'I do what you said with the last one. Think of her as the package. When we're talking, when we're in bed. In my head she's the package. The package says this, the package likes that. Somehow it makes everything easy. That was good advice.'

HuaGua was standing in the doorway, with a hand nonchalantly on the frame and one foot out of a slider. The guest was out of sight in the hall. They were laughing about something, she could not hear what. Now that it had come to it she was not careful or stealthy. She was too hasty and her hands were trembling. She opened the balcony door and slipped out into darkness then she slid the door back behind her. It did not close quite properly but she did not dare push it home for fear of the noise it would make. She fled to the bedroom and got shakily back into bed. The sheets felt like metal as she lay curled tight, scrunching the duvet in her fists.

59

Tom could hear breathing. Someone was with him. He felt fingers on his neck, then his bindings loosened and tape was yanked away. The blindfold was tugged down. He blinked tears from his good eye. His captor stood looking down at him. The sole of a red shoe pressed his cheek, pushed his head into the metal floor, mashed busted lips.

The lad said, 'That was a fucking turn-up.' A click was followed by a sharp intake of breath. He'd started smoking. 'Smacked you about a bit when I snatched your boyfriend, gave you some of those bruises, I think. You look filthy, did you have a rough weekend? I couldn't believe it when I saw the bag. Kiddy racing cars on a red pillowcase. I was like, no, it can't be, then I was like, of course. You know what you only went and did? You will not believe it. You robbed me to pay me. It is very funny, when you think about it. Hilarious.'

Tom realised he had seen those trainers before, at the gambling den, underneath the big money table, jittering up and down while Paulie swept blocks of cash from above. He recalled their owner. A tubby Asian teen in hip-hop gear.

Hot ash settled in Tom's hair. The lad knelt on him, crushing arm and torso, and leaned forward to whisper in his ear. 'Don't concern yourself with the what-ifs. I was never going to let the queer go. The, what does he call himself, butterfly. He is useful to me dead.' The burning end of the cigarette trailed around Tom's cheek, doodled up and down, stopped an inch from Tom's eye. Tom shut the eye and felt the heat on his eyelid.

'Where's the other robber? I want a full name and address. Postcode, if you can remember it. Might save your eye. You're going to die anyway, but you probably don't want to be tortured before.'

Tom was numb. It was as if he had lived for so many hours with his nerves tuned to a shrill pitch that they had now burnt out. He no longer felt more than a passing interest in his own fate.

'He's called Paulie.' Tom's voice was so hoarse he could barely recognise it. 'And he's dead.'

'Stop covering for him. I'll hurt you really bad. You got ten seconds. One elephant.'

The lad held Tom's ponytail with one hand, jamming his head in place, and with the other kept the cigarette poised. Tom said, 'It's the truth. That's what happened. There was a fight. Over the money.'

'Three elephants. Four elephants…'

The burning sensation on Tom's eyelid grew more intense. The sing-song voice trilled on. 'Seven ele-phants… eight ele-phants…'

'I can't tell you it's not true when it is.'

'Nine ele-phants.'

'I can't make anything up. I'm too tired. That's the truth.'

'Is it though? Is it really?'

A snatch of rap music blurted. A ringtone. The lad let Tom go. He answered his phone, listened, then said to the caller, in Mandarin, 'It's the first building on the left. I'll come and open the door. Hang on.'

He ended the call. He tapped his palm on Tom's cheek. 'I was just messing with you. To pass the time. My dad won't, though.'

He pulled Tom's hood back down.

60

All the buildings in this area looked the same and Jian took several false turns before he found the development, a cluster of six multistoreys around a walled garden. One block was unlit, standing black and monolithic against the purple sky. He parked and carrying his bag strode to the front door, where he peered through glass at a dark lobby, empty desk.

The door would shatter after a few blows, though no doubt an alarm would ring and half the neighbourhood wake. He bent to his bag and grasped his crowbar. But, as luck would have it, a building on the other side of the street had an alert concierge or nightman, who half-opened the door of his building and stood at the threshold watching, walkie-talkie raised.

Jian picked up his bag and walked on. He would try his luck at the gated side entrance, in an underpass around the corner. The gate should give to the crowbar, and attract less attention.

61

WeiWei lay taut and alone in the dark. She imagined HuaGua in the living room, counting the money again, smelling it. Or rooting in her bag for her house key – she remembered the putty she had glimpsed in his drawer – a key he would not find because of course, lol, she had no house. Eventually he would come back to bed. And when he did, it was vital that she give no clue of what she'd overheard. She'd pretend to be asleep. If he woke her, just act normal. Keep being sexy and pliable, and, what else had he called her, naive and foolish. She just had to get through this night. In the morning she could flee and never see him again, and that would be the end of the dreadful episode. Why did she always pick so badly? What a talent to have, the ability to get entangled with vile men. Well, that might be a conversation to have with herself another time.

What if he wanted to have sex again? The thought repelled her. How revolting too, to be the patsy in the situation. Why couldn't it be him? A blast of righteous anger blew out the shame and humiliation. Before she quite knew what she was doing she had thrown off the duvet and was out of bed, standing straight and crackling with wrath. She should just go find him and smack his smug fucking face in. With his stupid minimalist furniture. Break a Scandinavian design classic over his perfect hair, smear pretty-boy make-up in his eyes. She caught her reflection in the glass of a framed print and it brought her back to a sense of herself – a big-eyed, long-haired girl, not built for fighting.

She wasn't pretending anything for anyone. She should put on her clothes and run. Go where though? She was a broke, homeless, illegal immigrant. Back to Mama fluffy loo? No, fuck that as well as this.

She and her father were in urgent need of money – well, what about that big wad of smelly currency she had glimpsed? Why not find a way to take it? Stealing the rich kid's cash would not only solve their problems, it would restore face and dignity. A plan was forming and she grinned at her audacity. Oh, was she bad. See how bad she could be.

62)

Tom heard two men. The Essex lad, now speaking Mandarin, with the exaggerated, clipped tones of someone who had learned it as a second language, and an older man with a deeper, gravelly voice, whose Chinese was harder to understand as he spoke rapidly and roughly: a native. The older man grumbled, 'You better not be fucking me about. I'm driving round with a body and a gun. I don't like detours.'

'A dead body?'

'I have to drive to fucking Epsom.' Pronounced E-pu-so-mu. 'Dig a hole.'

'Why?'

'Dump body and evidence, leave it a week, phone the police.'

'For that Chinese cop?'

'Fucker turned traitor. Has to pay.'

'Why are you doing it? Why not delegate?'

'When things go wrong you take the reins. See through every step until it's all put right. Look, I got these two helping. Give them a wave. Another two fat old guys who didn't think they'd be seeing this kind of action again. See, you're not the only one in the doghouse. Everyone is back to school this weekend. It does us big brothers good to get our hands dirty once in a while.'

'Why do you think the cop turned? You were generous to him.'

'He must have had a spasm of weakness.'

'Not an attack of conscience, surely. Whoever heard of a Chinese cop with one of those?'

'Maybe he couldn't stomach taking orders. Come on, this better be worth it. Show me what you're so excited about.'

The van door was opened. Through the doors Tom glimpsed bare concrete walls and floor, white markings. They were in an underground car park. Empty but for one other vehicle, a black SUV, with a couple of figures sitting in the front.

The lad said, with a flourish, 'I present you… the thief. One of them. I caught him by myself, got half the money, too.'

The older man was stocky, dressed in a tracksuit. He peered down through thick glasses, intense but dispassionate, as if at a specimen prepared for study. 'You sure?'

'Ask him.'

'Does he speak Chinese?'

'He does, I heard him bellow at the robbery. All the money now, all that stuff. Doesn't look so fearsome now, does he?'

The man knelt beside Tom, poked him on the cheek, and said, in Mandarin, 'On Saturday you robbed the Lucky Day Leisure Association?'

Tom croaked, 'Yes.'

The man nodded, pinched the skin under his neck, muttered to himself. 'How about that.'

The lad called to his father. 'There was that other robber working with him, we need to get where he is out of this one. I don't think he'll be tough to break. Can I be there when you work on him? I want to see how it's done. I think that's fair, cause I caught him.'

Tom looked from one to the other. The lad's cheeks were smooth and rosy, the man's cut with wrinkles, but they had the same wide, square faces, the same stocky build.

The father said to Tom, 'Where's the jewellery you took?'

'I don't know. The other robber got it. I don't know what he did with it.'

'I see. And what happened to him?'

'He's dead.'

The man sighed, paused, stroked his neck again. His voice was quieter as he said, 'Let's not worry about all that a moment. How did this lad find you?'

'He kidnapped my boyfriend. I had no choice. I had to do it. I'm not a thief. I mean, not normally. I'm a student. I robbed your place so I could pay the ransom.'

'He kidnapped your boyfriend? This lad?'

'Yes. I didn't know whose place it was. It was the only way I could think to get the money.'

'I see.'

The man yanked the bag back over Tom's head, and smoothed the tape down to secure it.

Tom heard him stand and leave the vehicle and as he was shutting the door he was saying, 'Son? Come over here. I want to talk to you.'

63)

The streets around HARBOURVIEW ESTATES were rather dark and empty, and Shan saw no other pedestrians. She felt increasingly foolish and exasperated. Did she really think anyone would answer to a stranger at this time of night? That was assuming she could find the front door, as there was no obvious way in and her phone was no help. Approaching the only side of the compound she hadn't tried already, she heard the clang of metal. She sidled up and peeked into a shallow underpass, at a figure trying to lever open a barred metal gate with a crowbar. Jian heaved his tool and grunted with the effort. Somehow it was not a surprise.

She shouted, 'Hey. Where's my son? What's going on?'

He turned to consider her a moment, nodded when he recognised her, then went back to work. 'Go home.'

She stalked forward. 'I will not. Tell me what's happened. Where's Tom?'

He tugged again but the gate still didn't move.

'He's been snatched. I'm sorry I let it happen.'

'Snatched?' Her legs weakened, and she steadied herself against the wall. 'What do you mean, snatched? Snatched by who?'

'The kidnappers took him.'

'Oh my God. So... they took the money, and then they grabbed him? But – that's...'

Jian pointed through the gate, at angular blocks. 'Unfortunate, yes. A boy in there is working with the kidnappers.'

'HuaGua?'

'That's the one.'

'I was just coming to see him.'

'He'll tell us where your son is. We just have to...' He tried yanking from a new angle. 'get in there.'

The garden beyond the gates was spottily illuminated by freestanding lights. She could see a figure on the far side, contemplating a water feature while smoking a cigarette. She wondered how he had not heard the commotion then saw the headphones.

Jian wiped sweat from his face. 'The gate is stronger than I anticipated. We can go in through the front but there's a guard watching it from another building, we'll have to be quick. Maybe I can take him down first...'

'Don't be ridiculous.' She turned on her phone's torch function and flashed it round until the smoker saw and slid his headphones down. She shouted in English, 'Hey excuse me? Excuse me, hello, yoohoo, sir?'

He shuffled up, his cigarette end bobbing in the dark. A night owl, in tracksuit and flip flops, grabbing a smoke before bedtime. She trilled, 'I'm awfully sorry, we've gone and done a silly and forgotten our fob. Such a nuisance. Would you be an absolute angel and pop the gate? Saves going round the front.'

He peered at them. She winched her smile wider, then he tapped a button and the gate clicked. 'Thanks so much.'

He ambled off and they walked in, Jian holding the crowbar behind his back.

Jian said, 'So? What are you doing here?'

'Your daughter's with HuaGua. I thought she could tell me where you are.'

'I told her to stay with you, I gave specific instructions. She doesn't do anything she's supposed to.'

'Is she in danger do you think?' It was reassuring to have someone to share her angst, after being alone with it so long.

He ignored the question and pointed at a dark block. All the windows were black but one, at the top level, where a dim yellow light burned. 'It's that one.'

'How do you know HuaGua is involved?'

'Whoever snatched Butterfly must have had a copy of his house key. Only an insider, someone who hung out with them, would have had the chance to get, or copy, a key.'

'How do you know he's the insider?'

'Before he was snatched Butterfly went out with a big group of friends. The insider would want Butterfly drunk before the snatch.'

'That makes sense.'

'At the restaurant, HuaGua was providing the drinks.'

'Right.'

A security light came on as they passed the water feature, and instinctively she hurried on into the shadows beyond. 'And?'

'And what?'

'What else?'

'Don't need anything else.'

'That's all you've got? I thought you had evidence. I thought you knew. All you've got is a hunch.'

He was no longer paying attention. He had his crowbar out, and was considering the plate glass door.

'Your daughter is sleeping with him, I expect, I imagine you know that and disapprove. Do you not think that might be colouring your judgement?'

'No.'

'You think you can smash that?'

He tested the edge of the crowbar against the toughened glass, then pulled it back, braced for a swing. 'Yes.'

'Be noisy.'

'Then we're lucky this building is empty.'

'What are you going to do, to make him talk?'

'Whatever I have to.'

She stepped away, mindful of flying bits of broken glass.

'Just to let you know, that's fine by me.'

64)

WeiWei browsed dressing gowns in the walk-in wardrobe, picked one of red silk with a dragon motif. Then took the handcuffs from the bedside cabinet and put them in the pocket. She went to the en suite. The mirror had recessed lights round the edge, and when she turned them on she flinched, unprepared for such a high-def version of herself. Seductive, she thought: she licked her lips then bit them, and they fell into a pout. Naive: she let her eyes widen and her features soften into an expression of artless innocence, which took off a few years and rather more IQ points. Then, making lots of noise so he'd know she was coming, she went to the balcony and knocked on the glass door to the glass living room.

He let her in.

'You shut me in. Are you afraid I'll run away?'

He was sprawled on the couch. There was whisky and two glasses on the table, cigarettes and ashtray, the half-eaten cake. No sign of the money.

He said, 'I thought you were asleep.'

She yawned and shivered. 'I just woke up. The bed got cold. I reached for you but you weren't there. Darling.' *Qin ai de* – it was the first time she'd used that term, a strong marker of affection. He registered it, and looked at her and grinned. *Ni shabi,* she thought, what a cunt. His teeth angled inward like a snake's. He had the doltish, self-satisfied look of the utterly self-absorbed. His eyes were the squinty piss-holes of a drunk. How blind she had been.

She sashayed to the couch and shimmied between his legs. He relaxed and it became clear that her gyrations were having the desired effect. His hand slid up and down her bare thigh. She teased him, leaning in, then out again.

She mumbled breathily, 'I dreamed about you.'

She took out the cuffs and spun them on a finger while composing her features into an exaggerated mask of desire. In these kinds of moments, you couldn't be too theatrical. The metal cuffs were lined with pink fake fur. They rattled and sparkled. She leaned in.

He said, 'Those? I thought they were too wild for you.'

'Maybe I can be wild. A little wild cat. Talking of cats...' She shimmied again and her dressing gown fell open. She glided up and down so that her nipples brushed his chest. 'How do you like these? Don't worry, I am going to take good care of you.'

The low-slung couch had a tubular metal frame and black leather upholstery with prominent white stitching. She snapped one cuff onto the bar that ran along the back, then pincered his wrist and raised it. It was quite strenuous, keeping this bending and wriggling going, she was feeling it already in her quads.

She got the wrist up to the bracelet. His breathing was quick, his mouth open. But perhaps he caught something off in her expression or the impatience of her movements, for he frowned, his gaze sharpened, and his arm stiffened. He was too late. She snapped the cuff closed and it locked with a satisfying click.

She retreated. He rattled his bound wrist. She took the handcuff key out of the dressing gown pocket, showed him, put it back. Then pulled the dressing gown closed and tied the belt. She picked up his cigarettes and got one lit.

'What are you doing?'

He could move his cuffed hand sideways along the bar between two vertical supports about eighty centimetres apart. She let him work it out.

'You need some colour in here.' She pointed at his shaggy black and white rug. 'Replace this with something colourful. All this monochrome is good for an outfit but not a home. There's nothing cosy here.'

'You want to redesign my place? I thought we were going to fuck.'

'Let's talk instead.'

'You want to talk interiors.'

She flicked ash on the rug. 'Actually no. I want to talk about kidnap.'

There was no flicker of alarm or guilt in his face. Maybe he was as good an actor as she was. He scoffed. 'What about it?'

'We both know.'

'I really don't. Am I supposed to have kidnapped someone? Why exactly would I get involved in anything like that? I'm rich, in case you hadn't noticed.' His free hand arced gracefully, taking in view, paintings, furniture. 'Look at this, look at all of it.' For a moment he appeared poised and elegant, then he ruined it by tugging irritably at the cuffs and snapping, 'You're being ridiculous.' He twisted his hand and the cuffs clanked. 'Undo these.'

It was good to have the cigarette. It allowed her to pause and contemplate the smoke, which seemed to annoy him. Languidly moving her arm up to her mouth and down would remind him that he couldn't, and annoy him too. And she could gesture with it, and that helped her to inhabit a role: the *hongyan huoshui*: charming, deadly beauty.

She examined him for signs of fear and distress. Nothing yet. She said, 'I don't know why you do it. Maybe for kicks. Just like bored, rich girls go shoplifting. You said it yourself, you need some risk in your life or it's all too easy.' She worked to keep peevishness out of her voice. That wouldn't do, and nor would jabbing the cigarette, frowning, accusing. She had to be ice.

She walked back and forth and his black eyes followed. 'Maybe because none of this is yours. It's your father's. You want something for yourself.'

His cuffed hand balled into a fist, and she knew she had touched a nerve.

'What do you want?' he said.

'Your friend just paid you half the ransom for Butterfly. I want that.'

The use of the name clearly surprised him. 'How would you... What are you? Are you a spy or something?'

'I'm your nightmare. Don't deny me. Where's the money?'

His eyes flicked aside. She followed his gaze to a shelf. She moved a vase and found a wall safe with a keypad.

'In here, yes? What's the combination?'

'Fuck off.'

She said, 'My father is a fugitive who can't go home. I'm an illegal immigrant with nothing to my name.' She pointed at the safe. 'I need that money and will do anything for it. Anything at all. Imagine if I left now. No one will hear your shouts for help.'

His face was pale and pinched, his eyes furtive. He had lost his cool now. She fixed a glass of water in the kitchen, taking her time, then stepped wide around him, savouring the muttered curses he spat at her, and out onto the balcony. Let him stew a minute. She heard a faint smash from the dark garden far below. She craned to look, but saw nothing out of the ordinary. Perhaps it had come from the street, some minor car accident: sound travelled strangely around tall buildings.

She could see the outer walls of five or six more balconies below. It reminded her that she was atop a stack of homes.

All empty. She looked at other blocks, so many of them, rising all around, and wondered how many flats in those were also unoccupied, used as investment vehicles by absent owners. And when so many people struggled to find anywhere at all to live, or had to suffer in shitty bedsits. Of course it was just the same back home.

She thought about her father. His mission concluded, he would be heading to the suburban house with the fluffy toilet seat. She should call and tell him of this development. He would be tickled to hear that she had tracked the perpetrators down, and had a bead on half the cash. No, better to finish her business here, then turn up later with the money. She would find them crammed in that little kitchen. The two boys holding each other. The mother with tears of joy at the return of her son. Her father standing a little aside. She would come in and dump the loot on the table, being very cool about it, but secretly relishing their astonishment.

Wait. No. This Tom might want the cash back, mightn't he? He had a valid claim. And, after working so hard for it, she quite wanted to keep it. New idea. As before, but let it play. Later, join her father in that pokey box room. Let him bluster on the subject of the ridiculous new living arrangements, and awkwardly broach the engagement he had arranged. Then she would say 'I'm not getting married and I'm not living here.' And boom, dump the notes. No one else needed to know. Sly perhaps, but fitting for her new role. They could even – a delicious and daring thought – discuss going after the other half.

65)

Tom was taken by his arms and hauled to his feet. The tape on his ankles was cut. He was dragged out of the van, then hands took his arms and frogmarched him across the car park, through a door and into a space where the sound of his captors' footsteps rang. He guessed a large, high-ceilinged interior with a hard floor.

The hood was yanked off. Tom blinked and peered. A couple of orange lights in the ceiling did little to penetrate the dimness. He stood at the lip of an empty swimming pool. It was oval, about twenty metres at its longest. He was over the shallow end.

Two men stood either side of him, holding his arms. They were unfamiliar, but they had the build and thuggish look of tongs. One had a bandage on his head.

The kidnapper was there too, and the other man, the father. The father pointed into the deep end. Tom made out a figure at the far end. A skinny naked lad with his head in a hood. One wrist was cuffed and a raised arm dangled at the end of a chain secured above, to the ladder at the pool edge. Dark marks swirled around the chest. Tom knew what they were. Butterfly tattoos.

Tom shouted, 'Butterfly,' and the figure raised his head, tried to struggle up.

The father said, 'This is your boyfriend?

'Yes,' croaked Tom.

The man gestured to his colleagues, said in Mandarin, 'Put him down there.'

Tom was chucked into the empty pool. He twisted as he fell and took most of the impact on his shoulder. He pushed the pain away, as he only had one thought. He wriggled along clammy tiles, helped by the slope, towards his shadowed lover. They would be reunited before they died.

He passed chicken bones and junk food wrappers, a water bottle, a stinking plastic bucket.

Here were those slim feet he loved, the toenails painted black. He slithered up to Butterfly and pressed his face against the pale chest and nuzzled. He said, 'It's me, it's me.' Butterfly's hood was wrapped with tape, securing his eyes shut, but his mouth was free. Tom could feel his lover's breath going in and out. He kissed the dirty, naked body, saying 'It's me, it's Tom.' His tears wet the filthy skin. Then the voice came, weak and quiet, speaking Mandarin, a vague mumble. 'Tom, is that really you? Are you here?'

'Yes it's me, it's me.'

Butterfly's free hand came down and the fingers dabbled in Tom's hair.

'It's me, I'm sorry I couldn't help you, I'm sorry but I tried. I tried really hard.'

66)

WeiWei stepped back inside, closed the balcony door, pulled the thick drapes across.

HuaGua had thrown the cushions off the couch, and now squatted on the frame. She said, 'That's too heavy to pull, I can see you've been trying. You are stuck, aren't you? Yes, I can see you've worked it out. Just you in here, all alone. A tap over there but you can't get near it. Food in the cupboard but it's out of reach. How long would you last, do you think? It's lack of water that does for you, I believe. You get weak, dehydrated, you pass out, then die and dry out like a grape in the desert. I guess you'd last about five days. They wouldn't be fun, would they, any of those long hours.'

She paced and his glowering eyes followed. 'Unless you gnaw your hand off. A fox will do that, when he's caught in a trap. I'm not sure if it's possible for a person. I think you would pass out from blood loss. And of course your teeth are not sharp like a fox.' She examined the back of her hand. 'It's the thumb, isn't it, that big bump there, getting over that would be the problem. Tell me the combination to the safe.'

'No.'

'It's not like money means much to you anyway. It's just a little extra for gambling with, right? Let me have it.'

'Let me go and I'll forget all about it. We can say our goodbyes, no harm done. But carry on and… I know people who will kill you for this. Believe me. Carrying on is a big mistake.'

'After I get the money, I throw the key down out of reach,' she mused. 'You can work out how to pull it to you using a cushion, or the belt of your dressing gown. Something fiddly that will take an hour to get right. Then, by the time you get out I'll be gone. That's the best way I think. Yes, that's how we'll do it. Don't try and find me afterwards, you won't.'

'I am… do you know who my father is? Do you have any idea how bad an idea it is to piss him off? You're upset, you feel betrayed, I understand. But this is going to be tough for you. It's going to go very bad. If you just think about what you're doing for a minute, you'll see it.'

'Okay well this has been fun.' She found his house keys on a console table. She dropped them in her bag and opened the door.

'Where are you going?'

'I'll come back tomorrow and ask again. When you've had a day to think about it you might be more cooperative.'

She started to pull the door shut behind her.

'Wait,' he called, and she was pleased to hear a pleading note in his voice. 'Come in,' he snapped, 'Come on. Stop being stupid.'

She pushed the door open. 'The combination.'

'How do I know you'll let me go?'

'Of course I will. I just need the money, I keep my word.'

He lowered his head in defeat, and it kept dipping as he said, 'The combination for the safe is four three six –

She didn't catch the last digit.

'Again.' She came to the back of the couch to hear him better. Then didn't retreat fast enough when he leapt at her. He grabbed her wrist with his free hand and yanked her towards him. She screamed. He let go a moment, lunged again and now his hand was round her throat and squeezing. He was throttling her one-handed as her fingers flailed and scratched.

'Bitch. I'm going to kill you.'

His nails dug in. She couldn't kick him and her flailing hands seemed useless. She fought for breath. Anger with herself as well as him gave a flash of clarity. She remembered a temple courtyard in the snow. A family visit to light incense at New Year. To her teenage eyes it resembled a wushu film set. Out of boredom, she'd started throwing kicks. Her father beckoned her over, said she should know some real moves. He'd shown her how to escape a chokehold, punch with an elbow. But that film stuff, he said, was mostly bullshit. In a real fight you gouged eyes and snapped fingers.

WeiWei groped at the hand on her throat, got ahold of the little finger, and yanked it back as hard as she could. It cracked, he yelled, then she was free. She stiffened her hand into a wedge and drove it as hard as she could into his neck. He jerked back.

She skittered away as he came flying over the back of the couch. He swung at her and clawed the air and the dressing gown flared behind him. The handcuff chain tautened. The couch began to tip over, slowly at first, then with gathering speed, and as it went it pulled him down with it. His skinny limbs flailed and his glaring eyes widened with alarm. The couch landed with a thump then his head smacked the floorboards with a sharper sound. He lay still and the gown settled peacefully over him.

She blinked tears away, rubbed raw neck and elbow, caught her breath. Only when she was sure he was going to continue not to move did she look to the door, where a lot of banging was going on. Soon there was splintering and cracking. Someone was trying to break in, and didn't care how much noise or damage they caused. Shouting started. 'WeiWei? WeiWei?'

Her father. She was getting used to him turning up. Generally just a little too late. It would have been convenient if he'd arrived a few minutes earlier. She looked forward to telling him about the money.

'*Baba*? Wait. I'm fine. Hang on. I'll let you in.'

Jian dropped the crowbar and cradled his daughter's face. 'Are you alright?'

'I'm fine.' He watched her smooth her dressing gown and rub at the red marks on her neck. Her eyes were bright, her colour was up, but her voice was under control. 'I'm fine. Was getting heated but I dealt with it.'

The lad lay spreadeagled. The wrist of an outspread arm was shackled to a toppled couch. Shan was examining him. She muttered, 'Unconscious. Head trauma. Fractured wrist. He's not going to be helping us for a couple of minutes.'

WeiWei said, 'I was working on him. He was working with the kidnapper. He's got half the money. It's in a safe here, we just have to get the combination out of him when he wakes up. Where's Tom, Butterfly? It all worked out, right? Didn't it… it's fine, right? Isn't it fine?'

Jian lowered his voice. 'No. The money was paid. Then Tom was snatched. Butterfly is still being held, far as we know.'

'Huh. Oh shit!' She glanced at the mother, then leaned into him. 'But… that doesn't make any sense. The kidnapper came here, and I listened to them discussing it. He said he'd let Butterfly go after taking the money, he said everything was fine and done. He described it… You're saying he was making it up? Why would he lie about that? To the guy he's working with. I don't understand.'

'What did the kidnapper look like?'

'Um.' Her gaze travelled upwards as she recalled. 'A young guy, just a teenager, bit chubby.'

'Red Shoes, big headphones, American cap?'

'Yes, exactly. You know him?'

'Yes.'

Jian remembered his last encounter with the Incense Master's wayward son. He had said he had business to attend to this evening. Some business. It seemed the pampered child was keen to emulate, or even outdo, his father, whatever the father's ambitions and expectations. Not a surprise, when you think about it. One vicious psycho begets another; chicken eggs don't hatch into cranes.

'Why would he say he did that when he didn't?'

Jian scanned the room, attentive yet open. Ash on the rug, a broken cigarette, scattered couches, closed curtains. On a low table, a bottle of whisky and two glasses. An ashtray. Two plates and forks. Half a cake in a box. Let it come, there was no hurry.

Jian pointed. 'Did the kidnapper bring the cake?'

'Yes. He said it was to celebrate.'

Jian examined the cake. Sponge, decorated with fruit slices. He tasted the filling with a finger. Jam and cream. A fresh, delicate construction. The lad would have had to buy it during the day, carried it around in its cardboard box, looked after it, made sure it stayed level. A lot of fuss to go to while running a kidnap operation. Cakes were for groups of people. There were only the two of them. They could never hope to eat it all. It was too sweet for his taste, and it was not much to the taste of one of the celebrants, either: someone had left about half his slice. HuaGua probably.

Jian had it. He started looking round and under the table. 'It was cut with a knife. Where's the knife? They haven't cleaned up. Why isn't the knife here?'

'You've lost me, I don't...'

'Who cut the cake?'

'I think… I guess… HuaGua cut it.'

'Fuck.'

Jian knew who had the knife, and he knew why, and he knew what savagery was intended.

He said to WeiWei, 'When was the kidnapper here?'

'Twenty minutes ago.'

'We need to know where he's keeping his captives. It is a matter of urgency.'

'Why Dad, what's going on?'

Jian bent to the lad, tapped cheeks. 'Hey. Wake up. Time to get up.'

68)

Tom lay in the shadowed depths of the empty pool with his head on Butterfly's chest and with his lover's tremulous fingers running over his face. He was aware of hollow voices and flashes of movement above. The father told his thugs to wait outside, and he heard them retreat. Then the father pulled his son down into the shallow end, and now their voices came clear and echoing.

The father said, 'You're supposed to be doing your exams. Not stupid kidnap schemes for gambling tokens.'

'It's not that. It's subtle and artful. Why don't you let me explain? A rich idiot lives upstairs. Mainlander. His daddy owns the building and he lives here on his own. He likes to gamble. He spends his monthly allowance in a few days. Likes to think he's tough. Thinks it's cool to have dark friends.'

'Dark friends like you.'

'We cooked up a scheme, very simple. He fingered a friend of his – someone rich, with a grey daddy, who can pay a ransom.'

'You go to prison for ten years. And for what, a few thousand pounds?'

'That isn't what it's about. I want to tell you, but you keep interrupting. I recorded everything, the whole scheme. On this.' From one of his many trouser pockets the lad took out and displayed a small device. 'A zoom dictaphone, the best portable audio recorder for the commercial market, you even get the sound of the figures adding up in his head. I've got him mouthing off about his part in the scheme, all along the way. Planning it, agreeing to get the key for the lad's flat and make a copy, discussing how much money to ask for, how to arrange the swap using anonymous crypto coins, the whole lot.'

The lad moved all the time, prancing, shuffling, rolling his shoulders, touching his hat. His father hardly moved at all. He was quieter and harder to hear. Now he said, 'Yes, blackmail. Is that all?'

'No, there's more. I have a knife with the rich kid's fingerprints on. I'm going to kill the hostage with that and keep the body, and the weapon, on ice. So he's not only involved in kidnap. He's a murderer.'

'That old trick.'

'That old trick, same one you used on the cop. Who taught me that? Look, this rich idiot, he's a princeling. He'll go home soon and fall straight into a plum government job. Lots of influence. Access to his father's fortune. Political connections. When he's set up, then I'll go see him. Tell him what I've got on him. Show him all the evidence I've got hidden away. Then squeeze him. What won't he give, then? You see, I'm thinking. I'm thinking long term. I'm setting up. Just like you did, in the territory.'

'You were going to show me this?'

'A little later. But having the robber – the cream on my cake – has forced my hand.' He twirled round, then presented his hands out, palms forward, in a showy gesture. 'Well?'

'Well what?'

'Look at it. I caught the guy who robbed you. You can see a gorgeous scheme about to come to fruition. It's time. I want it.'

'You want what?'

'My tattoo. I want a great big circle right here.' He put a hand on his chest. 'You have to admit. I deserve it.'

'I'll give you what you deserve.'

The father pulled his son towards him and butted him in the face, and a dull crump resounded. The lad reeled, slipped and fell. The father stood over him and his voice was loud and distinct as he snarled, 'What is wrong with you?'

The lad was on his knees, clutching his nose. 'You did it. How often have I had to hear it? Extortion and kidnap and robbery... The crazy man in the territory.'

'I did it so you don't have to. I had nothing. Look at you. You went to good schools. You learned the language. The best tutors. You're supposed to go into politics, business... Not this. Dumb thuggery. Oh how very clever you are. You stupid fuck.'

He made to kick him, then stopped himself, stamped his foot, ran hands across his head.

Tom lifted his head, now attentive to the unfolding drama. The powerful father was furious with his son: could it be possible that he demand the captives be released? Tom strained to hear, and catch all nuance.

The father was pacing, grumbling indistinctly. Then he turned and walked straight towards Tom, his shoes ringing on the tiles. He stopped and regarded the captives. Tom looked beseechingly back, concentrating on the man's chest rather than his face, as he didn't want to look like he was committing the man to memory. Perhaps there was something he could say, that might help? He carefully formed a statement in his head. Just let us go, we'll tell no one, all we want is to go home. We're decent, trustworthy people, we'll be very grateful and we'll never tell. He opened his mouth to speak, found it too dry, swallowed, then before he could get any of it out the man turned abruptly and stepped away up the slope.

He said to his son. 'I can't believe this hasn't fucked up already. This stupid scheme is getting shut down.'

'But...'

'Shut down. No arguments.'

What did he mean? Might it be – here it was – fluttering to the surface, a faint, tormenting hope. Could they walk free?

Just... wake from this nightmare. If only they could just be left to leave, forget this ever happened, everyone would be happier. The boy would have learned his lesson and no harm would have come to anyone. If there was even the slightest possibility, he had to help coax that future into being. There were words, he was convinced, that would assist, if only he could find them. Tom pushed himself up and called, 'Please. Excuse me. Please.' It was sad how small his voice was. He coughed and tried again, louder, 'Please. Please just let us go, we won't tell anyone.' He meant it, was as sincere as he had ever been, and he hoped that the man would hear that behind the words, and that would help nudge him towards what was, surely, the sensible course of action, to untangle this whole awful situation, which was that everyone just went home and forgot all about it.

But they did not even look at him. The father said, 'There will be no evidence left. Those packages...' – he waved a dismissive hand at Butterfly and Tom – 'will be disposed of.'

The dismissive term, the blank gaze. The father was as cold as the son. Hope died and the despair was worse than before. Tom could hear weeping from below the hood. He pressed his face against the material, and felt the heat of breath and body, explored cherished contours: the line of cheek, soft lips, the neck's curve.

The father put out a hand to help the son to his feet. The lad batted it away and raised himself. He was holding his nose. A little blood was dripping from it. The father had a mobile out. He was talking as he led his lad away. 'I'm calling the road boys. They'll come and take these two and burn them up in a tarmacker. Those things brew at three thousand degrees. They'll be vaporised completely, even the fillings in the teeth. There must be nothing left of this stupidity. When we leave this is never spoken of again. Understand? It is vaporised from your memory and from mine. And after… no more gambling. No more running around and acting the thug. You go back to your studies. I know you find it hard. I'll get a tutor to help you. But you'll also get a bodyguard to follow you around, twenty-four hours. I will know everything you get up to.'

'But Dad...'

'Silence. There will be no more schemes.' He put a finger on his son's chest. 'And no tattoo.'

69

Jian hit harder. But it was no use. HuaGua was not coming to, not yet.

He stood. 'We haven't time to wait.' He addressed WeiWei. 'I need you to think. Did you hear them talk about it?'

'Yes I heard them, what a pair, talking about people as packages. They talked about me, it was horrible, the way they…'

There was a catch in her voice, her mouth twitched. If she started to cry they would lose time. Jian squeezed her shoulder and turned her to face the blank wall.

'Did they mention where they were keeping Butterfly?'

She took a deep breath, swallowed, and her eyes fluttered. But her voice was level. 'They said… HuaGua's job was getting the target's house key, and providing a place to keep him captive. Oh, oh.' She clapped. 'I guess one of his father's empty flats. Here.'

She went to the coffee table, opened it, and showed him a jumble of keys. Each had a label attached, with an address printed on it. He sifted. Fifteen or so sets.

He said, 'We need to find a list of the addresses. Compare that with the keys. Find the missing set.'

WeiWei shook her head. 'Maybe it's not that. Cause he said they, were all new builds. Those places have lifts and concierges, you couldn't keep a captive in a place like that, you couldn't get them in and out. You'd worry about noise too, when they were there. Waking the neighbours. It's not practical.'

Jian thought about the journey up here: all those blind windows, the vacant lobby.

'This building is empty. No concierge here. There are basements, I saw the buttons in the lift. You could jail someone right here, no problem. Especially if there's an underground garage. Come in and out and no one would see you. Very convenient. That's what I'd do.'

She had her hands in front of her face, tapping her lower lip with her little fingers. The few times he'd helped with her homework, when she was a lot younger, she had made just that gesture.

'When I was here before, and I was trying to get out, I accidentally went to the wrong floor, a basement health zone. It was closed up and stinky like night soil.'

'That's where he is. Locked up with a bucket to shit in. What level?'

'The first basement.'

Jian picked up his crowbar.

'You two stay here.'

Shan had been watching them, listening. Now she spoke, loud and strident, her voice creaking with strain. 'What about Tom? He might be there too. We need to call the police.'

'I am the police.'

The ladies kept talking but Jian didn't listen, he was already out of the door.

FAMILY BUSINESS

70

The father was making a call, saying nothing Tom could hear. The sullen son perched on the edge of the pool, feet dangling, a hand over his face. This scene dragged on for minutes, in which Tom found his enmity for his abusers dulling. He had come to see them as bland, implacable agents of fate. Hating them would be like hating the sea for drowning you. It was strange to know you were going to die soon. And without ceremony, like a stray dog. In what was nothing really but a dark and stinking pit. Strange and barely credible.

The father put his phone away and the son stood and said 'Well? For how long?'

'How long what?'

'Treating me like a child.'

'Until you've graduated.'

'But that's years. I...'

'Silence. The matter is closed. We go now.'

The lad pointed. 'You told me you didn't feel a man till you'd killed someone. I want to kill one. '

'You're not killing anyone. That one who's chained up, where's the key?'

The son took a key off a ring and the father took it, put it on the poolside.

'Leave it here? Why?'

'Otherwise they'll have to cut his arm off, won't they?'

The father called to unseen colleagues, 'The clean-up boys will be half an hour. They know what to expect. They'll deal with everything. Just see they turn up, then get on.'

He stepped up onto the pool ladder.

Someone called back, 'We still driving to the woods?'

'You go ahead with that after.'

'Yes sir.'

The son muttered plaintively, 'Let me see it to the finish. At least that. It's my plan, let me see it end.'

The father was up on the poolside now. He went down on one knee to hiss. 'Be quiet. Any noise from you I hit you again. And next time will be in front of those guys, you want that?'

He strode away. The son lingered for a last look at his captives, then clambered up the ladder and hurried after his dad and out of sight, and their footsteps faded into silence.

71

Shan said, 'So where's my son? Where's Tom?'

'I don't know,' said the girl. In the red dressing gown, she looked a callow, fragile thing, unsuited for any of this.

'What did your father say to you, just now? I saw you whispering.'

'He said Tom had been snatched.'

'Snatched!' She was pacing. If she stopped, she felt, she would collapse. 'It's just one kidnapper? A teenager? Really? You saw him?'

'Yes.'

She had held Tom and he had promised it would all be over if she let go and went home, and she had obeyed, and it wasn't over: it was worse. She had trusted him and trusted this Jian too, and look where that had led. She should have remembered what her mother used to say: you have to cook your own rice. She said, 'I'm going down.'

'Don't be stupid. My dad is sorting it out.'

'What if your father's been snatched?'

'I think you're a bit hysterical.'

'Not at all. Everyone's being snatched, aren't they? It all comes down to one silly boy. It's a vicious boy, that's all there is, isn't it? I'm not afraid of a boy.'

HuaGua groaned, and they both looked at him a moment. As he came round he curled protectively round his pale injured arm. Shan glared at him. 'Hey. You. There's just one kidnapper, yes? Your friend?' She kicked him in the side. 'I'm talking to you.'

'My wrist hurts, I need to go to hospital.'

Shan said, 'You're not going to hospital yet. People are in danger.' And then added in English, 'God sake!' She shuddered, gathered herself, and stopped. She did not collapse. She drew herself upright. 'I'm going down there.' She opened the gouged front door, looked at the dull, silent hallway.

The girl called. 'Wait. You might mess it up for Dad.'

'I don't care.'

'We should stay and wait. Like he said.'

'I'm going.'

'To do what?'

'You can't stop me.'

'At least take a weapon. You're a liability, aren't you, if you can't defend yourself?'

Shan got out her spray. 'He can get a faceful of this.'

'Perfume?'

'Pepper spray.'

'He's got a knife, you know that? Come on, my dad... this is his job.'

The lift might make a noise when it arrived, and alert the enemy. She opened a door and looked at a dark staircase. She could see a light switch but she would not put it on, she would descend into blackness. She said again, 'I'm going. I'm going down there.' She did not quite trust her body and it needed to be bossed about.

The girl sighed. 'I'll come with you. Wait. Wait a moment. I just want to put some more clothes on. Have you got any more of that spray?'

'No. I'm going now.'

'Wait for me. Please. I'll grab a knife, hang on.'

She had traipsed back and forth, worked herself into frenzies of worry, been assaulted, witnessed a violent death then covered it up. She was not about to falter at this final unknown. Shan started downstairs, stiff but resolute, with one hand on the banister to steady herself and the other holding the spray.

72)

Jian opened a door on the empty lobby. One more storey to go. He took another flight of stairs and came to a hallway and swing doors. A bike chain hung off a handle. It seemed the lad was here. He was careful not to disturb the chain as he slipped through. The space beyond was dark and close, the air fetid. He slowed, to give his eyes some time to adjust.

He was in a lobby and to the right lay a wall of frosted glass. The pool must be behind it. To the left he could see through clear glass into a gym. There were grey plastic covers over the machines, racks and treadmills. He was surprised to see two guys in there, their backs to him. They had taken the covers off a rack and were lifting weights, comparing biceps as they did curls. Baldie and Lanky. They hadn't even changed their clothes. If they were here, something must be happening. They could turn and see him at any moment. He would need to be quick and vicious.

Unbidden thoughts trilled as Jian calmed himself. I would like to say to the committee, and to the public, that I have been venal, callow and lascivious. He strode in holding the crowbar low and with a hard swing cracked Baldie's head. The man sprawled and his weights fell and rolled. I have betrayed the oath I made to party and country. Lanky swung a dumb bell. Jian stepped into the clumsy arc, jabbed the curved end of the bar into his face. Blood spurted and the weight clanked. I plead guilty to all the crimes with which I have been charged. He struck over and over till the bar bounced on bone.

Jian stepped back, breathing heavily. Blood spattered his shirt, dribbled down the crowbar. His shoulder was sore from the impacts. Both men were dead or dying. He had made a lot of noise, so no longer had surprise. Speed was his only advantage. He stalked out and through a frosted glass door and into the pool area. It was even darker here and the empty pool was a trough of shadows. Tom was twinned with another figure in the deep end. Moving fitfully, so alive. No one else seemed to be around, though Jian peeked in the changing rooms and shower cubicle to make sure. He called down.

'Hello?'

Tom struggled upright. 'There's two men.'

'I dealt with them.'

'That was you? The noise? Are they – dealt with them how?'

'Where's the lad who caught you?'

'He's gone. Just now. Him and his father. They sent... some-one's coming to kill us. Get us out of here, quickly, please.'

Jian clambered down a short ladder and jumped the remaining distance to the pool floor. Tom would be easy to free, he only needed to cut the tape but that chain around the other lad's wrist would require a bolt cutter to remove.

Tom said, 'They left the key, it's up on there.'

But before Jian could act a dark figure stepped up onto the ledge at the side of the pool, and coughed for their attention.

Uncle Seven was aiming a pistol. The deep end of an empty swimming pool was an unfortunate place to be cornered. It was more than two metres to the top. Jian had nowhere to go.

Uncle Seven said, 'Inspector. We were in the car, in the car park below. About to head off. I was just about to turn the engine on when I heard the faintest of clanging sounds from above. Should I check it out? I thought no, it will be the boys messing around. Oh, better check it out, I thought, you never know. Bring that gun, just in case. And here you are. You know this weapon of course. We were going to bury the Lucky Day Manager with it. To make good on our threat – remember. But it seems you have saved us the trouble.'

The son stepped up beside his father. He turned his beaked cap round and round as he said. 'Dad, he's killed the other two. You should see. It's... blood everywhere.'

'If you'd been thirty seconds later, you'd have got away with it. I would say, Inspector, that this weekend, your timing is off. I think you may be the world's unluckiest gambler.'

73)

Shan pushed open the door to the health suite and stepped into the lobby. The darkness was intimidating but she forced herself on, spray held before her with a rigid arm.

She grew aware of splatters of blood, dark but edged with red, dripping over the glass walls of the gym, and when she peered and shuffled she saw two men lying prone. Blood trickled down an outstretched arm to a dark puddle. Her stomach roiled and her arm shook. But they were stolid, unfamiliar figures: not Tom. Not Jian either. She felt so relieved that her arm dropped and she shuddered. She remembered the crowbar in the cop's hand. She had seen horrific injuries before, but always in a professional capacity, in a medical environment, not as a squalid crime scene. She reminded herself that they were strangers who she did not have to care about, that the cop killing them was good for the prospects of her son.

The girl came up behind her. She tugged her arm. 'I think we should go.'

But she had come so far. She said, 'No,' and headed for the wall of frosted glass. Tom was right behind there, she knew it. She pushed the door open.

74)

'Well?' The son said, 'Shoot him.'

'I want to talk to him a minute.' Uncle Seven walked around the pool and got down into the shallow end. He kept the gun aimed at Jian. He pointed with his other hand at the captives.

'That's one thief there. I have been told you killed the other.'

'Fuck your mother.'

'The money is not of particular importance but I would like to retrieve the jewellery that was stolen. All those family heirlooms. We return that and I'd say we've got our face back. I told you before, we're not animals, your end will be quick. But you have to help me with this. Where is the jewellery?'

'Fuck your mother.'

The son trotted down and sounded more boyish than ever as he said, 'Do that thing you said you did before. You shot him in the leg to see how fast he would die. Then the arm. Then you shot his face. Do that.'

'Be quiet.' A twinge of distaste passed over the father's face then the familiar mask was back. 'Tarmackers are coming to clean up. You have heard of this trick, I'm sure. You, and those two, will be annihilated, and no evidence will remain. You can spend your remaining time making peace with your ancestors or you can be in agony.'

'Fuck your mother. And your sick and twisted kid can fuck her too, he'd like that.'

'That's what you want? You want to be tortured?'

He gave the gun to his son and took his jacket off. He laid his jacket on the side of the pool and rolled up his sleeves. He said,

'Such a mess, Inspector. I thought I could use the situation. Recruit an ally. Just goes to show. You can't turn every situation to your advantage.'

The son mused, 'I'm not so sure.'

'Give me that back,' said the father.

The son held the gun two-handed, in an awkward sideways grip. He stepped back.

'How does it work? Is it cocked?'

'Of course it is.'

'The safety is off?'

'Don't mess around. Give it to me.'

The lad fired and Uncle Seven cursed then folded and fell. Blood flowered on his shirt as the flat hard sound of the shot echoed. He clawed at the tiles. Then another shot came and he was still.

75)

Shan, just inside the doorway, lay down on the cold tiles. The flat hard cracks made her ears ring. She crawled forward and peeked over the edge of the pool and saw her son below, tied up, and another captive, filthy, naked – that would be Butterfly – and there was Jian too. Other figures: a fat lad bouncing on the toes of his red shoes, holding a gun. He had shot another older man, who lay still. Blood trickled from him down the slope.

The lad was talking to the bleeding man, speaking English.

'I can say the cop killed you as well as the boys. Before I took him out. I'll be a hero and a leader. I'm taking over. And you say I don't learn. Look what I learned. Learned from you. I made one thing serve two purposes.'

He skipped closer to the body. 'I want that tattoo. I deserve it.' Blood was approaching his shoes and he stepped away again. 'It didn't feel… Now it feels like… it feels weird because I feel like it should feel like something and it doesn't feel like anything. Maybe the second feels different. Maybe you only really enjoy it after a few.'

He switched to Mandarin to address Jian, aiming the gun. 'Maybe it's different if they know it's coming and you can look into their eyes. And they look at you knowing they are going to die. What do you think, is that your experience?'

'No.'

The lad considered the captives. 'I'll try that next. Maybe them first.'

He held the gun out and planted his legs, and as he concentrated his tongue poked through his lips. With the other hand he blocked an ear. He was aiming at Tom.

Shan only knew that she could not let this happen. She jumped down and landed on the hard bottom of the pool, screaming, 'No, no. No.' She was aiming her bottle, pressing the toggle of her spray furiously. A foggy spray cloud hissed limply out. It travelled barely a couple of feet. As a weapon it was pathetic. Her rage was replaced with a spasm of despair. She was such a stupid woman. She screamed and cried, 'No, no. Take me, take me.'

The boy was looking at her and laughing.

76)

Jian snatched the shit bucket and hurled it. It span and hit the lad, spattering him, knocking him off balance. Just long enough for Jian to grab the crowbar, launch himself and swing. He caught the lad on his gun arm and he staggered but managed to cling onto his weapon. It was rising and Jian knew his chance had gone. The next swing would come too late – then something flashed from above and thunked the lad's shoulder. A dumbell. The lad staggered, the arm dropped, and the gun fell.

WeiWei was looking down from the pool side. She had another weight effortlessly raised.

Jian stepped into the boy's guard, grabbed his arm and twisted it. He yanked down, pulled the lad off balance, and they both tumbled. The lad fumbled a knife from inside a pocket on his trousers. He lunged and Jian smacked the arm aside, grabbed it. He rolled, controlled the arm by the elbow, turned it, rolled on top of the lad. He put all his weight on the arm and got the blade pointing at the lad's chest. He leaned in. The lad grunted as the knife thumped into him. Jian's weight drove it deeper. Jian waited, panting, listening to his own ragged breath, the lad's gasps, the scraping sounds of his protesting feet scuffing tile. I am guilty of all charges and offer no defence. The lad stopped moving, breathing. Jian detached himself, rose.

The space was quiet, a ghoulish tableau. Two men dead in the tiled pit, two trussed-up, two women peering down. Then Shan was running to her son and WeiWei was clambering down into the pool and Jian was puffing his cheeks, rubbing his back.

There was more work to do. Jian clapped his hands for attention and said, 'There are people coming. We have to be quick.' He pointed at Tom and Butterfly. 'Get them upstairs.'

WeiWei said, 'What are you going to do?'

Two bodies in the pool, two in the gym. The Manager of the gambling den in a vehicle in the car park downstairs, apparently. Hefty fellows, all of them, it would be quite a workout. He hoped his back was up to it.

'Bit of heavy lifting. See you in about half an hour. Go up and wait for me.'

77)

The gouged penthouse door hung open. HuaGua lay, pale and sweating. He looked pleadingly up at Shan as he said, 'I can't feel my arm.' She had assessed his injury: a simple fracture, painful but not life-threatening. He would have to wait.

She was helping Tom and the girl was helping Butterfly. They got them down a hallway and into a bedroom. She sat the boys down on the edge of a bed and put the light on. She told the girl to get scissors from the kitchen and when she came back she cut filthy clothes and bonds away.

She addressed Butterfly. 'Are you okay?'

Shallow cuts were slashed across his body. He said, 'I think… I'm okay.'

'Are you in any pain?'

'What?'

'Are you in any pain?'

He had the doe-eyed sluggishness that came from shock. Flashes of anxiety crossed his face, and he'd jerk and look round, as if he could not yet allow himself to believe his ordeal was over. She repeated her question and he gestured with a shaking hand.

'Right there? Let me see your arms. Lift your arm. Does it hurt? Is it tender?'

He began to cry and his gaze wandered. 'I need you to look at me. I need you to calm down. I need you to breathe. Deep breaths. There you go. I want you to sit there and keep breathing.'

She moved her attention to Tom. There was less blood on him, no cuts but a lot of bruising, some swelling.

'Mum? I'm sorry.'

'What happened to your head? Can you tell me what happened to your head?'

'I got hit. Punched. I got kicked. I don't know.'

'And here? What happened here?'

'Punched. People died. Mum. I'm sorry. This is Butterfly. I love him.'

'I want you to breathe normally while I put my hand here. Do you feel any pain?'

'Yes.'

Juddering blubs seemed yanked from his chest. The crying hurt him, so he would grimace between sobs. She laid firm hands on him, found broken ribs, a fractured collarbone.

'It's okay, it's okay. I want you to breathe. Sit and breathe.'

Blood and faeces had been present at the site, the wounds needed to be cleaned. She checked the en suite, found a shower stall, came back to address her charges. 'We are going to put you in a place where you can be washed. You will like it. We move you together and place you together.' She and the girl helped Butterfly and Tom into the stall.

Butterfly kept saying, 'Is it over? Is it over?'

'You are safe here, you are safe now.'

'Mum, I'm sorry.'

'You're doing great, you are okay. That's right. You're good.'

She got them both sat down in the shower. She turned on a showerhead and played the water on her wrist till it was warm.

'Mum, I'm sorry.'

'You are safe now you are okay.'

With a little soap and tepid water she began to wash the boys.

'Thank you.'

'Thanks, Mum.'

'You are welcome. You are safe now. You are fine.'

WeiWei was at the kitchen sink, washing blood away. Not her blood: it must have come from one of those skinny, disoriented boys. She was running the water cold as the sharp sting of it helped keep her in the present and away from lurid recollections of the awful things she had seen in the basement.

It had all happened so quickly, and in the dark, and there were details she was unclear about. She could not quite get it all straight in her head so she could not be sure it was really over. Could more vengeful tongs have arrived, and need fighting? Might they come up here? What was her father doing? He had been away for long tense minutes. It was unnerving to be up here alone and defenceless. She would not rest easy till she was out of the building.

'I can't feel my arm. I need medical attention.' HuaGua wouldn't stop grouching. Whining about his pains, how badly he needed to go to hospital, the various ways in which none of this was actually his fault. 'I can't feel the other arm, the cuffs are too tight.'

She was ignoring him, thinking of him as a package, albeit a noisy one. But now something he said caught her attention.

'You still want the money in the safe? If you let me go I'll give it to you.'

She turned the tap off and stepped over, careful to stay out of reach. He was pale and sweating and his wrist was red where he had tugged on the cuff. She threw a tea towel to him.

'You've proved you are not to be trusted.'

He wiped his clammy face. 'I'll give you the combination, you give me the key to these cuffs. I know what it looks like, and you're right, I've been bad, but I'm a decent person underneath. I'm just wayward. You must have sensed that, WeiWei, or you wouldn't have chased after me. We shared something special, WeiWei. We had such intense moments.'

She did not want to be reminded, and the way he kept saying her name was very provoking. She snapped, 'We didn't share anything. You wanted me for your sick criminal game. And I'm a gold digger who wanted your money.' Saying it made it true, or truer. All previous equivocations, all her mixed feelings and romantic projections, were lies to keep her from seeing herself.

So be what you say you are: focus on the money. How to get it from the safe? The exchange he was proposing sounded simple, but there didn't seem any easy way to arrange it. If she gave him the key, his motivation to give her the money vanished. Conversely, if he helped her get into the safe she had no incentive to give him the key. He would know that, so his only rationale to play this game was to find a way to cheat her at it.

There seemed just one method that guaranteed success: force the combination out of him. She was not a killer, she'd have to leave the key somewhere he could reach after some time. She put her imagination to work on the problem: place it on an ice cube on a gentle downward slope? Or leave it in that distant slipper and give him cutlery and tape to painstakingly construct some kind of grabbing device? Or – oh, of course – forget the key and source a hacksaw blade to give him, so he could painstakingly, and very slowly, saw through cuffs or sofa rail. She looked at his wounded arm, white and bent at a distasteful angle, decided that was the weakness to target for the hurting, then realised that she had put so much effort into thinking through the second part of the operation because she could not bring herself to consider the first: call it what it was – torture.

She felt revulsed. What was wrong with her? Very well. Could she tell her father the situation, then stand by while he did the necessary? She wearied at the prospect of thinking that one through, and wished she was a normal person again, that is, one with money. Being poor just seemed to throw up one shitty dilemma after another. HuaGua interrupted her musings. 'You don't know what you're getting into. Do you know who my father is?'

How pompous and absurd he sounded, it made her laugh. 'Threats now. I don't think you're in much of a position to be giving those.'

'You wouldn't believe me if I told you. Go have a look at my namecards.'

That might be another angle. The father was very rich. Could they do to him what he had intended to do to her, and hold him for ransom? She had seen how easy it was. The tricky part was over, as the hostage was locked up and desperate. It would only take a phone call back home. But of course she was known to him... maybe it was not realistic. It was something she could think through when she had the time and energy, or could discuss with her father. In the spirit of a girl who was merely exploring her options, she opened the drawer in the coffee table and took out the namecard book. It was the first card in there. Thick, off-white, with a raised print in a conservative font. She read the name and job title and said, 'Oh.'

'Yes, see?' The cuffs rattled as he craned forward. 'That's my father.'

79)

On hearing the hum of the lift, Jian struck a posture of studied boredom, leaning on the health suite wall. He lit a cigarette and flattened his features to blankness. To look more like a tong, he wore Baldie's watch, the fat lad's red cap, and sunglasses he had found in Lanky's shirt pocket. His hands, shoes, shirt and suit were spattered with blood. Maybe that helped.

The lift door opened to reveal four whites dressed like forensic officers, in plastic overalls, thick rubber gloves and overshoes. The hoods were pulled up and fixed below the hairline, and respirators obscured most of the rest of their faces. Two carried buckets full of chemical bottles and cleaning materials and a third lugged a plastic barrel. The tallest, at the front, carried nothing: Jian picked him for the leader. He walked up to Jian and said something. Jian puffed smoke, peeled from the wall, turned and walked away. After a moment they were following, overshoes squeaking.

Jian had turned on the lights around the pool. All the fittings and the tiles were shades of blue, which made the blood stand starkly out: rich and black in puddles, crimson where it had been smeared and tracked messily around.

Five bodies lay in the shallow end: the unfortunate manager of the gambling den; the two tongs, Baldy and Lanky; Uncle Seven and his son. Each was swaddled in grey plastic sheeting – sourced from the machines in the gym – held in place with liberal wrappings of duct tape. Jian had used up all his tape, and found more in the lad's van downstairs. He had taped crowbar and gun in there too. He had been scrupulous in covering and taping heads, just in case any of his specimens were known to the clean-up crew.

The whites gestured and jabbered. Jian was alert for any sign of hesitation or uncertainty. If they sensed anything untoward and made a call to check, his deception would be uncovered. But the discussion soon ceased, the leader gave orders and his colleagues stepped down into the pool.

Jian watched them pick up the first cocoon-like body. Then gave a curt nod to say goodbye, and returned to the lift. He could hear them grunting and their shoes squeaking, then the doors closed and he was in silence. It seemed he had got away with it. He set the lift to ascend to the top floor. He wanted never again to get into a fight, shift a body, or hear the irritating screech of industrial tape being pulled. At least such eventualities seemed reasonably unlikely, for the moment, anyway. With a bit of good fortune – and surely he was owed that – this barbarous episode was behind him.

He took off the sunglasses and rubbed his eyes. In the mirror he looked old, tired and beaten up. He pressed his back against the wall to stretch it. The motion caused a note, a cheeky twenty, to poke out from between shirt buttons. He undid the buttons and tucked it back into the racing car pillowcase, which was squashed snugly in there, taped to his bare skin. He'd found the plump bag of cash on the passenger seat of the young lad's van. A rare pleasant surprise, and some compensation for his aches and inconvenience.

80)

WeiWei squinted through the front-door spyhole, at a bulbous distortion of her father looking absurd in a red baseball hat. She took the splintered door off the chain, opened it and said, 'Is it over?'

'All done.' In the kitchen area he took off hat and watch, and set to briskly washing gore-spattered hands. Soapy water foamed and turned pink in the basin. He was moving freely but he looked as tired as she'd ever seen him. He said, 'The lads are alright?'

'Good enough, I guess. They're in the bedroom, The mother seems to have it under control.'

When he was drying his hands on a dishcloth, she said, 'We've got something to discuss,' and motioned for him to follow. She thought HuaGua was lost in his pains but when they stepped close his lolling head froze and he tracked them with sullen eyes. She skirted wide around him and led her father out onto the shadowed balcony. She showed him the namecard. 'Look who his father is.'

He tilted it so that it caught the narrow shaft of light spilling between the curtains and read the name.

'You know what this means. I think... well, I think he could get you a pardon.'

She was hugging herself for warmth. The black city beyond the balcony glittered, looked unending. 'What do you think? There's an opportunity here. I don't know how we'd work it. But... you'd come up with something, right? I don't know... it's worth thinking about. Isn't it?'

'You're suggesting we release the princeling, help him out of this mess, cover up his crimes.'

'Possibly. Just… It's worth thinking about. Isn't it?'

'That would entail, what, trying to ensure the silence of the mother and her son, and the lad who was kidnapped. Go to the father. Get him to work on my behalf, arranging for all charges against me to be dropped, with the threat that if he doesn't help, we reveal all concerning his son's scheme, and of course he would know the scandal will end his career.'

'Well… yes. A scheme. We get to go home.'

'A blackmail scheme.'

'Call it that if you want. Or you could call it being smart and making the world work for us for a change. All it is… It's just… we help him, he helps us. Or rather gets his dad to help us.' She said again, 'We could go home.' It sounded more plaintive than she had intended.

He was looking down at her sidelong, chin tucked, his eyes raised. A look she remembered. She was a little girl who had cheated on her homework.

He said carefully, 'Do you think this is what we should do now? Keep this scumbag in our lives? Hanging round like a bad smell?'

She shuddered. 'No. I guess… Now I've said it out loud it seems like a stupid idea. I mean… complicated and, well, wrong. I just… I want to go home.' She sighed and her shoulders sagged.

'Me too. Maybe one day. Don't give up.'

The Thames River was black but for ripples of acid colour where the city lights were reflected. Someone could get on a boat down there and sail it across oceans and all the way to China.

Jian said, 'Do you have the key to his cuffs?'

'Here. The kidnap money is in the safe. We need to get the combination off him.'

'Leave that to me. Stay a minute. Enjoy the view.'

81

Tom was out of the shower, with a towel wrapped around his waist. Butterfly lay on the bed and Tom's mother fussed over him, dabbing with cotton wool and a solution at his scars. Butterfly looked up at her and mouthed 'Thank you' and Tom squeezed his hand.

The gambler appeared at the door, gesturing. Tom limped over.

He said, 'We're going. I have some instructions. First, I want you to keep the police out of this. Can you square that with your mother? With your boyfriend?'

'I guess. But...' He gestured at HuaGua and lowered his voice. 'What about him? He needs to be punished. I mean, they won't want him just to get away with it.'

'He's paying now. Maybe he'll never use that hand again. And.' The gambler showed a dictaphone. 'I found this on the fat kid. He was collecting evidence of the scheme.'

'I heard about that. He's got everything recorded.'

The gambler pressed play. The voices came out distinctly and Tom shivered as he heard the lad say, in dull Essex tones, 'You did half. You were most thoroughly involved.'

The gambler stopped the device, pressed it into Tom's hand. 'Leverage. To make sure he stays honest.' He added a little key. 'The keys to his cuffs.' Then a namecard. 'This is his father. Make it clear you've got the recordings, you have copies stored in a safe place, and threaten to tell the lad's old man, and that'll keep him wrapped around your finger. Might help get your boyfriend's dad out of jail maybe. Or just suggest he might want to go home sooner rather than later.'

'Thank you. Look. I don't see why you can't move in right away. And the marriage. Soon as you want. My mum will be fine about it.'

'Forget about all that. Go back in there with your mum and your boyfriend, who need you. Close the door. And if you hear a bit of screaming, out here, tell them not to worry about it.'

82

In the kitchen Jian pocketed a spoon, then found himself a knife – a twenty-centimetre length of wicked steel, with a Japanese logo engraved on the handle. He tested its point on a finger, knelt to show the blood bubble to HuaGua.

'Back in the old days, the operation was performed in a hut outside the palace. It was popular, surprisingly.' He spoke in a conversational tone and held the knife loosely. 'The pain was temporary, and when you recovered, if you recovered, you were set up for life. A plum job in the Imperial administration. Of course you had no progeny, and I believe there were difficulties around leakage and the like. They had to wear nappies.'

'What are you talking about?'

Jian straddled the lad's upper thighs, and with his free hand pressed his head to the floor. 'Hence the old expression, maybe you have heard it, to be as stinky as a eunuch.'

He leaned in to speak quietly into his ear. 'Normally, the abdomen and upper thighs are bound, then the parts washed in pepper water. After the blade has flashed, the wound is plugged and covered with paper. The plug is taken out after three days. If piss gushes out the operation has been a success. We can't run to any of that, unfortunately.'

'Fuck you.'

'You were going to kidnap my daughter. You think I will let you get away with that? You have no idea what an angry father can do. Be grateful you're only going to lose your balls, not your head.'

The lad seemed to grow even paler.

'You wouldn't. Come on.'

'I would. Kidnap my daughter? I would do anything, everything. Stop wriggling. I don't want the knife to slip.'

Jian put the knife aside and took out the spoon. He touched the cold metal to wrinkly bollocks.

The lad tensed and shrieked. 'Please no, I'll give you money.'

'How much?'

'Twenty-five thousand pounds. Right now.'

'Now? Money in my hands?'

'There's a safe,' said the lad. 'Twenty-five thousand pounds, take it all. Back of the shelf, over there. Combination is four threes.'

'You'd better be telling the truth.'

When the safe door opened an earthy smell wafted out. Jian found a black leather satchel to keep the money in. He put the stash from the pillowcase on top. A pale slither among the untidy bundles of notes drew his eye. His namecard. He plucked it out. Detective Inspector Ma Jian, Qitaihe Public Security Bureau. The foxed, tatty thing meant nothing really. There was no reason to hold a card for a job you no longer did, in a country you could never return to, especially if you prided yourself on your lack of sentiment. It occurred to him that if only he had dumped it earlier, this entire business could have been avoided. There was a lesson there. He supposed he should get rid of it. But not now, not here, not when there was a chance of it falling once more into the hands of people he didn't want knowing his name. He slipped it into his inside jacket pocket. Perhaps he would be a sentimental fool and keep it.

He called WeiWei from the balcony, told her to gather her things.

'Let's go.'

'Go? I thought – aren't we going to live with that lad and his mum?'

'Let's try our luck elsewhere.' He showed her the money. 'We have options.'

'What about saying goodbye to them?'

'They're busy. They will understand.'

As they descended in the lift, she said, 'I worked out what your scheme was. I was not impressed. I decide who I marry.'

They were standing side by side looking at themselves in the mirror.

'Okay.'

'You can express an opinion, but it's my decision. My life is mine to mess up.'

'Very well.'

They stepped through the hush and darkness of the lobby into the bracing chill of the placid street. He said, 'I don't want to stay in this city. I would like to live somewhere with clean air and a view of mountains.'

'That would be nice. Do you really think we will get to go home?'

'One day.'

He set off at a brisk pace. 'Where are we going?'

'Get something to eat. I made you a promise.'

'It's three in the morning.'

'We'll find a place.'

Chinese slang glossary

666

Modern Chinese number slang derives from internet forums and textspeak. *Liu* (6) sounds a bit like *niu*, meaning smooth, and is easier to type – so 666 has come to mean 'awesome'. In the same way, 88 (*baba*) means 'byebye', and 520 (*wuerling*) sounds enough like 'I love you' (*wo ai ni*) to have become a term of affection.

Bao Ma

Foreign brands use a Chinese name that sounds vaguely like the original and has a positive meaning. *Bao Ma*, 'Treasure Horse', is 'BMW'. Coca-Cola is *kekou kele*, which means 'happiness in the mouth', and Samsung is *sanxing*, meaning three stars.

Colour wolf

Selang (literally 'colour wolf') means 'lecher'. The word 'colour' is often used in phrases around the subject of passion.

Comrades

'Comrade', *tongzhi*, once the term of address for all good communist cadres, has been co-opted by the Chinese LGB community to mean 'gay', much to the annoyance of the Party. Its literal meaning – 'people of the same will' – is genderless and positive, preferable to the traditional word for homosexual, *tongxinglian*, which is rather medical and has a pejorative overtone.

Dongbei

Literally the 'east-north' – the northernmost province of China, bordering Siberia. Once the home of heavy industry, it's now China's rust belt. According to Chinese stereotypes, Dongbei people (such as the leads in this story) are tall, hearty and direct, with good looks and a pure accent, if perhaps a little behind the times.

Jia you

Jia you means 'add fuel' and is used in the same way as 'go for it!' It can be heard at all sporting events.

Kill chicken scare monkey

Chinese has a treasury of four-character phrases that

distil history or legend into a pithy idiom. 'Kill chicken scare monkey' (*sha ji jing hou*) refers to a tale concerning a street entertainer who discovered a bloody way to motivate his pet monkey to keep dancing. Other memorable idioms include, 'horse horse tiger tiger', which refers to a story of a lazy painter whose image of a tiger-horse amalgam caused fatal misidentifications when the real animals turned up – it means to half-arse something. 'Point deer make horse' means to deny reality for political gain, and refers to the story of an evil courtier who tested the loyalty of his colleagues with a deer he asked them to affirm was a horse.

Laobaixing

Literally, the 'old hundred heads', a somewhat derogatory term meaning people of no particular account (like 'proles').

Laowai

A colloqial expression for 'outsider', used to refer to anyone who's not Chinese.

Little Fresh Meat

A slang phrase (*xiao xian rou*) to describe cute boy idols, well groomed, effeminate and not afraid of make-up, who are swooned over by teenage girls. Their androgynous looks have sparked consternation among the older generation, who would prefer a manlier ideal to have taken hold.

Princeling

Taizidang in Chinese. The pampered children of the political elite, generally unpopular at home thanks to their reputation for flouting the law and benefiting from nepotism.

Sajiao

To act like a girlish spoiled child, specifically in a dating context. It's a social game to establish gender roles: the male partner is supposed to weather the little tantrum with equanimity, then, when it is over, offer indulgent support and reassurance.

Tuhao

This slang phrase – 'dirt rich' – is used to refer to a fairly new class of people who have wealth but no sophistication, whose taste for throwing money around in ridiculous ways leads to much mockery and envy.

Author Q&A

Simon Lewis discusses the cultural context of his work and why he chose to write crime fiction from the perspective of a Chinese detective in London.

◆ Your novel *Bad Traffic* and now *No Exit* are crime thrillers steeped in the mindset of a hard-boiled Chinese detective and his daughter, an immigrant student. What gave you the idea and confidence to write from these points of view?

I went to China by accident. Having run out of money in India, I had to earn enough for a ticket home, and the only place I could feasibly make money that was also cheap to get to was Hong Kong. For some months I tended bars, taught English and delivered sandwiches, while living in a tower block in a cupboard-sized room. I shared with a friend, and we slept top to toe on a single bed. The whole city seemed, like me, frenetic and cramped and overly concerned with making money.

When I had enough to leave, I decided to go home overland, which took me through China, which seemed even more dynamic and alien. It was just shrugging off communist dourness in favour of something messier and more vital. Everyone seemed in a hurry or on the make. The food was great, the hotels awful, the people friendly, curious or helpful. That trip was the start of a lifelong fascination.

When finally I got home, I decided to study Chinese as a way to keep some connection with this place that I had found so baffling and fascinating. I was living in a squat at the time in south London and up the road there was another squat full of Chinese illegal immigrants. They were fun to hang around with. They spent their spare time cooking (brilliantly) or gambling (badly). They would feed me tremendously well and we would watch the football, and I would try to show them parts of London they wouldn't usually see (Pride, the ICA), or help deal with the drunken punk who would turn up pretending to own the property and demanding rent. As well as improving my Chinese, I started trying to see my world through their eyes. London must have been just as intimidating and strange to them as Beijing had seemed to me.

Some time later, I had the good fortune to be hired to write a guidebook to China. I did that job, on and off, for fifteen years and covered a lot of ground, though I don't think I ever lost the sense of being a slightly bewildered outsider. I certainly never stopped being surprised and intrigued. When I tried to write fiction using my experiences it didn't seem to work when I wrote about myself. I ended up being more inspired to try writing from the point of view of my Chinese friends.

◆ What attracted you to crime writing and what are your influences?

I always wanted to write crime. Literary fiction is usually psychological, dealing with personal and individual issues close to the writer, whereas the best crime fiction is sociological – it's about all levels of society, the more diverse, broad and sprawling the better, and its issues are often ripped from the headlines rather than the author's neuroses. I think if Dickens were around today he'd write crime fiction as it is the modern form most aligned to his ambition to paint pictures of his world in dynamic hooky stories where every chapter ends with a cliffhanger. I think it's important for writers to take a stab at writing about important events, to innovate by mixing and matching cultural norms and forms, and to write about what's urgent, not just what they know about, and crime fiction has always been a great genre for this.

For me, the greatest modern exemplar of that approach was Elmore Leonard, whose crime stories paint an incredibly vibrant picture of modern America. So I was very pleased when he wrote a puff for the first book.

My specific influences are cinematic. I've spent an awful lot of time bored in cheap Chinese hotel rooms, so often resorted to TV for entertainment. Which led to my discovery of one of cinema's great genres, the Hong Kong gangster film. These stylish, bloody tales of cops and robbers, betrayal and vengeance, were made with such panache that I was hooked despite not understanding the Cantonese dialogue. Back in the UK I worked out what I'd been so impressed by – films like Ringo Lam's *City on Fire*, or John Woo's *The Killer*, *Hard Boiled*, and *Bullet in the Head* – and rewatched them with English subtitles.

Later I became a fan of the gritty, down and dirty crime stories and social commentary made by the so-called 'fifth generation' of bold young filmmakers from the mainland – films like Jia Zhangke's *Xiao Wu* (about a doomed pickpocket) and Yang Li's *Blind Shaft* (about conmen coal miners). Great noirs deserving of a wider audience.

I wanted to create thrillers as dynamic, urgent and kinetic as my favourite Chinese films, to capture that style and verve in prose. I thought it would be fun to take the tropes and characters, and the cops and robber stories of betrayal, revenge and family, and plonk them in the UK.

◆ In a sense are you still writing a guidebook?

Yes. Writing for a Western audience, I try to explain aspects of Chinese life and mores. People might be interested in discovering, for example, that some Chinese people visiting the UK feel more at home in Canary Wharf than in Chinatown, or develop a taste for builder's tea and pork scratchings. It amuses me, as it amused my Chinese friends, to try to teach some slang and swearing (encourage someone with a *jia you!* but don't ever call them a *shabi*). I think it's vital for people to start paying attention to, and trying to understand, Chinese perspectives, as it's a hugely influential aspect of the modern world.

◆ How do your books differ from a thriller by a Chinese author?

I ask Chinese friends to check the text for anything that doesn't ring true. Still, Chinese writers' insights on what it means to be Chinese should be trusted over mine. But, as Chinese writers have pointed out, I do have one advantage over them: I don't have a government propaganda department breathing down my neck. The censorship in China is very hard for Chinese artists to navigate, and it's getting worse not better. A bar owner friend of mine once hosted a Japanese band whose lyrics included something ambiguously nationalistic. Someone reported this to the police, and the next day the bar, along with every other venue the band had played in, had been shut down. Censors are ridiculously over-sensitive to anything even vaguely political or critical of social conditions, and it's impossible to know what will upset them. That is one reason why many Chinese writers choose to write fantasy, history or science fiction (and do so very well); it's just safer. Say the wrong thing and you'll end up in prison, along with your publisher. Which means there is a dearth of honest writing about contemporary life in China. When Chinese friends read *Bad Traffic*, they remarked how unusual it was in dealing with contemporary rather than historical China (which is what foreign writers usually write about), and how lucky I was to have licence to do so.

I am also interested in writing about London, where I have lived on and off for thirty years, and writing foreign characters with different expectations and attitudes gives me the chance to try to write a fresh perspective on the city's charms, peculiarities and inconveniences. Observing the reactions of Chinese friends helps build that perspective – noting that, say, the parks seem to impress them more than the buildings, that the musuems make some cross – why have you got all this stuff of ours? That Big Ben is smaller than expected and the Thames bigger, that the absence of grandiose monuments at Karl Marx's grave causes genuine bafflement.

◆ **What Chinese Crime writers would you recommend?**

If you are interested in crime with Chinese characteristics written from an authentic perspective, look out for the excellent crime novels by overseas Chinese writers Qiu Xiaolong, Lisa See and Diane Wei Liang.

Qiu and Wei Liang both grew up in China but went into exile after the Tiananmen massacre in 1989. Indigenous crime writing is beginning to take off too. For most of the twentieth century it suffered, first from being looked down on by literary intellectuals, then, after 1949, it was banned as 'bourgeois' by Mao Zedong. The only crime fiction during his era dealt with unearthing counter-revolutionaries and foreign spies, though Chinese crime fans could still enjoy Conan Doyle, whose descriptions of Victorian poverty were seen as ideologically uplifting. Now, new works by Beijing-based He Jiahong (*Hanging Devils*), and great procedurals set in China by Mi Lei (*Profiler*), A Yi (*A Perfect Crime*), Chan Ho Kei (*The Borrowed*) and Zhi Wen (whose works are yet to make it into English) are becoming known. Mainland Chinese crime writing is beginning to find its feet.

Thanks

Thanks to Noe and Hana, Mark and Nat, Xiaoshan Sun,
Veronica Chan, Ivy Ngeow, Na Dong, He Kaiyun, Qing Qing and Charles,
Du Yingnan, Mayguli Manap, Pan Yin, David Leffman, Mark South,
Michael Nakan, Tim Draper, Yoojin, Chris Geary, Ali Finn, Hsuan Fen Chen,
Svetski, Tat, Cici, Li Qiongmei, Sam Mills, Tim Pan, Yen Yen, Ileana Chan,
Will Peterson, Jason Underhill, Andy De Emmony, Charlie B, Bill Maud,
Mark Hawtin, Alex Spears, Duncan McA, Liam, and last but not least,
Aunt Jen (sadly missed), Gareth, Mum and Dad.